Green Man Resurrection

Nick Brown

Published by New Generation Publishing in 2017

Copyright © Nick Brown 2017

First Edition

The author asserts the moral right under the Copyright, Designs and Patents Act 1988 to be identified as the author of this work.

All Rights reserved. No part of this publication may be reproduced, stored in a retrieval system or transmitted, in any form or by any means without the prior consent of the author, nor be otherwise circulated in any form of binding or cover other than that which it is published and without a similar condition being imposed on the subsequent purchaser.

www.newgeneration-publishing.com

New Generation Publishing

Nick Brown is a writer with an archaeological background. He is the author of the highly praised 'Ancient Gramarye' and 'Luck Bringer' series. He lives on the fringes of Skendleby and is currently working on the film script for Skendleby. He was appointed OBE in 2006.

With thanks to Jill for her constant love and support.

Also by Nick Brown

<u>The Ancient Gramarye series</u>
Skendleby
The Dead Travel Fast
Dark Coven

<u>The Luck Bringer series</u>
The Luck Bringer
The Wooden Walls of Thermopylae

With thanks again to Danielle Wrate of Wrate's Editing Services

Praise for Nick Brown's Ancient Gramarye series.

'Exquisite dialogue creates such an involving story that you will find it hard to tear yourself away from the pages. Much like a Roman Polanski Movie the narrative will unnerve and shock you to the core.' Horror Cult Films

'Gripping and genuinely creepy.' New Edition

'Echoes of the ghost story master, MR James.' I like Horror

'An autumnal must read.' Manchester Evening News

'It's crying out to be made into a movie.' Spectral Times

'A fantastic genre bending experience.' Web Weaver

'I wish the book had been longer.' Sexy Archaeology

'An imaginative thriller, mixing horror and thriller fiction with a pinch of quantum strangeness.' Author Land

'Nick Brown is the Hemingway of the ancient World.' Lucy Branch, author of 'Girl in a Golden Cage.'

Visit Nick Brown's author page
https://www.amazon.co.uk/Nick-Brown/e/B00FOM9E1A/ref=ntt_dp_epwbk_0

Or follow him on Facebook
https://www.facebook.com/NickBrownAuthor/?fref=ts

Or on Twitter
https://twitter.com/NickBrownAuthor

For Esther, Tony and Pippa and Steve and Judy.

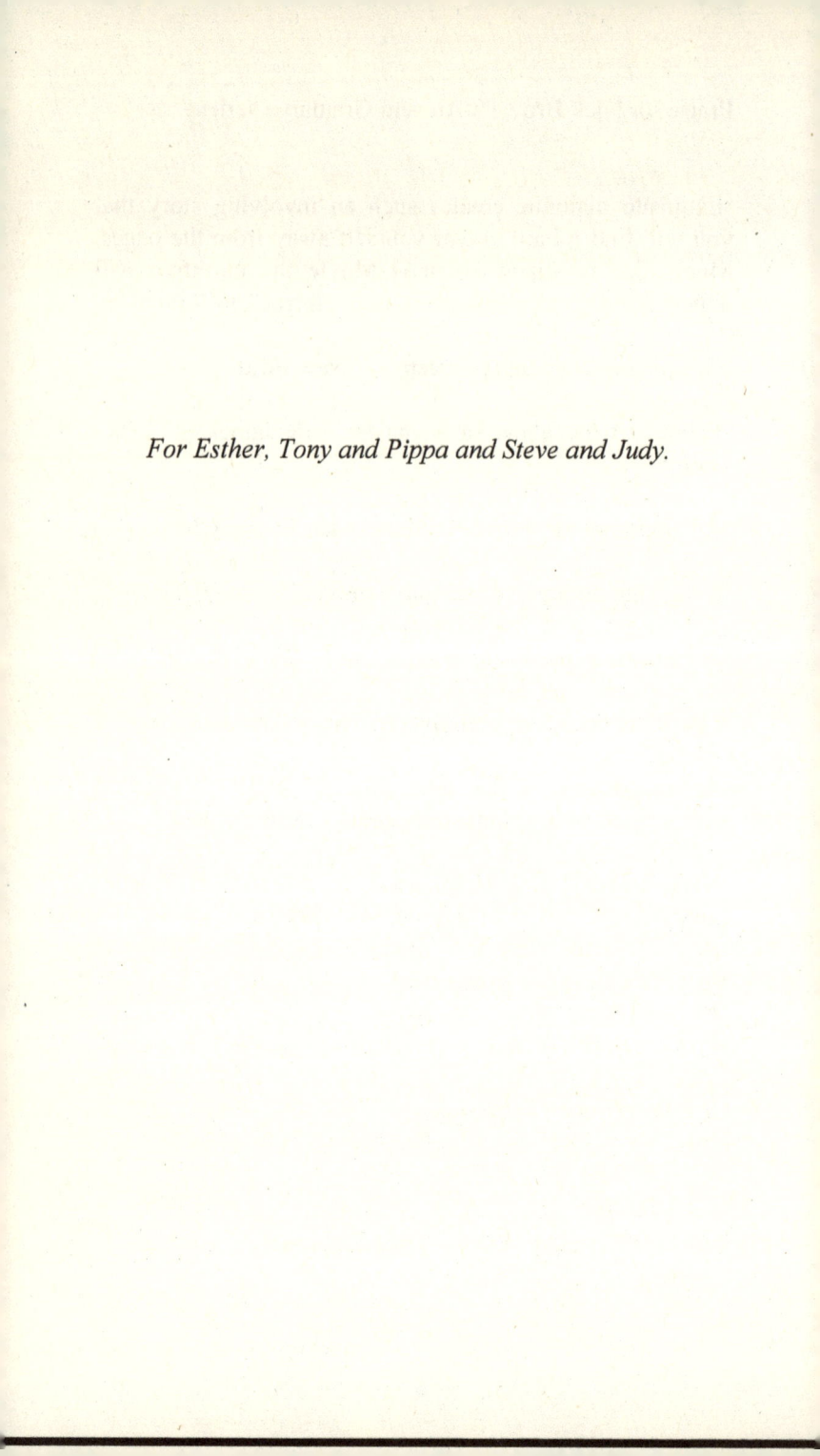

'At one point midway on our path in life
I came around and found myself now searching
Through a dark wood.'

                                        Dante Alighieri

'Scattered we were when the dark night was breaking
But in bright morning converse again.'

                                      Robin Williamson

Green Man Resurrection

Damaged Messages

He found her beneath the shade of an awning in a bar at the foot of the Plaka. She was easy to recognise from the description he'd been given, slender and graceful with black hair cut in a bob, but maybe a little older than he'd been expecting. He'd resisted trying to make contact ever since he'd drifted into Athens some days before thinking it as good a place as any to lose himself in.

She glanced up from the book, saw him and he wondered what her first impression was; he was still sufficiently engaged with life to care about such matters it seemed. He picked his way through the jumble of tables to join her. Half were empty. Greece had never quite managed to convince the tourist market it had settled down to a reasonably secure state since the troubles and the subsequent military coup. She stood to greet him and he was surprised she was almost as tall as he was.

"Thanks for agreeing to meet me."

She didn't reply, merely lowered her eyes. He signalled to a bored looking waiter leaning against a wall and ordered a coffee.

"Can I get something for you?"

Again no reply, but she slipped back into her seat so she was at least prepared to listen.

"I'd like to ask you a few questions about..."

She cut him off. "What are you doing here? Why have you tracked me down?"

"I made a promise."

"A promise to him."

"If you mean to..."

"Of course, who else would I be interested in?"

Despite a career based on asking questions, he didn't know what to say next. She solved the problem for him, asking, "Is he still alive then?"

"Alive? Yes, I think so, but not in the way you mean; more like he continues to exist, it's hard to explain."

"But he won't be coming back?"

"No, I don't think he can leave."

"Did he talk to you about me?"

"A little, towards the end."

"Yaya Eleni told me this would happen; she saw it in her visions."

He had no answer to this, didn't know what it meant. He gazed blankly across the table at her grief-ravaged beauty.

She prompted him, "So, she was right, it was real?"

"I think so, I don't really know."

"Real enough to drive you here where you hide like a dog."

"Perhaps, but someone else suggested I come to Greece."

She gave no reply just stared at him. He sipped at the cooling sludge of coffee in the tiny cup. A light military truck packed with soldiers traversed the street at the end of the lane, heading towards the old Agora. There were tiny tear tracks running down her cheeks as she asked in a soft voice, "Who was it? Who told you to come here?"

"I don't really know him. I only saw him once, and then under strange circumstances. He had a Greek name, I can't quite remember."

"Vassilis, was it Vassilis?"

He nodded. "Yes, something like that."

The light olive skin paled to chalk white.

"Of course, it would be. I will answer your questions but only after you tell me what happened over there in that cold place with the evil name."

"Skendleby?"

"Of course, where else but Skendleby?"

She paused as if making a decision, then said, "But we can't talk here, they will listen."

She dropped some coins onto the table then stood and walked away. He hurried after her. Behind their backs, the waiter made the sign that wards off the evil eye.

She led him through the web of alleys flanking the side of the Acropolis then turned upwards into a warren of small lanes left over from an antique age. At the blind end of one of these they came upon a single-story building with cracks in the walls and a few tables scattered outside. He couldn't work out if it was a struggling cafe or a soup kitchen for the workless poor and stranded migrants.

The sullen, oppressive silence was broken only by an occasional creaking made by the new growth on an ancient pollarded olive tree brushing against the corrugated iron roof. She sat at one of the tables, lit a cigarette and said nothing. He sat too and waited. After some moments, a powerfully-built man with a wild brown beard brought two bowls of thick bean stew and a jug of thin wine, placing them on the table.

"It tastes better than it looks. We can talk here, he's my brother."

It did taste better than it looked, but he wasn't hungry and after a few spoonfuls he watched her eat. When she put the spoon down and had taken a sip of wine he asked, "Tell me, what was it on Samos that sent him to us? I have to know what we missed. I need to know why my life was destroyed."

She ignored this, replying, "I have a message for him, it might help him understand. You can take it for me."

"How do you know I'll be going back?"

"Because you wouldn't have come looking for me if you weren't and, of course, there's someone waiting for you back there. Although she won't wait forever."

He wondered how she could know but put that to one side and repeated, "Tell me about Samos, what happened there?"

"No, first you tell me about what befell him in that place where the evil grew."

She spat the words out, he was taken aback. But she hadn't finished.

"What is it there preventing him from ever leaving? Tell me about that place of dread. Tell me about Skendleby."

Chapter 1: Signs and Portents

Beyond Devil's Mound, in the fading light, Anderson could see the evidence of Carver's development: site huts, heavy diggers and high fencing. The original sheds of the old bomber command airfield had been demolished and replaced by a city of Portacabins housing the construction workers.

That was phase one of the project. He was standing on land designated as stage two, staring at 'Devil's Mound' or, to be accurate, staring at the growth sprouting from it.

Of all the things he had to disturb him, and there were plenty, this was the worst. It had taken the top slot the moment he'd set eyes on it fifteen minutes earlier, driving the atrocity he'd been sent to investigate from his thoughts.

It wasn't only the thing itself; it was how it had grown so quickly, and the speed he could verify because he'd investigated a similar act of cruelty on the mound little more than a month ago, and it hadn't been there then – hadn't even been a trace of it. Now it stood at least nine feet tall. Nine feet of unnatural life.

It was a young tree of some genus he'd never set eyes on. The wood (if that's what it really was) of the trunk and branches was a sickly shade of white. It reminded him of the leprous-looking suckers, grown firm and strong, that grew out of potatoes left for too long in a dark cupboard. It looked dead; there were no shoots of green on the branches, just clusters of withered, black, berry-like objects.

But it couldn't be dead. It was growing at an almost palpable speed. It wasn't only Anderson it was disturbing; it was disturbing the mound itself, literally disturbing it. He could see fissures and lesions were opening in the surface of the mound, exposing the dark earth beneath the grass. He was sure the tree was causing this. He had a mental image of an unhealthily vigorous root ball expanding into all the crevices of the mound, its root tips probing into the cracks in the stone chamber and unsettling the earth.

Down in the heart of the mound, Anderson envisaged bone-white tendrils forcing the mound apart like the airfields hangars had been forced apart and destroyed by the industrial diggers. He tore his eyes away from the tree and was relieved to see a diminutive figure picking its way across the damp, claggy field surface towards him. Whatever the nature of the investigation, it was now firm police procedure never to send single officers to investigate Skendleby.

In fact, each investigation had to include Anderson, his boss, Viv Campbell, or Theodrakis. This evening, two of the three was present. He knew that Theodrakis was as uncomfortable about the place as he was, and this was confirmed by Theodrakis while still a few feet away.

"Strange, isn't it? The mound feels different, as if it has become a victim."

Anderson didn't have an answer to this, but he empathised. Theodrakis joined him in scrutinising the tree. Then continued,

"Yes, definitely different. The mound itself feels empty, purged. But everything around it feels worse."

Anderson nodded in agreement. He understood, but six months ago he would have regarded such a statement as madness. He asked Theodrakis, "Find anything over by the estate wall?"

"No, nothing. All we've got is here, just like last time."

"The tree wasn't here last time, it has grown in less than five weeks."

Theodrakis looked at the tree and Anderson knew it repulsed him as well.

"Can we be certain that it's here now?"

Anderson had grown used to Theodrakis, come to like him even, but he wasn't in the mood for metaphysics.

"If you don't mind, Sir, let's just concentrate on what we're here for, on the joker who left this."

It wasn't a joker who'd left it, he knew that as much as Theodrakis did, but a pretence of normality helped. They turned their eyes towards the object lying on the ground next to the unnatural tree trunk. It had been difficult to identify when they'd arrived because of its orientation, but now they understood it had been deliberately placed upside down they could see what it was.

A badger's head, no sign of the body, and that didn't come as a surprise to either of them. In fact, it was all too familiar, as if time were reversed. Since Christmas, there'd been no more murders, no more attacks on people, and even the death of the old woman in Shrewsbury, although linked to the case, was clearly suicide. Instead, there had been a steady trickle of sick incidents, perpetrated on animals, like those registered through complaints to the police before the Skendleby excavation.

There was one difference, however; this time, instead of following the route of a major arterial road south out of the city, the incidents were limited to two sites: Devil's Mound and Skendleby Hall. The police realised this was a significant shift in modus operandi, but had no idea of the nature of the significance. What those close to the case shared, however, was a griping feeling in their gut that there was worse to come.

Anderson wanted to leave this place.

"Done all we can now, Sir, we can leave the locals to clear this mess up."

Theodrakis, if he heard, ignored it, and Anderson was amazed to watch this normally fastidious man walk across to the mound and scramble up onto it. Anderson couldn't swear to it, but he felt certain that the branches of the tree began to twitch, as if reacting to the intruder. Once on the mound, he picked up the bloody head of the badger, turned it round and set it back the right way up. Then he climbed back down, mumbling to Anderson, "Didn't seem right to leave him like that."

Embarrassed at this gesture from his superior, Anderson averted his eyes and found himself staring back towards the mound directly at the badger. It wore a forlorn and surprised expression on its face and he felt a shiver of pity pass through him. They turned their backs on Devil's Mound and trudged across the wet fields back to the car. Behind them in the trees surrounding the Hall, the noise of crows started up. By the car, as they were changing out of their wellingtons, Theodrakis said, "You go on back, Jimmy, I think I'll visit the rectory, find out the perspective over there, and then maybe look up Mrs Carver. I'll make my own way back."

Anderson was happy enough with this and replied, "Ok, Sir, I'll…"

Before he could finish, the noise from over the mound made both of them turn back to look. It wasn't easy to see from the car across a few hundred yards, but there was a commotion over the mound. Crows were swirling round it, swooping down in pairs, as if hunting prey. They seemed to be pecking at something in the branches. It was hard to be clear because of the rapid movements, but it became apparent that it wasn't just the crows moving.

The thin white branches with their dead berries were moving too; scything and swiping at the birds – the tree looked alive. The crows weren't hunting anything, they were attacking the tree and the tree was defending itself. A crow fell to the ground; the others drew back out of range.

They circled above the tree, carking and cawing their fury as the vicious branches described arcs in the air surrounding the trunk. Then the birds left and the tree relaxed back into its original inanimate state.

Anderson, who'd dropped the car keys in shock, blurted out, "Did you see that, see those branches, they were moving?"

Theodrakis patted him on the shoulder. "Are you sure? Perhaps we did see that, perhaps we only thought we did. Believe me I've seen much worse."

It was meant kindly, but Anderson wasn't listening. He'd recovered the keys, opened the door and started the ignition.

Theodrakis watched him drive away then turned his gaze back towards the mound. It was still now, with its skeletal branches outlined against the fading light. He murmured, "So it begins."

****

Viv opened the door to the office of the chief's PA and was greeted by a warm smile.

"He's expecting you; I've just taken in the tea and some of those chocolate biscuits you like. He only allows himself them when he's with you, so he must be in a good mood."

Since the success of her investigation into the Skendleby murders and the announcement that she was now permanently attached to the Greater Manchester police she'd shed her pariah status and achieved a type of popularity. She was almost feeling at home but despite the sunny greeting she suspected that the chief wasn't in a good mood and she had a premonition of what the subject of the meeting would be. She was right.

"Sit down lass, have a biscuit; in fact, better take two, you'll need something to fortify you."

He leaned back in his chair to observe her, leaving her to wonder what was coming next. She didn't have long to wait and hadn't managed to unwrap the biscuit from its gold foil when he said,

"Now, while we're both sensible enough not to mention the Skendleby murders, let alone question if we actually did crack the case, we can't pretend the problem's gone away."

He paused for a swig of tea then asked, "Have you spoken to Jimmy?"

"Not since yesterday, why?"

"How did he seem? Is this getting to him?"

"No more than to the rest of us, Sir. Why are you asking?"

"Because when he came back from Carver's construction site at Skendleby he looked like a man who'd seen a ghost and his report made no sense."

She didn't reply, just looked at him almost teasingly.

"Well, it may have made sense to you, possibly even me, but to anyone else, anyone untainted that is, it would have sounded deranged. Didn't help you sending bloody Zorba with him. What made you do that?"

"You know perfectly well, Sir; he's more experienced than us."

She knew better than to prolong this opening salvo of the conversation; it was his way to begin with grumbling, she knew it acted as a type of fine-tuning or foreplay to the real burden of his meaning, which would come later. Let him talk himself out, get the irritation off his chest then a dialogue could commence. Despite her apparent coolness and the acute brevity of her analysis, she dreaded the conversation to come. But there was no way of putting it off and she sensed it coming like distant thunder on a sultry day.

"Jimmy's no fool and no soft touch. He held things together for you and Zorba last winter, and he watched both your backs. So when he asks to be excused from any part in the Skendleby investigation, and puts in a report that's all about a bloody tree and which makes no sense, I begin to wonder what's really going on that I should know about."

She knew where this was going and didn't really know what to say so deflected it by throwing something else into the mix.

"Before we get to that, Sir, I need to patch you in on something that Zor...that is Colonel Theodrakis told me this morning."

She saw from the chief's eyes that hearing what Theodrakis said was the last thing he wanted, but that he was gripped by a horrified fascination at the prospect, so she used the pause to press on.

"He said there's a game changer on the way."

She could see from his expression he was hooked.

"A game changer?"

"Yes, something's coming, coming from Greece."

She paused.

"Something, or perhaps someone."

The chief swallowed some tea the wrong way and began to cough.

****

Waves crashing on rock, the sound filled the small, bare cell. Like part of the rock from which it was hewn; a pallet bed, small table, candle, chamber pot and a jug for water. A tiny window opening out onto nothing but sky, waves a hundred metres below waging an unceasing war on the cliff base. Not a prison cell, but a house of religion, and yet there were many similarities – although those imprisoned here came through choice. A choice not to face the world but to punish themselves and live the most ascetic life possible under God.

The man in the cell was on his knees, hands clasped over his ears trying to keep something out. White hair cropped close to his skull, face careworn and lined, left ear mutilated and partly missing. He had moved here to the most remote and austere monastery he could find, but it wasn't far enough, he couldn't escape.

It seemed God, who to his surprise he'd found, didn't want him to live a life of anchorite poverty and silence. He had other ideas, otherwise he wouldn't let this happen. It wasn't the noise of the storm and the sea he was trying to drown out, it was the voice. The voice he recognised, the voice he'd thought was the Devil's but couldn't have been because it was here in the monastery with him.

He took his hands from his ears - perhaps it was all in his head - and tried to pray. The sound of the mass weight of the storm-driven waves grew louder, each surge an explosion. The candle guttered and died leaving the cell twilight grey. But now he could see. He could see Skendleby and feel the living death in it stretching and growing. He knew it sensed resurrection, knew it was conjuring the forces that would release it.

The scene changed and he saw a house of women, a spiritual community; the traces of ritual scattered about. They too were waiting for something to arrive, but death was closing in on them, those useful idiots. Then, like a freeze-frame, the picture stopped and the voice started again, bitter and mocking.

This time he recognised it; the honeyed voice he'd listened to the day he'd lost Alekka. It was worming its way through his ravaged ear into his mind, planting its poisoned seed of the future. But it wasn't him it was trying to seduce this time. It was them, the women welcoming death and something far worse into their lives. A death that she carried with her and which no power existed to defeat. But he retained enough self-control to realise that this dream wasn't meant for him. He was eavesdropping on another wavelength.

But if this wasn't for him why was he hearing it out here so far away where he could do nothing? He knew the answer: he could never get away – he was doomed to watch as history repeated itself with increasingly terrible consequences. Or, even worse, it wasn't finished with him. He threw himself onto the bed, pulled the rough blanket over his head and curled up in the foetal position.

But it didn't help because in his mind the frame unfroze and the tragedy rolled on as the Aegean Sea continued to tear at the rock outside. There was no peace for him here anymore he was being summoned. There was logic to this in a way, he'd started this tragedy and, if for no other reason, he had to return to expiate his guilt.

After a few moments of wretched indecision he got up off his pallet, dipped his face into the water bowl and began to stuff his few belongings into a backpack before walking out of his refuge. The main hall of the monastery was deserted, looked as if it had been this way for centuries, languishing under a thick dust canopy.

Come to think of it, he couldn't remember the face of a single monk he'd shared the monastic vigil with. Ahead of him was a crack of daylight where the great iron-studied door leaned open on its hinges. He walked through it and followed the steep path down to the sea. To his surprise, the sea was now calm.

On the jetty a small boat waited with a hooded monk seated in the stern. He wasn't surprised. He stepped down into the boat, the monk slipped the cable and the fragile craft pulled away. He neither expected nor received any greeting from the helmsman so looked back up the cliff towards the monastery for a last glimpse of his refuge from terror.

Perhaps there was some particularly opaque, low-lying cloud because he couldn't make out the monastery at all, just a few blocks of fallen stone. Then the creeping sea fret swallowed them up.

Chapter 2: The Cruellest Month

Claire was blooming. Her swelling filled the house, sustaining it through the tempests of spring that blew away the daffodils and shredded the tulips. The storms of late April made no impression on the women of the house, who were warm and secure in their purpose. In the 'Gathering' room where they convened, all eyes were on Claire as she spelled out the role they were to play in the glorious future that would follow the birth.

Margaret sat slightly outside the circle looking on, feeling marginalised, peripheral. This wasn't the way she'd expected things to develop; the house was changed and she missed the loving support of Olga in the meetings and the security of her presence in bed.

She'd been dazzled by Claire, seduced by her in every way, but Claire no longer visited her bed. She was less bothered by this; Claire's brand of loving was physically punishing and more than a little frightening. She was very bothered, however, by the fact, apparent to all, that she'd been replaced as leader. It seemed the house and its purpose were no longer hers to guide.

She wasn't sure when or how this happened, but she was aware that the glamour Claire had cast over her in those first days had begun to slip. When she thought about this, which she did constantly, it seemed the strangest aspect of it was that Claire, whose control seemed absolute, was unaware of it. She was terrified of Claire and did her best to remain as inconspicuous as possible; she stayed at the margins and watched.

The more she watched, the more frightened she became. Claire had changed the house, starting by her veto on replacing Jan and Olga. Claire insisted their present number of Leonie, Rose, Ailsa, Jenna and, of course, Margaret, was the optimum. They would remain as a community of six until Claire decided otherwise. Margaret suspected Claire didn't like women very much.

She tried to refocus her attention on the meeting but couldn't because the more she looked at the others, the more she was struck with a horrid fascination. Whatever it was she saw, they obviously saw something different. They sat in silence, their eyes fixed on Claire, almost drooling with something akin to subservient lust. Even Rose, who Margaret suspected had no feelings except malice and envy, sat gazing at Claire with adoring, cow eyes.

She suspected her housemates were also unaware of the other changes in the house, changes that she tried desperately to block out. Although there were now only six of them living here, Margaret suspected there were others; it certainly sounded like that, particularly at night when the corridors echoed with footfall and voices. Sometimes she caught a brief glimpse of these others, but they quickly faded. She dreaded the nights.

She tried to think about something else but couldn't. She suspected Claire knew about these others, in fact, at times she'd seen Claire disconcerted about what she could obviously see and hear, as if her control was momentarily shaken. The house was haunted: haunted by Claire. But almost worse than that, there was something haunting Claire.

If she were capable of being certain of anything in this house, where the rules of reality were warping, it was this. Claire too was haunted. At night, lying awake in the large, cold, empty bed, the noises tormented her. In her bedroom, the largest and most beautiful in the house, she spent the nights in a sweat of terror.

The noises began in the room next door; Claire's room. They started with a whimpering sniffle, like a small girl crying out in a nightmare, then gradually grew in intensity to full-blooded shrieks, not just one voice but many, sounding like the dormitory of the damned. The first time this happened, Margaret got out of bed to investigate. She got halfway across the floor when she heard the sound of the next-door bedroom bursting open.

All resolve gone, she hurtled back into the refuge of her bed and lay in the dark listening to the sound of next door's occupants dispersing along the corridor and spreading throughout the house. Their murmured, distressed chunterings seemed to reach her from every angle: above, below, even outside the window. She waited to hear the screams and footfall of her housemates but these never came. Instead…

Instead, a threnody of grief and terror seeped through every pore of the building. Then, after a time which she couldn't gauge, it ceased. The door of Claire's room shut with a bang and silence regained dominion over the house.

She lay shaking in bed, wishing Olga was there to calm her, stroke her hair and kiss her. But Olga was gone, replaced by Claire. Claire, who'd driven Olga away and seduced Margaret, used her brutally and then discarded her. Eventually she dropped into a dream-tormented sleep. The morning after the first time this happened she'd eagerly asked the other women about their experience of the night. She'd been met with blank looks and incomprehension. They'd heard nothing.

From then, Margaret knew she was alone, a prisoner in her own realm. The others showed her no hostility, but showed her no regard either. It was as if they inhabited another dimension, one where she was of no account. When Claire entered the kitchen their eyes switched to her with a gaze of needy anticipation.

She could see that gaze on their faces now; they stared at Claire with adoration as she talked to them about the glorious future that would follow the birth of the miracle child. They murmured and cooed over every utterance that slipped from Claire's bright, scarlet lips. Margaret found this particularly chilling as, for much of the time, Claire didn't bother to say anything, just sat smiling as if amused. So what, Margaret wondered, was it that the housemates thought they were listening to?

Occasionally, Claire turned her head towards Margaret and smiled, as if at some shared joke. Margaret hung her head, trying to be invisible. While she was doing this, Claire began to speak again and, to her horror, Margaret realised that she was speaking to her.

"Are you enjoying this little show, Margaret?"

Margaret raised her eyes and stared back speechless.

"Such a hoot, isn't it? Just look at the poor little lambs, look at the way they gaze at me with such love. I could make them do anything I wanted, Margaret."

Margaret still couldn't speak.

"Don't worry about them, they can't hear us, in fact, they have very little individual will left. I've taken it all. No, there's only you and I who have any inkling of what's going on and believe me, Margaret, you have no idea about what's really happening. If you had, I'd kill you."

Claire ceased smiling and Margaret felt her bowels turn to water.

"Which, believe me, I soon will do if you carry on with this sulky behaviour and don't begin amusing me again. You can't sit there all day moping because that big lunk, Boxer, left you."

Claire paused, realising that Margaret didn't understand. She trilled with laughter then explained.

"Oh, didn't you know, that's what they called her in prison? Boxer, because she liked to use her fists, liked to hurt people. You didn't know, did you? I'll bet you didn't even know she'd been in prison. Oh, how delicious, I can see she never told you. Boxer was Olga's prison name, you silly goose."

She laughed again and Margaret felt sick. Claire shrugged her shoulders and continued.

"Sorry to keep breaking off but every time I inhabit one of these bodies, I can never resist a bit of fun. Only ever a bit though, because human bodies don't seem to last very long once I get inside them, so I suppose it's as well this is the last one.

Anyway, where were we? Oh yes, I remember. I'm telling you because, after all, this was your house and it seems only fair to share a little of what's going to happen here with you. You should feel grateful I've not reduced you to their state of feeble subservience."

She nodded her head in the direction of the other women.

"And while we're on the subject, Margaret, I have to tell you that you're a very poor judge of character. What on earth drove you to choose some of them for a place in your little Eden? I mean, what sane person would let her into their home for five minutes, never mind as a resident?"

Claire pointed at Rose.

"The nicest thing anyone could say about her is that she's a treacherous, venomous, psychotic who likes inflicting pain, and that one's not much better."

She indicated Jenna.

"Sour, bitter and poisonous and as for the others, well, they make negative energy look dynamic. Leonie is the only one with anything about her. I imagine that apart from her dreadful taste in men she must have been quite good fun before her rather disastrous brush with Skendleby. You know, now that I'm tired of your rather feeble efforts in bed I might restore her functionality and try her out one night."

Claire paused and silence filled the room; the women sat staring at Claire and listening to what they imagined she was telling them. Margaret couldn't tell if she preferred the silence to the awful things Claire was saying. After a spell, the silence broke.

"You know, Margaret, the only women of real worth here are the ones who've gone. Poor little Kelly who it was such a simple pleasure to kill. Sweet, loyal Jan and, of course, Boxer. Sorry, Olga, she was the best of the lot really, I almost miss her."

Claire may well have carried on but Margaret, urged by some sudden compulsion, blurted out, "What happens to you at night? What goes on in that room? What are those noises? Who are those other..."

"Stop it."

The voice was a scream, shattering the windows. Claire's face a mask of fury; horrid in the way it changed from a human face into something unrecognisable and terrible. The transformation took Margaret's breath away; she felt the blood draining from her face.

Then Claire's normal visage was back, the spell was broken. Her housemates laughed as if Claire had made a joke, then they began to clap; Claire was transmitting again.

Feeling Claire's attention shift, Margaret used the opportunity to slip away; she slipped out of her seat and scuttled up to her bedroom where she sat in the gloom, primarily just trying to breath regularly and then to think. It wasn't really thought, rather horrified speculation on the nature of the foetus that Claire carried within her womb. What manner of fright must it be? What was its purpose?

Then, gradually, as her deep breathing restored a vestige of control, she considered the interchange and the way Claire could control reality. However, this engendered hyperventilation, driving her back to the breathing exercises.

Strains of music seeped up from the room below, perhaps they were dancing, celebrating whatever Claire had told them. In the days before Claire, when Olga was still here, before Kelly was slaughtered, they danced sometimes. Danced to celebrate the joy their life in the house gave them, danced to celebrate their empowerment.

Margaret was pretty sure that any trace of empowerment was long since departed, so they must be dancing to some illusory fantasy that Claire had impregnated their minds with. Then a wave of terror struck her, so immobilising that she cried out loud.

If Claire could do all this then she must know Margaret's thoughts. It was then it struck her that Claire wouldn't have opened herself to her if she intended to let her live. Claire was toying with her before she destroyed her.

She sat on the bed disabled by morose speculation. Outside, the light began to fade over the bleak and sodden fields lying in the lengthening shadows of the Edge. Spring wasn't meant to be like this; it was intended to bring relief from winter and the magic of renewal – it was meant to be about rebirth.

That was when the full horror of her situation hit her for the first time. What was the purpose of this birth soon to be loosed upon the unsuspecting world, and what part had she played in it?

She'd always been unsure of the exact motives that had led her towards divorcing Ken and setting up the community of women. Ken hadn't been a bad man, not even that bad as a husband. All she could remember was that one day she'd woken up with the vision of the community fully shaped in her mind, along with the steps she needed to take to achieve it.

Now it felt like all this had been decided for her in order to facilitate the needs of some other purpose. Something very similar must have been driving the movements of all the other women in the house, but it would appear that they were still of some use and hadn't reached their sell-by-date.

She remembered the thing that Rose and Leonie had fetched up from the cellar and wouldn't let her see, but which she knew they'd handed over to Claire. What was that? Not something they'd enjoyed doing as Leonie had been sick for days and not eaten anything and Rose had taken time off work.

The shadows growing over the fields were now mirrored by the shadows in her room, as the sickly daylight bled into twilight. She needed to contact someone, needed help, needed to raise the alarm. But outside the community who could she trust? This thought led to hysterical laughter; who inside the community could she trust? No one.

Once she calmed down and began to think she'd narrowed her list of options down to two. DI Campbell, the austere but strangely desirable policewomen leading the team who'd investigated the spate of killings last year, and...

And this gave her a real surprise, the scruffy looking vicar who'd turned up offering help after Kelly's death. The police wouldn't take her seriously so it would have to be the vicar, more his line of work, she decided. But first she needed to get out of the house. The house that now terrified her.

She put on an expensive country-style hooded coat, which she'd ordered off an exclusive fashion site and quietly made her way downstairs. She wasn't sure what she'd do when she got out but noticed that by the time she reached the front door she had the car keys in her hand. There hadn't been any need to keep quiet, the noise of music and laughter from the 'Gathering' room drowned out any other sound.

The front door was curiously reluctant to open, maybe it was locked. But it wasn't, it just wouldn't shift. Margaret began to panic. Then, when she was about to give up and sneak round to the back door, it suddenly and of its own volition swung back on its hinges, and she was outside.

But then it seemed she wasn't, or certainly not in any version of the outside she recognised. She'd arrived somewhere that wasn't anywhere. That's the only way she could describe it to herself. A limbo of opaque, grey light, but nothing to see, nothing to hear and no sense of touch. In fact, she couldn't even feel herself, she'd ceased to exist. Perhaps this was what it felt like to be dead, perhaps she was dead.

She turned back towards the door. But of course it wasn't there either, just the extension of limbo. Now she knew she wasn't dead because of the surge of panic immobilising her. What had she done? Was she in hell? A cold hell of grey nothing, no distance and no perspective, just absence. She started to scream, but there was no sound.

Then she was back in her bedroom putting on the expensive coat and preparing to go out. She put it back in the wardrobe, there was no point. She knew what would happen if she tried to leave the house. She sat on the bed to think.

What was happening couldn't be real. Maybe she'd been drugged, maybe this was all a dream. But somewhere deep within she knew neither of these was the correct answer. Despite her dabbling with the occult, she had never truly believed, it had been more of a lifestyle option; real magic had never entered her life. So she was left with only one explanation for her predicament: Claire was exerting some psychological hold over her, something akin to hypnotism.

This seemed the most logical avenue of causality. It was also the most frightening. Without thinking about it, she looked in the bedside draw for the card that the vicar of Skendleby had given her on the day of his unfortunate visit and rang the number of the rectory.

The phone was answered immediately.

"St George's Rectory, Reverend Edmund Joyce speaking."

Margaret was flustered; she hadn't expected so quick an answer and blurted out, "Reverend Joyce, I need to talk to you..."

His answer cut her off.

"Of course, Margaret Trescothic, I've been expecting you to call, why have you waited so long?"

Had she been thinking clearly, she'd have wondered how he knew it was her, but she wasn't so gabbled, "I need to talk, but please can you come here, can you come now?"

"Last time I called you weren't very pleased to see me, perhaps you should come here."

"I can't, I can't"

"Why, Margaret, why can't you come?"

"Someone's preventing me from leaving."

There was a soft chuckle at the other end, followed by, "You make it sound as if you're being held prisoner in your own house."

"I think I am, I think I am a prisoner."

She was in floods of tears now. Why did he sound so calm? He must think she was mad. She tried again.

"Please, please come here now."

She had another thought.

"I know you're in touch with Olga, tell her, please tell her, and ask her to come."

He replied with a question. "Who is holding you prisoner in your own house? Tell me."

"She is, Claire is, she's taken everything."

There was a peal of laughter at the other end. She recognised the cruel, mocking cadence and her analysis was quickly confirmed as the owner of the laugh spoke.

"Oh, you are priceless, Margaret, so much fun. How could you be stupid enough to think you'd be able to call out? Haven't you understood anything?"

Claire laughed again as Margaret sat speechless, trembling like a terrified fawn in a car's headlights.

"You silly booby, it's lucky for you that I find your antics so amusing; they're all that's keeping you alive. You know, it's getting a bit dull down here with your idiot housemates, I may visit you later tonight. Can't promise that you'll enjoy it though."

The phone went dead. Downstairs the music and laughter increased in volume…

Chapter 3: Season of Rebirth

A damp, late afternoon just before Easter and Ed Joyce was trying to light a fire in the chill drawing room when the phone rang. His hands were still filthy from trying to coax the split logs, obviously still too damp, into something approximating a flame. It had been a disturbing day.

Not the least cause for this was a cryptic reference he'd teased out of the final and most opaque section of the hidden diary of Dr John Dee, erstwhile necromancer at the court of Queen Elizabeth I. Finding these toxic papers concealed in the archives of the John Ryland's Library had taken considerable effort. Ed wished he'd spared himself that effort.

It wasn't that the revelations weren't interesting enough to tempt the appetites of any academic and, had he been unaware of and untainted by Skendleby, he'd have been tempted. But, and it was a big but, in his present context, what they imputed terrified him.

From an academic point of view, their knowledge of the 'Book of Enoch', a mystical addendum to 'Holy Scripture', assumed that Dee must have been familiar with the fragments discovered in the Dead Sea Scrolls. Dee died in the 17th century and the scrolls were discovered in the 20th century.

Ed remembered from his studies at Cambridge that there were Enochian allusions to be found in the scriptures for savants who knew where to look. But here Dee quoted verbatim from a text that included details only recently uncovered by modern archaeology.

Not only that, but the passages Dee quoted in a Skendleby context pertained to beings Enoch called 'The Watchers'. To Ed, the very idea of watchers was sufficient to raise his heart beat to an unhealthy level. For him, the

'Watcher' was the spectral presence that haunted the churchyard and held strange communion with the crows.

The crows whose presence he could feel every moment of his conscious thought and who swam through the dark material of his dreams. The crows whose fetid carcass breath he couldn't shake off.

The ringing of the phone was therefore a welcome intervention. A welcome intervention up until the moment he lifted up the handset and answered the call.

"Ed Joyce here, how may I help you?"

Sound from the other end of the line but no words.

"Hello, Ed Joyce here, can you hear me?"

Still no words, but a sense of someone there. Ed began to wonder if this was a prank call, clergy were subject to these from the disturbed and malicious. But on the other hand, it could be a soul in need and Ed would never turn away from the desperate and despairing.

"Please, do speak, I'm here for you."

It seemed that this might work. There was a babbling at the other end that sounded like a woman crying, no discernible words but palpable fear. Strangely, it also sounded like a recording that had been speeded up. He was about to speak again when the sound changed.

Changed to a sharp, shrill peal of laughter, then the line went dead. It wasn't so much the icy malice of the laughter that stopped him in his tracks, but that he felt he knew the voice. Something very wrong was stirring. A year ago he would have panicked and reached for the tranquilisers, now he dialled ring back. The number was withheld.

He glanced over his shoulder at the window that looked out across the graveyard towards St George's, the Christian centre of the parish of Skendleby and, Ed suspected, the pagan centre before the church arrived. It was a gesture conditioned by nerves and his knowledge that something just within perception shared the graveyard with the restless dead. But there was nothing to be seen amongst the graves standing forlorn in the fading light except the withered vestiges of daffodils. It began to rain.

Later, as the fire was catching, he was disturbed again, this time by his mobile whose screen identified the caller.

"Ed, are you able to talk?"

"Olga, I thought we agreed you'd text and I'd ring you if I was alone."

However, it seemed she'd forgotten any agreed protocols, either that or this was urgent.

"Ed, I can't contact Margaret. Have you heard from her?"

Now Olga's trepidation embraced him and, without thinking why, he remembered his strange call and the laugh which terminated the exchange and reminded him of Claire.

"Ed, I've a bad feeling about this, I can't get her on her mobile, house phone, social media, nothing. It's like the house and everything in it has vanished."

Ed wondered why she said everything rather than everyone when he realised from the silence at the other end that a response was required.

"I suppose that I could pop over there on a pastoral vis..."

"No."

She cut him off.

"No, don't you go."

"Then how can I set your mind at rest?"

"Ask your neighbour to go for you."

For a moment this puzzled him and he thought of Davenport who was now too ill to leave the house. Olga must have sensed this.

"Mrs Carver, Suzzie-Jade, she's as hard-faced as they come, nothing would stop her, ask her, she owes you."

Ed wasn't sure what it might be that Suzzie-Jade owed him but understood Olga's description. However, there was a side to Suzzie-Jade that he suspected no one other than he and Theodrakis had ever seen, but there was no point relating this to Olga. Instead he said,

"Ok, I'll talk to her about it. What do you want me to tell her?"

"I doubt you'll have to tell her anything, Ed. I imagine she already knows what we're worried about."

Before Ed had time to work this out she delivered her final conversational surprise.

"When are you going to find time to take me for a drink?"

He made a series of ambiguous suggestions and ended the conversation. But he was now pretty wound up and knew he wouldn't be able to settle down to anything productive so decided to go out. Once outside the rectory door, to his surprise, the sun came out and picked out, in flashing brilliance, the wet slate roof of Skendleby Hall. He stared across the graveyard and the estate wall at it until the brightness became too much for his eyes to bear.

It was then that he made his decision to visit Suzzie-Jade. He knew, of course, that Carver may well be at home but realised that he was no longer frightened of him. Any encounter would be uncomfortable and perhaps far worse, but it would at least shake him out of his present mood. He'd hardly seen Suzzie-Jade since the surprisingly intimate Christmas dinner she'd attended at the rectory and, as Olga had intimated, there were things he wanted to ask of her.

The sun had breathed some warmth and life into the evening and he meant to make the most of it. Following the path from the rectory towards the lych gate, he saw the verdant new life of spring: buds stretching out from branch and stem towards the light. Easter, resurrection and hope, all these circulated in his thoughts and percolated through his feelings.

Things improved further as he was walking the short stretch of road towards the Hall. The gates swung open and the Range Rover with smoked glass windows and the SI 2 number plate pulled out of the drive and headed, with considerable acceleration, towards the main road leading into the city. So, any contact with Si Carver was, at the very least, deferred.

He slipped through the electric security gates before they managed to fully slide shut and began his walk along the drive towards Skendleby Hall. The land was waterlogged, not knowing what season to expect after a series of false springs. The trees scattered across the untended and unloved parkland were in a varying state of bud, early leaf and winter dormancy, as if there'd been a dispute amongst them as to the time of year.

As the hall drew slowly closer he had time to ponder two questions: what would he ask Suzzie-Jade and what was he doing here? He knew he was being guided towards some purpose and this, and the fact he was no longer frightened, bolstered his resolve even though he had no plan or strategy.

Then he was at the Hall door and, after a prolonged wait leading him to wonder if the bell was working, the door opened. He found himself confronted by a woman of advanced middle years. She was clad in a plain, ankle length black dress.

He'd expected a much younger woman, remembering the murdered Marika and the variety of dancers from Carver's clubs who it was rumoured were mandated to help out at the hall as part of their extra curricula activities. The woman squinting at him was certainly no dancer. He enquired about the whereabouts of Mrs Carver.

"Not here."

"Do you know when she'll be back? By the way, I don't think we've met, I'm the priest of Skendleby, Ed Joyce, call me…"

"Not here."

"Would it be possible to leave a message?"

"Not here."

Ed accepted that this minimalist conversation had reached its limits and was wondering if he'd be able to persuade her to open the electronic gates so that he could get out when he returned to the end of the drive.

Then he sensed a change and, looking past the left wing of the Hall towards the estate wall, he detected, rather than saw, movement. He ignored the tutting of his monosyllabic interlocutor and tried to focus his gaze.

Seconds later, something blackish, moving at the speed of a jerky trot, emerged. It was heading for the Hall. He removed his glasses to wipe clean with his handkerchief but on replacing them realised any optical impairment hadn't been the fault of his specs. He sensed the housekeeper had withdrawn, a feeling confirmed by the sound of the door slamming closed, but that didn't seem to matter now.

Something was happening, something numinous, he felt it shivering down his spine. He recognised what this meant, it was back.

But as he watched the thing lurch across the broken terrain it began to change. The progress steadied as if modified by the local laws of physics and the black shroud morphed into a pastel shade of pink. Within moments the transformation from threatening spectre to show-pony jogger was complete.

"Hiiyaaa, been expecting you, innit. What took you so long?"

He took a deep breath.

"Mrs Carver, I mean, Suzzie-Jade."

She laughed and he relaxed.

"You don't like calling me that, do you? Good news though, vicar, don't think I'll have to call myself that much longer."

"You mean Mrs Carver?"

"No, silly, I never use that anyway. I meant Suzzie-Jade, think she might have had her day."

A couple of years ago such an out-of-kilter and ridiculous exchange would have reduced him to a state of blushing humiliation. Now he played it with a straight bat but realised that behind the screen of banter something deadly serious was being imparted.

He smiled and waited for the next move. She unlocked the door and beckoned him to follow her into the Hall. Once inside though, instead of heading for one of the receiving rooms, she moved at a rapid pace up the stairs. He hesitated.

"Come on up, Ed."

He ascended while looking around. He'd never got this far into the Hall before. The place was a mix of expensive, if tasteless, refurbishment, patches of half-finished alterations and a few vestiges of fading elegance. He felt a stab of sympathy for Davenport. What would the old man feel if he knew what had been done by Carver to the ancestral home? She was a good distance away from him, about to enter a room at the end of a long corridor.

"In here, hurry up, haven't got all day."

He speeded up and followed her through the door. He was in a bathroom almost as large as a small bungalow, but it wasn't the opulence that gobsmacked him. Suzzie-Jade was wriggling her way out of the tight-fitting, fetishised running gear. As he stared in a mixture of shock and fascination she stood for a moment posing. She lifted her hair, then pinned it up.

"Don't be silly, Ed. It's not as if any of this is what it seems, is it?"

She deliberately twitched her rump at him and walked into a shower the size of a bedroom, giggling. He sank onto a small Ottoman beneath a decorated mirror.

Who'd be a vicar, who'd believe him? He listened to the splash of water while surveying the double sink, double bath, hot tub, bidet and gilded tables covered in cosmetics. Then she was out, glowing and rubbing herself down with a huge fluffy bath towel.

He asked the question he knew he shouldn't but couldn't refrain from. "What if Mr Carver returns early?"

When she'd finished laughing, she said, "Why ask that? Not as if we're doing anything, is it?" She studied him for a moment, "Unless that's what you want, Ed, in which case."

It must have been his expression that set her off laughing again. "Oh, Ed, you do cheer me up. Don't look so worried, I'm teasing you, and anyway, Si wouldn't dare come in here if he knew I was in the house. I scare him too much for that."

That Ed could understand, she was beginning to scare him too. She shrugged into a soft robe.

"There, that make you feel better? We can talk now. Don't think there'll be any more laughing."

She was right, things once said can never be unsaid and some words change lives forever. The doors of perception, once opened, never close on the same space. Suzzie-Jade opened a door painted with the same design as the mirror and walked through into a bedroom. She sat on the bed and patted the space next to her. Ed dutifully sat. She took his hand in hers, which felt strangely cold. There was nothing sexual in the touch for either of them, the contact was about sharing comfort and strength.

"You've come to talk about the house, haven't you, Ed, Claire's house?"

He nodded. "Yes, I've a bad feeling about what's going on over there."

"Wherever there is, Ed."

"What do you mean? You know perfectly well where it is."

"We know where a building is located, that's not the house. The house is something else, something very different."

"What do you mean?"

She didn't reply just asked him, "Margaret been trying to contact you then? She can't though, can she?"

"I don't know, someone has, and Olga's worried. No one can contact the house. Olga was wondering if you would be willing to visit it, see what's going on."

"Can't do that, Ed, I'm not strong enough to confront Claire, not yet anyway."

He tried a different tack.

"What did you mean before when you said the house is something else?"

Aware he was babbling, he came to a halt. He felt her increase the pressure on his hand.

"I can't really explain, I just know things, don't know why I know them, but I do."

Ed could tell she was struggling. He also noticed how her accent and vocabulary altered. He sensed metamorphosis in her and he clung onto her every word. The walls of the bedroom seemed to recede and fade.

"Can't explain, Ed, except it's like what we can see when we're here, you know what I mean by here? I mean the bit of life we can understand is only a small bit of what there is. But in that house it's all there, all the bits we can't see, can't know about. Stuff from the present, past and future, stuff that's never been here and never will be. Stuff that doesn't belong here, shouldn't exist here, doesn't exist here. But all the same it's there and Claire controls it."

"That can't be right, I know Claire's been a bit strange of late but what you say makes no sense."

What he meant was that he didn't understand what she was saying, although he felt in some strange way she was speaking a type of truth. A truth he couldn't believe but which nonetheless he felt. So he asked, "How do you know all this?"

"Don't know, it's like there's two of me. Sometimes I'm something else and then I find I'm at the estate wall looking out over the mound and there I see things differently."

She stuttered into silence. Ed couldn't think of anything to say. So they sat together on the bed, her cold hand holding his. The temperature of the room was rapidly dropping and he felt himself on the brink of some terrible, new understanding. Then she said, "Did you know Claire talked to Si at Christmas?"

Ed's face spoke more eloquently than words would have.

"I've heard him talking to her and guess what? She's going to show him how he can destroy the mound. Why do you think she'd want to do that?"

Ed didn't want to guess. He didn't have to.

"Because once that mound has gone then she can never be put back into it. Once the mound has gone nothing can stop her."

Chapter 4: Haunted and Deserted

He'd made his way through a mental fog; a dreamy, trance state, along shadowy roads and obscured towns, drifting along insubstantial ghost streets flickering and fading in and out of focus. No sound, no sense of smell, no feeling. He thought that maybe it had been like this in the womb and this idea of rebirth, the chance to try again, slowly crystallised in his unconscious where it lay sustaining forward momentum.

There was purpose. He knew where he was going and why, maybe not how, but, wandering through a strange world, two out of three wasn't bad. He knew that when he got there all the tricks of being alive he'd lost would return, if only for a short time. Travelling hadn't been easy, he'd no money but cars stopped, took him to airports and bus stations for which, to his surprise, he had tickets. The last stretch was familiar. He decided to walk, give him time to think.

Chorlton Street bus station, lying shabby in the drizzle beneath the concrete high-rise parking, was like an old friend. This surprised him until he realised he was beginning to remember. Also he felt hungry, but his revived memory couldn't tell him when he'd last eaten. Must have been some time ago, he was so thin and his stomach felt tight as a drum and wouldn't stop rumbling. He considered trying to negotiate some chocolate from the kiosk before realising he'd already set out on the walk.

It was several degrees colder here than where he'd started from, no glimpse of sun through the low grey cloud that hung over the rooftops spitting rain onto the gum-encrusted city streets. He turned south and headed towards the vast, shared campus of the Manchester universities. The students hadn't changed, crowding Oxford Road, its bars and shops packed out, the buses crawling slowly along the narrow road restricted by the largely empty but spacious cycle lanes.

But now he felt alive, flickers of recognition and nostalgia sporadically disturbing him. He walked past the Neo Gothic courtyard of the Victoria University, where the archaeology unit had been housed, then cut through the building sites and new developments towards his destination.

After about half a mile he turned into a street of much older buildings, large Victorian houses once inhabited by the wealthy, now by students and families too poor to live elsewhere. Other houses had been boarded up but some of these showed signs of having been reoccupied as squats or doss houses for crackheads.

Then a door he remembered in a large old house that had seen better days. This wasn't a squat or crack house but it radiated the same melancholy feel of neglect. This was a house nobody loved or could be bothered to care for. Peeling paintwork, cracked glass in a couple of window panes, gutters leaking water that debouched from blocked drainpipes to dribble down damp brick walls. There was a downstairs light on, a bare light bulb dangling. He climbed the three steps up to the front door and knocked.

Giles was slumped on a broken-backed sofa facing a pile of unwashed plates and mugs on a coffee table and a bag of unwashed laundry on the floor. His domestic life was in another period of shabby dislocation. This one perhaps the most damaging of all.

Claire had been the solution to his life plans. For her he'd suffered more things than he'd thought himself capable and dredged up courage and honesty that he never suspected he possessed. And yet...

And yet it had all gone wrong, or, as he now thought, it had never really existed. It had been a chimera, an illusion of everything he needed, and now he'd been dumped. Worse, she was pregnant and with his child. It must be his, he was sure it must be his. And yet...

And yet if it was his, why had she walked out on him to live in that house? But that wasn't the only thing confusing him. Towards the end she'd begun to frighten him. He couldn't tell what he was looking at anymore. It-she changed, seemed to change so that he couldn't be sure who or what he was living with. He was certain, however, it was no longer the beautiful and caring psychic healer who'd saved him from the horror at Skendleby. And yet...

And yet, it wasn't just the cruelty she inflicted during their love making, scaring him physically and mentally. There was something far worse than that which he didn't want to think about. But the baby, why had she left him as soon as she was pregnant? Wasn't it his baby too? This thought always stopped him dead in his tracks. Was it his? He thought so, but it wasn't this that troubled him so much as the question of what type of baby it would be.

He knew this was mad. A baby was just a baby and like all babies it would enter the world with a blank account, blameless. And yet...

And yet there was something deeply not right about this, something that frightened him more than did Claire. This time, though, it hadn't been his fault – he couldn't be blamed for the baby. He'd even moved back into the despair and wreckage of his own house, leaving the Lindow cottage for Claire and the baby in case she wanted space for herself. So no guilt attached to him this time. And yet...

And yet, that wasn't quite true either, there was Viv, the DI leading the Skendleby murder case. The woman who'd fitted him up for a crime he hadn't committed but who now...

He got no further with the mental self-examination as the soft knocking sound he'd not noticed became louder. Someone was hammering at the front door. Relieved to be shaken out of hurtful introspection, but not thinking sufficiently to question who would be pounding at the door of a house believed to be empty, he left the sofa, left the room, took six steps towards the gloom. In the hall he pulled at the front door, it was stuck, damp had entered the wood and it had swollen up.

Outside, the knocking grew louder until eventually, with a vigorous jerk, he wrenched the door open. He saw what stood beyond it and gasped in shock.

He must have looked like he was about to faint because the visitor held him with both hands. So they stood like that for some seconds, clasped in an embrace while staring at each other's faces. Giles was trying to place who it was. There was a familiarity but also something alien. The visitor seemed to be taking stock, counting off memories.

Giles found his voice first, perhaps because the visitor displayed no evidence of possessing one.

"Steve, it is you, isn't it, Steve? I thought I'd never see you again."

There was no reply and it was Giles's turn to be physical. He took the visitor's hands in his and drew him into the house, sat him on the sofa then sat himself on the coffee table gazing at him. He couldn't think what to say. The visitor looked round at his surroundings then broke the silence.

"Your housekeeping hasn't improved I see."

The features had changed and aged but the voice was the same.

"Steve, what are you doing here?"

****

About three miles away, in the police headquarters, an unusual conversation was taking place. The chief had walked into Viv's office and asked her to get hold of Theodrakis and Anderson. This had taken some doing. Theodrakis was, as a rule, notoriously difficult to locate and Anderson was believed to be on a lunch break with PC Gemma Dixon. This latter detail was meant to be a carefully kept secret but was common knowledge in the 'nick', with bets being taken on either an engagement or a pregnancy as an outcome by June at the latest.

So it wasn't until three that Anderson, Theodrakis and Viv presented themselves at the chief's office, by which time he wasn't in a particularly good mood.

"What the hell's going on over on Carver's site?"

This was obviously a rhetorical question, which no one bothered to answer. Instead, Viv sat watching the chief with a look of rapt and respectful attention. Anderson stared down at his feet and Theodrakis gave the impression of not having even listened to the question. Following the intervening silence, the chief supplied the answer he'd intended to all along.

"Well, I'll bloody well tell you."

He then proceeded to make a number of points, picking them off on his fingers as he went along.

"First up, bloody nothing as far as we're concerned, we've done nothing."

He paused, looking round for any challenge to this. None was forthcoming.

"Second, not a day passes on site without some act of a bloody, filthy vandalism and let me tell you, your bloody badger's head has got nothing on some of the things these sick bastards are coming up with."

Again he looked at them. Viv and Anderson stared back in contrition; Theodrakis inspected the contents of his wallet.

"And third, the protests against phase three have gone too far this time."

Phase three was the final piece in the development jigsaw and was to be built over the fields surrounding the Skendleby mound. Before the chief could continue, Theodrakis, who apparently must have been listening, interrupted him. "It's not meant to be built on. History has shown us that, so perhaps it would be wise to listen to them and leave the place alone."

Not best pleased at being interrupted, particularly from that particular source, the chief made a heroic effort to keep his temper. "Not the first time you've made that observation, Colonel Theodrakis, and as I've told you before, that type of decision is nothing to do with us."

He glared at Theodrakis who looked away, leaving the field to the chief.

"Which brings me to number four. What have you been bloody doing, what do we pay you for? And please don't tell me again that we don't pay you, the Greek government does, please Colonel."

Viv knew that this was the time she was expected to speak.

"I know how frustrating this is for you, Sir, and I appreciate you taking the political pressure for us."

She paused and smiled at him, giving him space to appreciate her diplomacy.

"But, there aren't any leads and it's very hard keeping the team working on Skendleby together. There's three times the sickness rate amongst them than in the rest of the force and because of some of the particularly nasty incidents, two experienced members are leaving on disability. At present, there's just the three of us who attend that site. I believe that even Mr Carver won't go near it."

This seemed to partially mollify him.

"I'm not saying it's easy and I know about the stress. In fact, it could have been three but that lass you're seeing, Jimmy...Gemma, isn't it? She has a bit more spirit."

Anderson continued to stare at his feet, but his normally pale complexion coloured up.

"Anyroad, it might be better if Carver gets permission to build over it, that'd get him off our backs and might put an end to the whole business."

Theodrakis cut in. "That would bring down something far worse believe me. A great deal of what we are dealing with at present is only metaphysical or psychological, to put it in terms you'd find acceptable. You let the developers destroy that mound and everything we're being warned about will happen. You need to believe that if nothing else."

The chief, genuinely angry now, snapped back, "Warnings? You think that's what these acts are? Well, in my book they're crimes, bloody crimes. Let me just remind you there's been murders, abuse and atrocities on animals. Skendleby is its own crime wave and we can't stop it. Manchester's crime problems are meant to be gun related, something we deal with. At least you know where you are with guns, but this?"

They sat in silence, thinking he was right. They knew that everyone on the local force would rather deal with gun crime than Skendleby. His next utterance, however, did surprise them.

"And it's not only Carver and some of the politicians wanting the development speeded up we've got to worry about."

Viv was pleased to see he had reached the stage where it was we again rather than just them letting him down. Usually when he employed the collective pronoun, the dressing down was over.

"It's what's going on in that house, the one we had all the trouble with round Christmas."

Anderson asked, "You mean the coven, Sir?"

"Aye, but that's not the term you should use. We've got a problem contacting Margaret Trescothic; you know, the one who owns it, whose ex-husband was murdered."

Viv thought to herself, "Here it comes, he's got to the point of all this."

"Well, we're having trouble contacting her, nobody there seems to know where she is."

****

Giles watched as Steve sipped his coffee then took another bite of the bacon sandwich; he seemed to have forgotten some of the basic principles of eating and almost all of the mechanics of speech. So Giles sat and watched him struggle with his food. He'd given up on any attempt at conversation, despite being tantalised by Steve's unannounced re-entry into the world.

Last time he'd seen him was as he'd been taken by an aged monk into an insubstantial monastery that even to Giles, in his state of shocked incredulity, didn't seem real. At the time, Giles had been pretty certain that no one would ever see Steve again. Now the Lazarus-like resurrection had him flummoxed. He sat, watched and waited.

But it wasn't a comfortable wait. He knew that whatever storm had blown Steve, or what was left of Steve, onto his doorstep was a harbinger. Whether of good or ill, he wasn't sure. However, time seemed to tick away and eventually Steve finished eating. He looked at Giles then stood up and left the room. Giles heard his footsteps on the stairs followed by the bathroom door closing.

Followed by nothing for what seemed like ages, so long that Giles began to wonder if Steve was self-harming or had passed out. He was about to go up and find out when he heard the toilet flush, so he sat back down. Some minutes later, Steve reappeared looking slightly better. He looked at Giles and uttered the first full sentence since his comment on the state of Giles's housekeeping.

"No point in me apologising, we both know this isn't a social call."

"Yeah, but at least tell me what's been happening to you, what you're doing here?"

"Doing, I'm not doing anything; this is about what I have to do."

The elliptical nature of this remark broke the back of Giles's patience.

"For fuck's sake, Steve, don't be so bloody secretive. You turn up here out of nowhere, uninvited, say nothing for hours then spout some crap about…"

Steve put up his hand, signalling for Giles to stop; he did.

"Sorry, Giles, I'm not used to being with people, certainly not back here, the place where everything went wrong."

Giles regarded him sympathetically. He looked like he was about to cry. His skin was almost translucent and that, combined with the lack of facial hair and bald head, gave him the appearance of a malnourished child. Whatever he'd been through it was obvious it hadn't stopped when he entered the monastery. Giles decided to ask him about his time in there as a gambit to get him talking. He was about to pose the question when Steve spoke.

"I'm here as a warning."

Giles sat waiting for what would follow.

"As a warning and perhaps something more. I'm not sure, it isn't clear, but I think something will be demanded of me."

There was a pause. The intervening silence seemed to stretch away into infinity, then, "It's all happening here now, moved on from Greece."

Given his recent experiences, this didn't come as a surprise to Giles, but what followed did.

"Do you know of a house of women near here? Some type of religious community perhaps?"

Giles thought about answering, decided against it and just nodded.

"I've been shown it in a vision."

"And?"

"And it's not what it seems, not at all."

After delivering this line Steve winced, as though the very words had come at a great price. He took a deep breath before saying, "That's where it's concentrated now, all of it from everywhere, everything there is, in that space. That's where it's gone to and that's where it will occur."

Giles couldn't help himself, he asked, "What?"

"The end, of course, terror first and then the end."

Chapter 5: Friends Old and New

Later, much later – midnight – Giles finally got him to talk like a human being, like the old Steve. Or at least a shade of the old Steve. He only managed this by dint of slipping a generous slug of whisky into a mug of tea Steve agreed to take before going to bed. Whether it was his exhausted state or the change to his metabolism, it did the trick.

Not that it produced a conversation, just an outpouring, a stream of consciousness, a flurry of hurt.

"My whole life, Giles, I've ruined everything I touched. I never committed to anyone or anything, just kept moving on and on. All down to fear. I've lived my life afraid and tried to avoid anything that could hurt me."

He paused for a sip of the alcohol-laced tea and looked up. Giles thought he was looking to make eye contact, but he wasn't, he was staring at something behind Giles's left ear. After a moment, he continued.

"My one chance was Alekka. I let her down, of course. I didn't trust her, I let her die. She needed me, risked everything for me, I ran away. When she died, if that's what it was, I'm still not sure she was capable of a natural death, I died too. Everything good in me died, any feeling or humanity."

For a moment, Giles thought he was about to cry. But he didn't. Maybe he was right, maybe he'd moved beyond that.

"Since then? Since then I don't know, don't know what I am. Not much more than a physical construct composed of sadness and guilt, nothing more. Fear maybe, I think that's still around."

He ground to a halt – silence – Giles assumed he'd finished. But he hadn't, he moved on to the bit he'd meant to say, his message.

"But they don't let you get away that easily, not when they have a purpose for you. In that place, whatever it was, wherever it was, I was given a purpose, but they didn't tell me what it was. Just said I'd know it when I saw it. Then I had the vision of that community of women and the next thing I knew I was here."

He shook his head, blinked owlishly then collapsed onto the sofa. Giles stretched him out, put a cushion under his head then went upstairs to fetch a blanket. When he'd covered him up, for reasons he didn't understand, he kissed him on the forehead then left the room, turning off the lights.

That night the house was disturbed by noises. It was as if Steve had brought others back with him. It was the house as it had been the night they'd made the mistake of opening 'Devil's Mound' at Skendleby. That night he'd panicked and fled to take refuge with Claire. For him it had been the first step on a long, slow road to redemption, but for her?

He'd rather not think about what he'd brought her into, so he lay awake listening to the noise of the house: taps turning themselves on and off, footsteps in the hall and a low pitched susurration of what might have been voices growling at each other at a frequency that was audible but indecipherable. However, this time he didn't panic and leave the house.

The past had taught him many things and he knew now that whatever he was hearing was happening elsewhere and the house was merely picking up elements of the disturbance at the fringe of its frequency. This was a minor haunting, insubstantial and unreal.

For a time, he worried about Steve and twice went down to check on him, but he showed no sign of stirring and at about two in the morning, a time when the taps were off but the shower on, he drifted into an uneasy sleep. Two things woke him, which in a way was lucky as he'd neglected to set the alarm. The house phone rang several times then cut out. Giles didn't bother to answer as he knew the landline had long since been cut off. Then his mobile whistled at him announcing an incoming message.

It was from Viv. "Hi, Giles, I can get home about four, please come round."

As with all his dealings with her, he wasn't sure if this was a good thing or not but he thought he'd better go. He went through to the bathroom, reassuring himself facetiously that he wouldn't need to operate the taps. After a quick and nasty instant coffee, no milk – he'd forgotten to buy any – he entered the living room to tell Steve of his plans, but decided against waking him after an initial whispered effort.

Steve was deep in sleep and breathing lightly. For a second, Giles considered the possibility he'd fallen into a coma, but sensibly decided that it was probably exhaustion. He left the coffee out, a twenty-pound note and two large scrawled messages telling Steve how to contact him and that he'd be back that evening, then he set off for work.

On the way he pondered the wisdom of contacting Theodrakis and Jan. Jan he wasn't sure how to contact and Theodrakis, it turned out, he didn't need to, as there was a message waiting for him at the Unit's offices. Sophie was telling him about it before he reached his desk.

"A Colonel Theodrakis called twice; he wants you to meet him at the Lindow site as soon as you can get there."

"But haven't we got to make a presentation about the survey for the airport relief road?"

"Norman and I are quite capable of sorting that out and, if necessary, we can reschedule. The Colonel was very insistent."

That didn't sound good and Giles didn't want to visit Lindow. He might be able to deal with whatever was messing with his house but the hyper reality of Lindow was something of a different order. Nothing good ever happened there and it had been a murder site long before the Romans arrived.

He knew that whatever archaeological context the police had blundered into would make no sense. Sadly he had plenty of time to think about it en route. The M60 was being upgraded to a 'smart' motorway and as a consequence was, as always, gridlocked, but this time it had proved sufficiently smart to cause queues on both the M62 and M56. So he sat in traffic, and having texted Viv telling her he'd be with her between five and six, he mulled over whatever grisly and illogical finds the police would have for him to look at on site.

In a way he was fortunate to be stuck in traffic because that at least put off the time when he would have to examine the evidence frightening Theodrakis on Lindow Moss.

****

Just about the time Giles hit the motorway gridlock, Jim Gibson was walking into Beard's butcher's shop in Bramhall. He was there so early because, like Giles, he hadn't slept well and for pretty much the same reasons. He enjoyed the familiar Friday morning banter as he ordered the meat for the weekend. Enjoyed it more than usual perhaps, as it was reassuring to be standing somewhere that had been performing the same function for so many years and where life followed the safe quotidian pattern.

He used to think the same about his house; old, comfortable and ringing with family noise. But last night, late when the others were asleep, it was a different type of noise he had to contend with. At first he'd tried to dismiss it as stress, he had plenty to feel stressed about and it all came from the same source, Skendleby.

He'd received some strange phone calls lately, he liked to think of them as strange, but they were actually threatening. He knew what was behind them, or rather who was behind them, Si Carver. Not that Carver made them himself of course; he had people who did that for him. He'd been under pressure from that quarter ever since the

Journal had published a couple of articles objecting to the scale of Carver's Skendleby development.

The articles made sense to Jim and he'd followed them up with a self-penned editorial suggesting that the last phase of the development be suspended pending an independent enquiry. The calls started shortly after that. Then yesterday he'd received a visit from a man who'd somehow managed to slip into the offices undetected and deliver a series of crude threats.

Jim had been in journalism long enough to know it could often be uncomfortable, but only once before had he felt so threatened. The other time had also concerned Skendleby. He'd tried to shake the feeling off but couldn't and it followed him home. He'd drunk more than he should the night before but it hadn't helped.

Particularly, sometime after eleven, when the phone rang. Any unexpected call at that time isn't going to be good news and this was no exception.

"Gibson, that you?"

The voice seemed distant but disagreeably familiar.

"Who is this?"

"It's all started again. Have you seen it lately?"

As an editor of a paper, Jim wasn't unused to crank calls and so put his usual procedure into operation.

"I'm recording this call and I'll be passing it on to the police, so if you..."

"Not if you've any sense you won't. This is..."

But Jim had already worked out who it was.

"Si Carver."

Carver was right, there was no point passing this on to the police, he'd have to talk to him.

"If you're going to ring up so late at night you could at least try to make sense."

"It'll make sense when you see it."

"See what, Mr Carver?"

"The mound, that bloody mound at Skendleby that the archaeologists set off."

"I've seen it plenty of times."

"Well, come and look, look at what's happening to it now, what's growing out of it. It even scares the bleedin' birds. Come and look, then see if you still think it needs preserving. Do it, Gibson, I'm telling you."

Before Jim could agree or argue the phone went dead and a shaken Jim returned to the whisky bottle. He'd better go and look. He'd been thinking about Skendleby too often over the last few days. Just when he thought he'd got out he was being pulled back in.

Carver was right about it having started again. The Skendleby poison was leeching out, feeling its way into the locality. Lying sleepless in bed that night, he listened to the aggressive and disconcerting rustlings and whispers running around the sleeping house.

****

The moss was its normal wet, claggy self and Giles felt it trying to pull his boots off and suck him down with every step he took. He was lumbering across the sodden, black surface towards the area cordoned off by police tape.

Strange that there was never a view of anything from the heart of the moss, even on clear days, even though the outliers of the Pennines were so near and the Edge lurked directly above it. It was closed in on itself, furtive and secretive, and, as both police and archaeologists had demonstrated, somewhere in its depths there lurked secrets best left undisturbed.

Theodrakis, wearing a pair of Wellingtons far too long for his legs, waddled a few paces to greet him.

"Sorry for having to drag you out here, my friend, but as you can see we've a problem and you may be able to help."

Theodrakis turned and they walked back together towards the scene of the investigation.

"Steve's back."

Theodrakis halted mid pace.

"How? Why? What's he doing? He can't be ready, isn't fit."

Giles didn't have time to reply before they'd reached the taped-off area. Anderson nodded a greeting, Theodrakis slipped away from his side. But Giles missed both of these movements.

"What are those? They weren't here last time, I was here a week ago, and they weren't here then."

Not a particularly elegant sentence, but the meaning was clear. No one answered.

Within the curtilage of the police tape, following its boundary, a circle of saplings was growing. Stick thin, bone white and without foliage save for tiny pricks of black colouration at the tip of the spidery branches. They looked unreal as they swayed to the rhythm of a breeze that wasn't blowing. Eventually Anderson said, "You have to walk through them, choose a big gap and try not to let them touch you."

"But what are they?"

"Do your work first, I'll tell you later when we're away from here."

"But?"

"Just try to ignore them, don't listen to the noise they make. Look, just follow me."

Anderson made his way through a sizeable gap and walked into the circle. Giles followed, as instructed. At the heart of the circle three scene-of-crime officers were on their knees carefully inspecting something. Giles noticed they were wearing headphones.

"We just need you to confirm something for us, the rest can wait until later."

He must have seen the blank look Giles gave him.

"We've had reports from local residents about screams and voices shouting for help."

"Local residents? There aren't any, no one lives in the centre of the Moss."

"That's why we ignored it for the first couple of days, then some nosy bugger came and had a look. They found bones, human bones. That's why you're here, to confirm they're ancient bones. After that we can escape from this."

"What's that noise?"

"Told you not to listen."

"That whining sound, they're making it, aren't they? God, it's horrible, sounds like a dying animal. Why don't you do something about them?"

Anderson grimaced. "They don't like to be touched."

Giles thought he was joking. He wasn't.

"Please, Dr Glover, the quicker you do your bit the sooner we can leave."

Giles saw the scene-of-crime nerds making room for him. He peered into the gap they'd created.

It looked like an occupation level excavated in a Bronze or Iron Age roundhouse, with many of the timbers preserved by the waterlogged conditions they'd been buried in. He could see the hearth and a variety of artefacts scattered on the floor. It was a hugely exciting find, and yet.

It wasn't possible, too near the surface, anything like this would be eight to ten feet down at least. He was trying to reason this out when Anderson's voice cut across him.

"What do you make of them?"

"Of what, this is incredible?"

"The skeletons, what do you think? Look there where the timbers are thickest."

Giles looked, saw. At the far edge of the hut circle he identified the entrance. There, jumbled beneath fallen beams, lay the skeletal remains. From this distance he couldn't tell how many and he certainly wasn't going any closer to find out. Partly from his archaeologist's reluctance to disturb evidence but mainly from trepidation.

"Are they old? Can you confirm that this is an archaeological site and not a murder one?"

"Not really without examining them and even then I'm not the bone expert, we'll need Jan for that."

"What's your first thought?"

"Well, it looks like late Bronze or more likely Iron Age. The bodies are under the timbers therefore of the same context."

"So, if the timber's Iron Age then the bodies are too?"

"Yes, but I've only glanced at them, I'd need to..."

He let the rest of the sentence drift away, realising the error he'd made as Anderson seized upon it.

"Be plenty of time for that later."

Anderson stood the scene-of-crime officers down and the five of them picked their way gingerly out from between the saplings. Outside, Theodrakis was waiting for him and took his arm to lead him away. Behind him, Giles heard Anderson saying to a uniformed sergeant, "I know they don't want to have to stay overnight out here, but this place needs watching, so double them up and let them bring one of the four-by-fours up here. They can stay inside with the engine running."

Chapter 6: Peering into the Abyss

Giles rolled away then paused a moment, looking down at her, wondering. His body was sticky and his nostrils filled with the conjoined scents of their mingling. How had this happened?

Under two hours ago he'd arrived at her flat, anxious and strung out. In the gloom of the vestibule he caught a glimpse from the corner of his eye of a black-clad janitor, but as he blinked and looked again no one was there. He blamed his paranoia. He didn't really know what he was doing here or even what type of relationship this was.

She'd even seemed surprised to see him, which was a bit rich considering he'd called at her invitation. But as she opened the door he was perceptive enough to realise from a single glance at her puffy eyes that she'd been crying and to recognise someone else who'd reached the edge and peered into the abyss.

He was about to fill her in on the bewildering horrors he'd encountered at Lindow when she turned and walked into the kitchen. He followed, saw her open the fridge, remove a bottle of wine and unscrew the top. She filled two very large glasses, far larger than the government's new sensible drinking advice recommended.

They both drank the first glass quickly and she refreshed the glasses, emptying the bottle. The problem with the sensible drinking advice was that it ignored the ability of alcohol, temporarily at least, to take the edge off anxiety and loosen the tongue. Viv said, "I don't want to know about whatever it was you dug up at Lindow."

He saw the precursors of fresh tears gathering in her eyes.

"I want you to tell me about you and Claire."

To his surprise, this came as a relief. He'd been waiting for her to ask about Claire for some time. In fact, he desperately needed to talk to someone about Claire. Needed to let some of the rage, fear and hurt building up inside him escape. So, instead of Lindow or whatever the return of Steve portended, he said, "She's changed. I don't even know if it still is Claire anymore. I haven't seen her for weeks, but…"

He hesitated for a moment but he'd started now, so he was going to finish.

"She terrifies me, I loved her so much, and I think she's carrying my child but…but I'm scared of her."

"Scared?"

"Yes, very scared. I mean it, Viv, physically and psychologically."

Instead of laughing, she said, "I can understand why, she frightens me too."

She finished her wine, took another bottle from the fridge and opened it. He didn't really like white wine, particularly cheap Pinot Grigio, but he needed the alcohol hit so finished his glass then held it out for a refill and settled down to listen to her.

"She thinks she knows me, has some deep inner knowledge of me, as if there's something hidden from the rest of the world that we share."

She paused and took a sip, Giles prompted her. "Go on."

"I'm trying, but every time I think about her I think I must be losing my mind; so much so that I can't even be sure that the next bit actually happened."

He could see she was considering whether to continue, worried that maybe he wouldn't believe her. Then she decided.

"One night, before Christmas, in the middle of the freak snowstorm, Claire invited me to join her at Oliver's Bistro near Skendleby. I must have been mad, the country lanes should have been impassable; the news reported a complete shutdown of the roads. I certainly felt mad once I arrived."

She paused and sipped the wine.

"That's another strange thing. I had no trouble driving. I listened to the local radio reports of traffic stuck in a total whiteout and yet I drove those roads without difficulty."

In the pause that followed, the silence in the kitchen was oppressive. He could see panic in her eyes and streaks of perspiration on her forehead.

"When I arrived, nothing seemed real. She meddled with me."

She must have seen from his face he didn't understand the context of meddled.

"Abused me, interfered with my mind and my soul. It's difficult to explain. It felt like she drew me into a different dimension and when we were there she subjected me to a mixture of seduction and psychological torture."

"And?"

"And it worked, worked on both levels. I was massively aroused like never before, wanting her but at the same time terrified, mentally dislocated. I was on the point of no return, about to succumb to the desire and the threat, swept away with lust for both the pain and the release. That's when it happened."

"When what happened?"

"Mrs Carver arrived."

"Suzzie-Jade? You're joking!"

"No, believe me, I'm not, she wasn't like herself, she was more like Claire. It's hard to explain, but I knew she was there for me."

She looked at Giles for some sign of understanding; there wasn't any, so she pressed on.

"For a moment the two sat facing each other locked in a strange conflict. It looked like a mime, they didn't touch but stared and moved their hands as if they were controlling a contest being held somewhere else, like Xbox. Claire got up and left. Mrs Carver talked to me, can't remember what she said, then she left too. I thought I must be going mad."

This time it was Giles who reached for the bottle to refill the glasses.

"I think you had a very lucky escape."

Then, without intending to, he pulled off his sweater and T-shirt in one movement. He pointed to some deep, recently healed scars across his chest and puncture marks on his shoulders and lower back.

"I think the ones on my back are worse but I don't get to see much of them."

She reached out to touch the scars on his chest and that's when they became lovers.

Now they lay entangled in her bed. She looked to him like a blend of the Williams sisters crossed with a young Michelle Obama; strongly built, strangely beautiful. He wanted to stay, knew she wanted him to. But he had responsibilities.

"Viv, I don't want to but I have to go. Steve's back."

This last utterance she obviously regarded as a complete irrelevance.

"Steve?"

"Yeah, the one who opened the Skendleby Mound."

"Zorba, sorry, meant Theodrakis, told me he was in Greece, locked up in some weird monastery."

"He was. I thought he'd gone for good but yesterday he showed up on my doorstep looking like death, all skin and bone, couldn't explain how he got there. But…"

"But what, Giles?"

"He said he'd come for a purpose, he'd been sent."

He could see from her face this made no sense. He tried again.

"Viv, I think the endgame has begun."

She got up and walked naked across the room to grab a robe hanging from a hook on the door. He watched, admiring the blend of flesh and muscle. Once robed she turned to face him.

"Can't believe any of this, Giles, but I feel it. Feel I'm being watched, I don't think I've been left alone since I was drafted onto this case."

She walked through to the bathroom. He began to dress.

****

Steve was still on the couch when Giles opened the door to his living room. He looked like he'd been there all day. He was contemplating waking him when he saw Steve's left eyelid peel back and realised he was awake.

"Had anything to eat, Steve?"

A mundane question for such unusual circumstances, but Giles was eager to preserve as much normality as he could muster. There was no response.

"You been there all day?"

Steve nodded.

"Taps been behaving themselves, have they?"

"Not sure, been asleep, what've you been doing?"

Giles made a pot of tea, took Steve a mug, then lowered himself into an armchair and surveyed the gloomy squalor of his house. It was so different from the modern, sparkling minimalism of Viv's shiny new apartment. He wished he'd stayed with her. He sipped the tea and was thinking about the nature of their relationship when Steve broke the silence.

"I'm coming back to work. I have to look at this stuff you've been finding. I think I'm beginning to understand why I'm here. There's something you need to do for me."

"What's that then?"

"I need to see Claire."

****

Margaret had become invisible; she'd discovered this in her own 'Gathering' room. Depressed and strung out by her isolation, she'd gone downstairs to talk to Leonie and Ailsa. They blanked her. This was the final straw, she began to shout and rage at them. There was no reaction. They continued the conversation they were having about a summer break. Margaret was about to grab Ailsa by her shoulders and shake her when Claire walked in smiling. Claire could see Margaret, she was looking right at her.

"Clever isn't it, Margaret? You don't exist to them. In fact, they've forgotten a time when you did exist. Such a giggle, isn't it? They believe this is my house and my community. Everything about this house before I entered it has been erased."

Margaret couldn't reply, she just stared open mouthed.

"And in a way, Margaret, dear, they are quite correct. This is my house now, I am the leader here, whereas you."

Claire paused and favoured Margaret with her most radiant smile.

"Whereas you, Margaret, are less than nothing."

Margaret blurted out, "But I'm here, what have you done to me? I'm still here."

"Oh bless, how sweet. Let me explain things in terms even you will understand. You don't exist, not anymore. Look at it this way, existence is only perceptual. You may think you exist but only to yourself. To your former friends, you're less than a ghost. At least ghosts, as you primitives so quaintly term them, can, under certain circumstances, leave some type of impression. You can't make any because you never existed."

"But you can see me."

"Of course I can, you silly goose. I arranged all this. Look, watch how pleased they are to see me, like little puppies wagging their tails. No point you being here, Margaret, it will only upset you, better go back to what you still foolishly believe is your room."

Claire turned away to begin an amusing anecdote for Ailsa and Leonie. She was like someone tossing a bone to dogs.

Margaret didn't return directly to her bedroom, partly because of Claire's remark about it only being what she believed to be a room. What was it if not a room? Perhaps she'd succumbed to some form of lunacy.

She wandered into the kitchen and felt tears welling up as she gazed at the chair where Olga used to sit. She even felt nostalgic about her time with Ken and would certainly have accepted an offer to return to her life with him.

But Ken was dead, had died violently, hunted down as a fugitive. This she knew was fact. She began to suspect that the same forces that had led to his death were responsible for what was happening in the house.

So she stood in the kitchen she had so lovingly designed, and where she and Olga had sat every night reviewing the day before retiring to bed. She began to whimper, and knowing it was a whimper no one else could hear made it worse.

What had she done to deserve this? She'd tried to forge a loving spiritual community of women. Then another thought struck her. Perhaps she hadn't, perhaps she had only played a walk on part in a plan devised by something else.

Nothing could be worse than this. If she was mad she wanted to die. If she was sane and this was happening and the rules that governed the world were so changed, she wanted to die even more.

She walked across to the work surface adjacent to the vast top of the range Aga. From the top draw she removed the razor-sharp filleting knife, tucked it into the sleeve of her cardigan and headed for her room, as Claire had instructed.

Chapter 7: Quantum Weirdness

Giles put Norman in charge of terrestrial archaeological duties while he headed for Lindow with Steve. In his conversation with Norman, Giles didn't really concentrate, his mind was on other things. He didn't respond when Norman, trying to give feedback on the inner city development rescue dig, said, "The work on the line of the new transport route is far more complicated than we'd expected. There are areas of burials all over the place under there, none of them documented or attached to any identifiable buildings or dating context."

After waiting in vain for a reply, Norman added, "There are far more bodies than there reasonably should be and the really strange thing is that preliminary dating suggests a huge discrepancy in the time periods. Something must have infected our dating process because what I've been looking at suggests remains way too old for a Manchester context; and it's not just isolated examples throwing us out, there are large quantities of…"

Giles wasn't listening, had he been he might have grasped the significance. Instead, he cut him off, just mumbling, "Yeah, Ok, good, take care of it will you, Norman."

With that he headed for the door his mind fixed on whatever the shifting Moss of Lindow had in store for him. In the car en-route, Steve, to Giles's surprise, talked a little without having to be prompted. There was something different in his voice, which Giles found difficult to place.

"We need to have a plan for this, Gi. Start with a trial trench through the section where the bone is most thickly scattered and where the churn and movement is greatest. It's not archaeology as we know it, so it's not as if we'll damage permanent features or the stratigraphy."

Giles was about to ask him why, but Steve's answer pre-empted him.

"At least that way, with any luck, we'll eventually find some type of ground zero, be able to separate what should be there from what shouldn't; give us a chance to establish a basis for stratigraphy. It worked on Samos, well sort of."

Giles nodded. Steve was the better archaeologist. He was thinking how to manage things when Jan joined them later to examine the bones. He hadn't wanted to involve her; she'd been pretty flaky since her return to work and subsequent expulsion from Claire's 'coven'. But he needed a specialist and, unfortunately for Jan, she was the only bone specialist apart from Rose, who he didn't want anywhere near the place. It had to be Jan.

Jan and Steve had last seen each other when he'd jilted her and run off to Samos. He was worried about Jan and her reaction to the changes in her former lover. His mind was circling round the problems he'd have to manage when, without noticing it, they'd arrived.

Anderson greeted them on the Moss, looking drawn and pale but relatively cheerful. The reason why was evident from his first words.

"This is all yours now, nothing here for us thank God, so we're off."

Steve asked, "What's that noise?"

Anderson pointed towards the area demarcated by police tape.

"That'll be only too clear to you when you get over there. It's getting worse, they don't seem to like us very much."

Giles looked across to the thin white saplings waving their branches in the still air. Anderson was right, the sound was louder, whining and insistent like the sound pulses used in some public areas to deter teenagers whose ears were sensitive to the frequency. This frequency made teenagers of everyone.

Anderson's expression changed, became concerned. "Be careful of those saplings, they don't like being touched and have a nasty sting."

Giles asked, "Why didn't you cut them down?"

Anderson's face formed a moue of distaste. "Oh, don't you worry, we certainly tried. Just the once mind, not after that, no one wanted to try again." He shook his head as if trying to shake out the memories before adding, "Don't let them touch you or get into your head."

Giles had tried to avoid looking at them. Now he gave them his full attention. They seemed taller and the thin, bare branches were certainly longer, twisting and turning in perpetual motion.

Anderson turned to leave, saying over his shoulder, "Remember, usual rules apply. Find anything you suspect is related to a modern crime, anything suspicious like that, then you stop digging and report in. We're off. Watch yourselves."

Steve was staring at the trees as if they were familiar to him; then he shrugged his shoulders and carefully picked his way between them. Giles watched as Anderson walked off the Moss towards the squad cars. The place already felt more hostile and desolate for his absence. Giles felt the first stirrings of fear. He thought he heard Steve mutter,

"Just like Samos, an impossible assemblage with no context."

The nine words, constituting Steve's initial appraisal of the site, brought Giles back to his senses and he remembered what a fine archaeologist Steve was when he bothered to put his mind to it.

Cutting the sample trench felt like grave robbing. The route Steve selected followed a line whose surface appeared to be strewn with the contents of a series of remains from ransacked funerary structures. Giles was surprised the timbers from the Bronze Age hut he'd noticed on his previous visit had vanished, to be replaced by a scatter of grave goods complete with ritual and fetish objects.

This surprised him less than it should have done, nothing surprised him much now, but he felt he owed Steve an explanation. He prepared himself to project his voice above the chatter of the saplings but, as he opened his mouth, Steve pre-empted him.

"Save your breath, Gi. I'm more familiar with this stuff than you're ever going to be so just be grateful for your good fortune."

Giles was about to question the validity of this, but Steve had taken over the leadership, as he tended to do on excavations, and for this at least he was grateful.

"We're going to start the trench by the Neolithic flint and Grooved Ware potsherds. There may be a little context there and we'll end by that mix of feather and bone. And yes, before you say it, I do realise that the feathers can't have survived in that condition and therefore can't be real."

He didn't wait for an answer and set to, marking out the proposed line of the trench. They worked pretty much in silence for the next three hours. This was a silence determined not only by their understandably laconic disposition, but by something more compelling.

On their patch of Moss, other than the sibilant whining of the saplings, there was no sound, no bird song, not even a faint hum of traffic from the main road into Altrincham a few hundred metres away beyond the hedge line. Even the immediate noise of their digging seemed to be sucked straight down into the damp peat.

Not that the gruesome and apparently random finds they collected lended themselves to conversation. These they tagged and bagged methodically, overcoming their distaste in the process. As they moved systematically through the layers, it became increasingly apparent there was no meaningful stratigraphy to study. This stuff hadn't been formed the way archaeological levels and deposits were. On normal digs, the evidence didn't shift about and reconfigure itself. At times it seemed the diggers were more static than the dig.

Shortly after noon, Steve established the floor of the peat, reality's ground zero.

Giles was tired, his spirits sapped. "Time for a break," he said.

They clambered out of the trench and lit cigarettes. Steve said what they were both thinking,

"Same as Samos, an impossible jumble of artefacts, a fucking cosmic joke."

"Talking about cosmic, you know anything about quantum theory, Steve?"

"What, Gi? You feeling alright?"

"No, listen, I mean it. I've been thinking about this stuff day and night for weeks."

"Ok, better get it off your chest; I'll give you as long as it takes to smoke this."

"It's complicated, but basically it sort of says that if the universe is infinite then eventually every possible combination of things gets exhausted."

"So?"

"Well, after that, because it's infinite and there are no more possible combinations, then everything just gets repeated."

"You're beginning to sound like Vassilis now."

At the mention of Vassilis, a picture of total misery covered Steve's face; Giles remembered how Steve had loved Vassilis's daughter. Giles ignored it and pressed on.

"Think about it, Steve, that means there are infinite versions of what we're doing here spread across the universe. Time and reality are meaningless, so what's happening to us could come from anywhere. Maybe somewhere where the rules are different, maybe all the versions of us have got muddled up."

"Giles, I know this stuff upsets you, but all this gets us nowhere."

"Steve, listen; that's what some physicists say too, they say it can't be infinite, but the only way to stop it being infinite is to have other universes, perhaps rolled up inside each other or stretched out next to each other like shirts in a wardrobe."

Steve held up his almost-smoked-down cigarette.

"Thirty seconds, Gi."

"Ok, so if there are other universes and pretty much the same things go on there, maybe they bleed into one another, infect or crossbreed."

He looked at Steve expecting sarcasm, but was surprised to see he was listening.

"And if that's true then a quantum glitch could be as real as what we see every day, except that normally the conditions for us to see it aren't right."

"So you're suggesting this comes from somewhere else?"

"No, I'm saying that according to some theories, a collection like this turning up may not be frequent but it's inevitable somewhere in the multiverse or infinite universe."

Steve ground out the glowing butt in the peat, but instead of killing the conversation as threatened, he took a deep breath as if it was taking a great effort and said, "In a way you're sort of right. Look, I've seen things you've haven't, Gi. The things I think we're dealing with understand how the universe works better than us, they can apply the laws. Us, we're little more than Palaeolithic cave painters trying to influence our environment. We can beseech and invoke but we can't do."

It was the longest utterance he'd made since his resurrection. Giles asked him the question he both wanted and feared an answer to.

"But why? Because this isn't just quantum weirdness is it, Steve?"

Steve gave no reply, just turned back towards the trench. Giles grabbed him by the arm and turned him back round to face him. He was easy to turn, as if there was no weight or heft to his body. For a moment, Giles thought he might come apart.

There was a moment's silence and in that silence Giles heard the chatter of the saplings becoming more urgent and, as much to drown out the impure noise as to elicit Steve's answer, he asked, "Steve, talk to me, I can't stand this and I know that you know much more than you're saying."

Steve said nothing but stared into Giles's eyes. In that gaze, Giles saw more than just the normal suffering. He also saw pity.

"So, just answer me this, because it's driving me crazy. Last question, I promise. Why is this all happening here and nowhere else?"

"Because I think whatever was haunting us in Greece is now here."

"How?"

"Maybe we brought it back."

"What?"

"I don't know, Giles, but from what I've learnt, going to Samos wasn't a lifestyle choice."

He registered the blank stare Giles directed at him.

"We didn't choose to go, we were sent, and it was no accident. All of us mixed up in what happened over there were directed by something."

Steve paused, then muttered to himself as much as to Giles, "But what was it that sent us and why?"

There was a silence. Giles didn't know how to fill it, he didn't have to.

"Whatever it was, Gi, I think the moment for that purpose has come. This stuff we're shifting through now is a symptom of the disorder."

He bent down to pick up his trowel. Giles thought he'd finished but there was a last, almost whispered, message.

"And I'm so sorry because it's worse for you, Gi, you still have a life."

Talked out, Steve turned back to the trench.

Giles was trying to work out what Steve's last phrase meant when he saw the diminutive, hooded figure of Jan picking her way across the claggy surface of the moss towards them. Jan, the kindest and most conscientious member of the unit. An aura of fragility and constant sorrow accompanied her and Giles felt a spasm of guilt.

****

Jan recognised the saplings as soon as she saw them, long before she could hear them. Had she heard their noise at that moment she'd have recognised that too. But it wasn't the unnatural trees or having to face whatever Steve had become that was freaking her, there was something else. Something she'd have to tell them before joining the excavation, which rendered seeing Steve again a matter of little, or no, importance. It was something she'd only just begun to dare admit to herself. Something that made her hope she was mad rather than correct.

Before she joined in the excavation she'd have to tell them about the entity which kept her from sleeping. The entity she believed had drawn her to the women's house for a purpose and then driven her away.

Chapter 8: Jan's Tale

It came tumbling out in a gabbled torrent, a cascade of fear, garbled and unhinged. But she'd chosen the right man as confessor; Ed Joyce had been where she'd been and worse, added to which he was a gentle, compassionate man. So he let her spew it out; all the anxiety, fear and loathing, there'd be time to digest and make sense later.

There came a pause and he passed her the – by now tepid – mug of tea and a tissue from the box he kept on his desk. They were in his study, appropriate really as it was here that Ed had first encountered the terror of Heatly-Smythe's journal. She took the tea and the tissue, wiped her nose and eyes then took a sip. She was still terrified but she'd found someone she could share this with, she'd taken the first step and it gave her a semblance of control.

What she couldn't share was where the idea to talk to Ed came from, that way lay madness. A dream, but it hadn't felt like a dream, and she'd been wide-awake sitting on a bus when she'd dreamt it. It had been more like a conversation.

She couldn't share it, couldn't even think about it in case it set her mind drifting again. Once it started to drift these things wormed their way into it. A man had sat next to her, she'd smiled because she thought she recognised him and hadn't ever expected to see him again because, because...

And that's when the horror gripped her; because he was dead. She looked again to be sure and during that terror-filled glance he spoke one sentence.

"Talk to Ed Joyce, go to St George Skendleby, Jan."

She'd rubbed her eyes to focus and when she opened them the seat was empty. It had all happened in a flash but the words stayed with her. She was tired and strung out but this act of necromancy felt horribly real and she believed in it.

Two stops later she got off, still shaking, and walked the few hundred yards to her new digs. She'd been staying there and sleeping on the sofa since her flight from the house. She didn't mind that, it stopped her being alone and company seemed to keep the horrors away.

She was pleasantly surprised the flat wasn't empty, both Lisa and Olga were in the kitchen. Olga made her a coffee, Lisa smiled then looked away so while she waited she let her eyes roam round the kitchen. The walls were mainly bare; Olga was a minimalist and Lisa? Well Lisa was a blank.

One thing was different, though, stuck out like a sore thumb. The whiteboard where Lisa wrote down her appointments had changed. Its usual appearance: acres of blank white interspersed with occasional black lettering had been augmented.

In the bottom left corner, Lisa had drawn a flower, then added at a later date, it seemed to Jan, the outlines of a man's head above it. Connecting the flower to the head she had drawn some green shoots stretching up from the flower to take root on the neck then curl their way up the face towards the shaggy hair. The face reminded her of Steve.

Olga placed the mug of coffee on the table in front of her. She sat talking with them, biding her time wondering at what a strange trinity they were. After twenty minutes, Lisa, who'd said nothing, only smiled and nodded, as if on an impulse, got up and grabbed her coat.

"I'm going to see Jim, I won't be long."

The moment she left Jan poured out her experience to Olga and as a consequence of her advice, that same evening she found herself inside the rectory of St George Skendleby with Ed. If both Olga and the dead man recommended it she had no choice and anyway, from what she remembered of Ed Joyce, beneath the pompous exterior beat a kind heart. She was right about the kindness and the pompous facade had long since been swept away. He'd made her tea, sat her in the armchair.

"You can talk to me, Jan, you can trust me, I won't judge but I think I might understand."

She believed him and the next minutes of tearful burbling were strangely cathartic. It felt like being a child again, taking all your troubles and transferring them to an adult. She'd needed that.

"So, you believe that whatever guided your steps towards that house was entirely different from whatever it was that sent Rose and Leonie there?"

With this he'd got to the heart of it, and Jan wondered why it'd taken her so long to understand. Right from her first day in the house there'd been something different about Rose and Leonie, she'd put it down to a consequence of their Skendleby experience. But it wasn't; they'd stayed in the house and succumbed to the evil seduction. Rose, in particular, had flourished like a poisonous hothouse flower. The effects on Leonie had been alarming.

"But how were we summoned in the first place, what's happening?"

She felt the tears, never far away these days, welling up.

"And now I'm seeing the dead, please, Ed, what's happening to me?"

He didn't answer. She was about to ask again but something had changed. The room felt unnaturally still, like during the swollen silence preceding a summer storm. Not merely silence, the complete absence of sound. She realised even the clock had ceased ticking. Outside the window, in the spring breeze, nothing moved. In the pregnant, permanent moment she awaited the inevitable. Ed was frozen, suspended in time, the teacup halfway to his lips. The dust motes caught in the shaft of sunlight laid static, their dance suspended.

Then it came, dropped into the void, softly spoken, nasal and slightly slurred as it had been when he was alive and they'd mocked him behind his back. There was a thin white gash across his throat which opened and closed as he spoke.

"Don't worry, Jan, nearly done now; tell him what you saw in the house, he'll understand, the crow voices inside him will help. Tell him to meet me in the Chop House in Blackpool Fold, Tuesday evening at six."

The room appeared to be floating, she felt the onset of a sick headache. The voice again, faint this time as if projected across a vast distance.

"Hope for your sake this is the last time we meet because if you see me again it means..."

Distance and sonic distortion swept away whatever last message had been intended. But a voice was speaking.

"I don't know, Jan; we are playing our part in a game with different rules to the ones we know."

She realised it was Ed answering the question she'd asked what seemed aeons before on the shores of a different galaxy. She let Ed speak, giving her space to recover her senses. After an indeterminate time she realised the room was silent again and that Ed was standing over her chair shaking her gently.

"Jan, are you ok? I think you fainted or experienced some mild seizure. Mary is making up the guest room and I wonder if you'd like me to call the doctor?"

"No, no doctor, I just felt a little dizzy."

And she did, more than a little, the room was spinning but beyond that she realised she was desperately tired and to sleep somewhere safe and protected was hugely appealing. Also, she no longer had the energy to talk, she was finished for the day, whatever she'd interacted with had sucked all the energy out of her. She was even too tired for fear now.

Ed, who would have been surprised and gratified to know he made her feel safe, helped her to her feet and with Mary's aid took her upstairs to the bedroom they'd reserved for the child who'd never arrived. Ed wondered what had impelled Mary to choose this rather than one of the guest bedrooms.

He left Mary to put Jan to bed and wandered back down and into the rectory's huge drawing room, where he sat down to wait for his wife.

****

Sunlight through the window and a late breakfast greeted Jan the next morning. In the warmth of the sunshine reflecting off the polished wood of the table it seemed a brighter, safer world. But that was an illusion. She sat across the table from Ed, trying to eat toast and honey, not with a great deal of success. There seemed more honey on her fingers than in her mouth and the sticky hands made her feel childlike. She took a sip of tea in an attempt to stall for time before answering Ed's question.

"How were you persuaded to join the community at the house, Jan?"

"At first..."

She faltered, took another sip, tried again.

"At first I thought the letter was from Steve, even though it wasn't signed and the writing was different; but it wasn't. I'd been tricked, lured."

She tried to choke back her sobs; failed.

"Take your time, Jan, we're in no hurry."

They sat in the sunny silence of a kitchen disturbed only by occasional sniffles. After some moments, he asked, "If not Steve, who do you think it was that wrote the note, you said it came from Greece."

"It had a Greek postmark but it wasn't from Steve, but I'm certain I was made to think it was."

"Do you know anyone else over there?"

"No, no, but I think the postmark was a trick."

"A trick?"

"Not that it mattered. I contacted Leonie like the letter suggested, made me feel less lonely and she got me into the house. At first I thought I was safe, thought I'd found what I was looking for. What a little fool I've become."

"You're nobody's fool, Jan, and if I'm sure of anything I'm sure your part in this will be for the good."

"So why lure me to the house? You've no idea what goes on there."

"No, but you can tell me when you're ready. First, try to tell me why you think it was a trick and if it didn't come from the women, and Olga's sure it didn't and it wasn't Steve, then who was it from?"

"I think now, and I wish I didn't, that it was from the same person who sent me here, the person who wants to meet you, Ed, a person I knew."

A year ago, Ed would have been flustered by a strange mixture of fear and social embarrassment. Now he merely enquired gently, "And what's so wrong with that, Jan?"

"Because he's dead, was dead long before the letter was written. Dead, yet he gave me a message for you; he wants you to meet him in the Chop House in Blackpool Fold. I don't think you should go."

A cloud must have crossed the sun because the sunlight brightening the table was replaced by shadows. Not knowing how to continue, Ed got up and began to clear away the dishes.

****

Later, after Ed had called Olga to research Jan's mental state and been told, in no uncertain manner, to follow his instincts, the conversation was reconvened but didn't commence as he'd anticipated.

Towards evening, after Ed finished work for the day, he stared out of the study window across the graveyard thinking about one of his older parishioners. She was an elderly woman, lonely, almost housebound and he suspected slipping into dementia. He was contemplating contacting her son, now based in London, whose visits had become increasingly infrequent, when Jan slipped into the room.

"Sorry about dropping that on you, Ed. I'll tell you the rest if you're ready for it."

He was as ready as he'd ever be so motioned her to the armchair. To his surprise, she joined him at the window, saying, "I see things now, things I never used to. It started in the house, I thought it would stop when I left, but I can't lose it."

He was sufficiently experienced not to interrupt.

"Things I'm sure you can sense but not see. I see things differently. Let me tell you what I see from this window."

Ed wasn't particularly sure he liked the sound of this but he sensed the offer wasn't optional so he watched and listened.

"The church and this house are safe enough, maybe your god sees to that, but the rest is dangerous and ancient. It answers to different powers, plays by different rules. You take a risk when you cross that ground, Ed, and there are evil things at the margins; peripheral, shifting, unknowable things. The women's house is like that but far, far worse."

This was far too close to his own experience for him to ignore and it took him off guard. So in spite of himself, he responded, "Not the type of observation one expects from an archaeologist."

"From a Skendleby archaeologist it should be."

Neither wanted to look out of the window now and almost as one they turned towards the chairs. Behind them, a red sun sank below the churchyard wall.

"So, what do you need to tell me, Jan?"

"That house isn't what it seems and the presence of those women is a temporary disguise. Soon their purpose will be done. The house exists in several dimensions and in all of them it's bad."

"Well, perhaps now that Claire is there it might..."

She cut him off, most unlike Jan.

"Claire? Let me ask you this. Have you seen that necklace Claire wears?"

"Yes, I think she brought it back from Samos."

"What would you say it's made of?"

"Some type of ivory, not very politically correct perhaps..."

He faltered to a halt because Jan was laughing, not a nice laugh.

"I used to think that too, Ed, but then I began to see differently."

He didn't reply, the room seemed to grow colder as the last glimpses of exsanguinated sunlight faded and darkness crept slowly up the walls. He knew something terrible was coming. Jan looked waif-like and diminished, lost in the depths of the winged armchair.

"Then, after I'd been there a short time, on the day Lisa arrived, we were in the 'Gathering' room before dinner, Claire walked in with the necklace. That's when I saw the difference."

For a moment he thought she'd finished and that was all she was going to say. But she'd been steeling herself.

"The necklace wasn't bright and shiny anymore, it was dark and stained. Sections of it looked ancient, but the most striking thing was that there were two links missing, or, as I now believe, two links that hadn't yet been added. I don't know what the others saw but..."

Ed couldn't see her face in the twilight shadows, but he suspected she was crying.

"But as I watched, the separate links began to move and flex and they weren't ivory, Ed, they were sections of fingers, jointed sections; flexing at the joint. Alive, they were alive."

Now she was sobbing, he stood up to comfort her but she waved him away.

"No, let me finish. That's why when Claire asked Rose, Leonie and me to look for something beneath the cellar floor I refused, because I knew what it was she wanted.

They found it and it freaked them. Now there's only one link to find and when she has it..."

She couldn't speak any more, just sat sobbing and he sat watching. Then when the dark was fully-grown he took her hand and led her into the kitchen, she didn't resist. Mary made tea then sat hugging her as Ed added slugs of whisky.

Sometime later, when she was calmer and Mary had left the room, Jan said, "That's why I have to join the excavation at Lindow because there's a connection."

"I don't think you should go, Jan."

"And I don't think you should go to meet the dead man in the Chop House. But I know you will."

Chapter 9: The Gathering of the Dead

She was of course correct and just before six on Tuesday, Ed found himself descending the curving stairway into the basement, which housed the timeworn Chop House. He threaded his way through the press of after-work drinkers thronging the bar, to the dark passage leading to the dining area. Here it was surprisingly quiet, in fact the restaurant was deserted. He caught a fleeting glimpse of a dark clad waiter who appeared to wave him toward a table in the far corner set for two.

Ed was about to question the man regarding the whereabouts of his host when he realised he was alone. He sat down to wait in the silence, his heart beating faster than he felt was good for it. The convivial noise from the bar was so faint that it sounded immensely distant. Then from behind a curtain concealing a passageway, a tall, dignified man appeared bearing a tray upon which lay a plate and a half bottle of wine.

"Complements of your friend, Sir, I think you will find this most satisfactory."

He indicated the wine

"A seventy nine Chambertin, quite rare these days, it should accompany the steak and kidney pudding rather well."

The man had an old-fashioned air about him and spoke with a vague Eastern European accent, which Ed couldn't place. As he was pouring the wine, Ed asked him, "When will the person who so kindly ordered this be here? Is he not eating?"

The waiter looked amused.

"Eating, Sir? Very droll. I'm sure he will materialise at some stage."

With that he turned and disappeared behind the curtain. Ed sniffed the wine, it was one he'd never expected to taste being far beyond his stipend. He sat for a moment sipping and looking round, and then, as there was nothing else to do, he began to eat.

The first cut into the plate-sized pudding released a stream of gravy and an aroma that confirmed Ed in his surmise that he was about to enjoy the comfort dish of choice from his childhood. It was served with fat chips, mushy peas and a small jug of jus; a gastronomic twist to a working-class feast.

About halfway through the steak and kidney and towards the end of the wine, he became aware of a prickling sensation on the hairs at the back of his neck. Something told him he was not alone and with a sense of trepidation, all appetite vanished, he turned around.

Lurking in the shadows behind his left shoulder stood a gaunt figure. Ed was wondering where the shadows had come from, he was pretty sure they hadn't been there a few minutes ago, when he realised there was something far stranger to fear. His new companion had a black fedora pulled down over his forehead and a large scarf resembling a bandage enveloped his neck. Between these two sat a papery-white face.

"Listen carefully, there is little time."

A scratchy, thin voice. The words forced out as if the vocal chords were unused to being used. Ed didn't like it, it unsettled him and he heard his own voice reply foolishly, "Aren't you eating anything?"

It appeared the vacuous nature of his response came close to amusing his spectral interlocutor, who said, "Eating, I used to. Let's say I ate earlier."

A hand appeared on the table at Ed's side, white skinned almost translucent, no flesh, dry, fraying skin over bone. Looking up at the man's face, Ed noticed that the bandage round the throat was stained, as if what it contained was leaking.

Ed stammered, his voice little more than a whisper. "What are you?"

After an indeterminate pause, by way of a partial explanation, it replied, "I've been travelling, searching, and the last place a living person could recognise would be Nice. That should tell you who I was, if not what I've become."

Ed didn't want to know who he was or where he'd been, he just wanted him to go back there and leave him alone. He was about to get up when he experienced a fluttering inside his chest. It felt like something was stretching its wings deep within him. He remembered the crows and what they'd told him.

A harsh, cawing voice in his mind told him to remain seated. He steeled himself for what was to come. He didn't have long to wait. From somewhere beneath the stained bandage covering the throat of his terrible host there came a dry cough, like the fluttering of dead leaves, and then, "Go to the Portico library, it will be open, ask for volume forty nine of the Manchester Oil and Coal Exchange transactions, 1887. They will have it ready for you. I pray that what it contains grants you more luck than it did me."

"And what, what should I..."

But he was alone, sitting by half a plateful of cold food and an empty half bottle of wine. Then the waiter was back.

"Fortunate for you that you managed to drink the wine before your friend arrived, wouldn't you say, Sir?"

Ed sat speechless.

"Better go now, you need to get to the Portico and this chamber is about to close. Don't worry, the bill's been taken care of."

Ed didn't need further prompting, he was on his feet lurching for the exit. Once back in the bar area it was another world, noisy but safe.

Outside, the weather had changed. The air felt fresh and raw and a fierce spring shower was beating down as he dodged between patches of shelter towards the Portico library. Crossing a major road junction, temporarily – as were so many major arteries of the Northern Powerhouse, closed by major construction works for the new Cross Rail – he saw a police cordon where he'd read in the local paper archaeologists were operating.

More police vans were approaching, blue lights flashing, sirens hooting. Then he was at the door leading up to the Portico. He rang the bell, the door swung open and he began to climb the creaking flight of stairs, his feet leaving footprints in the dust.

Despite the Portico being a membership library and Ed not being a member, no one challenged his entry.

A woman of indeterminate middle age, drinking from a paper mug of Costa coffee, looked up and as he began to stammer out his request. She handed him a thick volume bound in a faded leather cover. "You can read it over there."

She indicated the far end of the room beyond the shelves, where a series of antique winged armchairs were scattered around some ancient looking tables. He'd been here before to a public art exhibition and been impressed by the atmosphere of an old London club, now it didn't feel so appealing.

He picked a chair in the corner, sank into the upholstery and looked at the book. It was a bound collection of foxed and faded papers detailing the transactions of a long-dead trading room. He didn't know where to start. Until, that is, an envelope slipped out as he was flicking through the pages. He knew who it was intended for and managed to catch it before it slipped off his knees and onto the floor.

For a moment, he sat hesitating over opening the flap. He didn't want to read it in here alone, didn't want to read it anywhere in the city. If he was going to read it, it would be inside his own church. He looked around, there was no one about; the librarian was nowhere to be seen. Slipping the envelope into his jacket pocket, he dropped the book on the table and left the library as quickly as he could short of running.

Outside, more police vehicles were gathering and the cordoned off area had been expanded. He rushed blindly past and was brought to his senses by a sharp jolt.

"Look where you're going."

Ed looked up and saw he'd blundered into a man wearing a hard hat and some type of overall. They recognised each other at the same time, but Ed's mind, occupied as it was, couldn't place where.

"Rev Joyce, isn't it? I gave a talk on the Skendleby excavations in your church hall, remember?"

"Yes, yes of course."

Ed remembered the archaeologist but was searching for the name.

"Sorry I blundered into you, should have been looking where I was going. It's er...?"

"Norman."

"Yes, of course, Norman."

They shook hands. Ed, now he was concentrating again, realised that the archaeologist was shaken up by more than their collision. He asked, "What's going on? Aren't you meant to be investigating somewhere round here before the Cross Rail gets built?"

"Not any more, been shut down."

Ed wanted to get away but the man looked so disheartened that he felt he should maybe stay and talk a while. He asked, "Why? Won't that delay things further? What did you find down there?"

"Bones."

"An old burial, I don't remember there ever having been a church here."

"There wasn't."

"I don't understand."

"Neither do I."

He pointed towards the police beyond the cordon.

"Neither do they. At first we thought it might be a plague pit, or some 19th century graveyard overspill, but..."

He left the words hanging. Ed was now genuinely interested. More than that, he dreaded what was about to be revealed, this was no coincidence.

"So, what's your best guess?"

"Haven't got one, not now. They stretch out over all that area and probably under where we're standing, packed together, huddled up – thousands of them. They shouldn't be here, not in these numbers."

"I see, but why the police?"

"They're not all old."

He started to laugh, not a humorous laugh, the nervous laugh of someone stretched to the limit.

"And they're not all young."

He'd stopped laughing now.

Ed said, "Sorry, you've lost me."

"We've lost everyone. What's happening here isn't right, isn't credible, I tried to tell Giles."

He stumbled to a halt then tried again. "A huge concentration of human bones and we've not even determined the limit of them. Some very old, before Homo sapiens from the look of them, others spread right through the ages, no context, impossible really."

Ed prompted him, "And the Police?"

"I had to contact them when we found new bones, contemporary, modern. Like a nightmare, no logical cause, had to call the police."

Ed felt the man's fear like an infection. He knew the envelope in his jacket was part of this. He needed to get home and was about to make his excuses when Norman said, "They've been placed there, it's quite deliberate. The dead are gathering, all across the ages they're gathering, and the police are welcome to them."

With that he was gone. The light had gone too. Twilight faded to a deeper grey, rain began to fall again. Avoiding the cordoned off area, Ed scurried back to his car along the side streets. Passing the police headquarters, whose brutalist, greying concrete contrasted so badly with the Neo Gothic of the Town Hall, but fitted so well with the sky, he saw a single window illuminated on the third floor.

****

The room the light was illuminating belonged to the chief. He was with Viv, Theodrakis and Anderson. They'd been there since the first reports about the bones had come in some hours ago. The chief was floundering, searching for an explanation to the inexplicable.

"How do you know it's not some type of bloody illusion like on telly? You know the Great Magico and all them others who trick people every day. If they can hoodwink the whole bloody nation on TV then it shouldn't be too hard to trick a few coppers and archaeologists, should it? Bound not to be long before criminals started using it."

He spluttered to a halt and looked around for support, there was none, not even from Anderson, whose expression showed his deep displeasure at being included in this parley. No one spoke, the chief read the runes the lack of response implied and sunk his head into his hands. They sat in silence, aware of the rain outside beating on the windows. When he next spoke it was in a softer tone. "I could have taken early retirement, become a non-executive director for security companies. Wish I had now. But I stayed on, wanted to see an end to the murders, make the city safe again."

There wasn't really an appropriate reply to this and no one tried to find one. Silence.

"Maybe it's not too late; maybe they'll still let me take my pension."

Anderson had never seen him like this.

Viv said, "That's the last thing you should do, Chief. We need you, Manchester needs you."

It sounded sycophantic but she meant it, without his support they were lost. It seemed to mollify him to an extent. He lifted his head and said, "Thanks for that, lass, DI Campbell that is."

He paused, maybe expecting a rebuke for patronising sexism, none was forthcoming so he pressed on. "Ok, well, before I go any further I'd like each of you to give me an opinion, brief mind, on what this is and what we do. Perhaps you'd like to begin, Colonel Theodrakis."

Theodrakis was unprepared, having been pretty certain that he'd be either kept until last or left out altogether.

"I'm not sure, perhaps it is all illusion but a much more dangerous one than the type you imagine, a type that none of us can imagine. But that doesn't help us, all I can say is it's part of the same thing I saw on Samos. There's a terrible purpose to this and it terrifies me."

They sat waiting for more. There wasn't any.

The chief asked, "DI Campbell?"

"I agree with Colonel Theodrakis, don't know what it is, but..."

She paused, as if uncertain what to say next, then pressed on. "But I think we have to assume that the women's house at Skendleby is part of it and, as we've unfinished business there, that's the place to start."

"What about the bloody bones across the road?"

"Obviously, when the evidence comes in we'll examine it, but you asked me for my opinion chief and I agree with Colonel Theodrakis that they're a symptom of something and the only something we've got is in Skendleby."

He sighed wearily, turning to Anderson. "Jimmy?"

"Something's going on but I can't buy into all this horror film stuff."

Theodrakis cut him off. "Where do you think those trees at Lindow and Skendleby Mound came from then, Jimmy? Remember how they made you feel?"

There was no rejoinder. Having got his feelings off his chest and let them have their say, the chief moved onto the thing he'd brought them in here to tell them. Not before asking his PA to bring in a tray of tea and chocolate biscuits. Once they were served he began. "Now, you may not like this, but it's come down from the very top, political like."

He paused to look at Theodrakis before adding, "Greek as well as British, I'm afraid, Colonel. I don't have access to their intelligence but this business has some very senior people across the world very worried."

He looked across at his audience for a reaction, but they kept their heads down, so after clearing his throat he continued.

"Apparently, Skendleby and Samos aren't the only places affected by these outbreaks. There have been others which they've managed to keep hushed up."

He paused before the bombshell.

"So, because – through bloody bad luck it seems – we've managed to bloody accumulate all the bloody experience of this type of thing up here, I've been instructed to set up a squad to investigate what they describe in their stuck-up, clever-bugger way as 'incidents that transcend the a priori.'"

He took a sip from his mug before saying, "So, that would be you three. Another biscuit anyone?"

Chapter 10: Church, Hall and Hell

The wind in the rafters of St George Skendleby caused the ancient timbers to creak like a ship in a gale. Ed sat in a chair, in the apse lit by the multi-coloured slanting sunlight streaming through the stained glass window. On his lap lay a small collection of timeworn papers with a more modern looking note atop them.

It was the following day. Ed hadn't wanted to read whatever it was these papers would tell him at night. Soon it would be twilight and he didn't want to be caught in the church with these tainted papers when the hour between dog and wolf arrived, so he could no longer procrastinate. It wasn't only dread of the documents tormenting him, though.

He wasn't alone, hadn't felt alone since the moment the crow flexed its wings deep inside his chest. Neither was the crow the only thing haunting him, there were others. Not crow, but nor were they human. They weren't present in their corporeal state, of course – that would be impossible – but all the same he could see them. Well, not see exactly, more sense them or capture a fleeting image from the corner of his eye.

Even here in the spiritual safety of his church, he felt their presence. How could they be here? Did this mean his church was defiled or that it sanctioned their manifestation? And if it did, what did that mean? Neither of these currently vital questions had been raised during his training as a priest, nor in his theological studies at Cambridge.

He thought he knew who they were. Two, oh dear, God help me, he recognised: Marcus Fox and the creature from the Chop House, who he now thought was the murdered archivist, Tim Thompson. The others? Heatly Smythe he was pretty sure of, his haunted predecessor from the 17th century and the most persistent of all, he thought, must be Dr John Dee. There were others, more insubstantial, decrepit and mouldy, infinitely older.

What were these revenants here for? He knew the question was dissembling and dishonest because he knew the answer. They were urging him to complete the task they'd failed. "Better get to it, Ed," he told himself and with trepidation settled to his studies.

First, the modern note, scrawled in some muddy reddish substance that Ed didn't wish to identify.

"Follow this trail, pray for my soul, God protect you from them."

That was all, disturbed and manic, hardly an inducement to peruse what followed. But he'd started so he'd finish. At first glance the other documents were, in appearance at least, less threatening. They dated from the 12th century, were written in an abbreviated form of Latin and dealt with events that occurred between the killing of William Rufus and the sudden death of his successor Henry I.

Oddly enough, Ed was familiar with two of the historians, although not with these particular extracts which, it appeared, had either not been intended for publication or had been proscribed. The first document seemed to comprise a commentary on a controversial section from the 'Historia' of Henry of Huntingdon. The text was rambling and unbalanced and claimed to substantiate a reference in the Historia that the death of William Rufus in the New Forest was the consequence of witchcraft. The most telling sentence had been underscored.

"The death was certain an act of malevolentia being practised by witches who travelled from divers parts for this one purpose. This being the first act in a greater purpose, the Lord protect us. 'Thou shalt not suffer a witch to live.'"

The second document, again a copy from a later period, was by Orderic Vitalilis, the author of 'Historia

Ecclesiastica', a work Ed was well acquainted with. Not acquainted though with the rambling and distressing diatribe that he now held in his hands. This passage had obviously never been intended for publication, but was more like a prayer for the author's soul. This passage dealt with the death of Henry 1, which it linked to the murder of William Rufus.

It spoke of a demon, something unspeakable to which the witches were subjugated. There was no doubt in the mind of Orderic he was witnessing the events leading to a satanic second coming. An apocalyptic event which had been foretold in a nightmare that afflicted the ageing King Henry. So compelling was this vision that Henry had fled to the religious house at Cluny in Burgundy, seeking spiritual protection.

The confused ramble came to a halt with an account of some monks at the abbey of Cluny whom Orderic, if he really was the author – Ed now entertained series doubts about this – believed had attempted an act of necromancy that took place in 1135, the year of Henry's death, to subdue the demon. This mission had been sanctioned, in desperation, by Peter the Venerable, Abbot of Cluny.

The third and most disturbing of the documents appeared to be original, so old and faded was it and written in a form of Latin Ed struggled to translate. He couldn't imagine what Thompson had needed to do to procure it. It purported to be authored by Robert de Torigny, the prior of Bec in Normandy. It wasn't dated but had been set down after the events it described when Robert was Abbot of Mont St Michel. It had been written when Robert was readying himself for death and needed to confess his sins.

It hinted at the events at Cluny that Orderic, or the pseudo Orderic, had described, except it ascribed the actions to a group of monks in the northern French hilltop city of Laon. The evidential section of the fragment was brief, but by the time Ed had read it he knew why it was meant for him.

When he finished reading he sat motionless as the light through the stained glass window began to whither and fade. He could never escape. Robert de Torigny had intended it for him and now it had found him. The monks at Laon had been skilled and brave, they'd known what they were doing and had stalled whatever it was that threatened them. But it was temporary and had come at a cost. He reread the last passage a final time.

"Having through cunning secured the knowledge they knew themselves in mortal and spiritual peril. For them, death must come before they were discovered. One kept a record of it with which he fled with to Quarrie Les Tombs, where he secreted that which the demon fears against a time when it might be employed. The Lord preserve him from what he has become."

Ed hesitated for a moment then reread the last passage, the message written all those years before and intended for him.

"Now you have knowledge of this, follow the trail from Laon to Cluny to Quarrie Les Tombs, there you will find those who will guide you. Use well what you find and may God protect you."

Who were 'they'? How would they help him? He felt the crows within him grow anxious. He knew without them telling that a hand had reached out from the past to bind him to this quest. History used to be an escapist pleasure, now it was life threatening and possibly worse.

Neither was St George's a refuge anymore. He remembered the finger bone he'd buried deep under the crypt following his unsuccessful exorcism of the mound and recalled the ethereal singing he heard as he scraped about in the cold earth. He remembered Jan's words about the haunted graveyard.

He used to love studying medieval historians, particularly the clerical chroniclers, it had been a form of escapism for him. No longer. In fact, nowhere and nothing was safe now, well certainly not for him. And if he was in danger, then so too were all those he loved. These he had to protect so he'd no choice, he had to follow the path laid out for him. As he reached this decision he felt the inner crow settling down to rest and the spectres dispersing into the ether.

For a time he sat in the darkening church bereft of either thought or the capacity to move. He was only brought to himself by the sound of knocking, followed by the noise of creaking hinges as the great wooden door swung open. Then a voice both loud and grating. "Hey, Joyce, you in there? I want a word with you!"

It brought him back to the world, and he was surprised the voice of Si Carver could serve as an agent of relief. Albeit temporary relief, as ideas of what Carver wanted in his church began to seethe amongst his thoughts. Before Carver could advance any closer or shout again, he was on his feet.

"I didn't expect you as a guest in church, Mr Carver."

"Yeah, well, I got reasons."

Although delivered with his habitual gracelessness, Ed noticed a lack of assurance in Carver's reply and deduced he was troubled. He felt a distinctly un-Christian frisson of satisfaction.

"Well, now you are here enjoying the shelter of God's house, perhaps you might care to enlighten me as to the nature of those reasons."

The reply had been deliberately couched in the manner that he knew Carver would most dislike and he chided himself for his childishness, but his animosity toward Carver overcame his sense of either manners or grace.

"I need a favour, need your help, tried everything else, nothing worked."

There was a childlike anxiety in Carver's tone and Ed's natural good nature reasserted itself.

"Ok, better tell me what's bothering you."

"No, not in here."

"Yes, it does seem to have grown rather dark, hang on and I'll turn the lights on."

"Nothing to do with lights, it's at the Hall, you need to come across to the Hall."

This was the last place Ed wanted to go, he prevaricated. "Well, when I return to the rectory I'll check the calendar for a mutually convenient date."

"Got to be now otherwise it'll be gone again."

Carver's distress was growing. Ed, against his better judgement, was intrigued but didn't have to wait for further elucidation.

"You need to come across now, the house needs exercising, I want you to come over and exercise it."

"Exercise it?"

"Yeah, like they do on telly, 'Celebrity Hauntings' and all that, you should know all about that, it's your job, innit?"

Exorcism, was that what he meant? Ed felt all relief at the mundane nature of this conversation and the discomfort of Carver's manner drain away. Exorcism was the last thing he wanted to think about. It was too close to what he'd been reading.

"I'm afraid the 'Service of Exorcism' is something the church rarely does these days and only then in special circumstances."

"Didn't stop you trying it on the mound though, did it? That was special enough for you."

How had Carver come to know about that? Who'd told him? Carver saw his discomfort and pressed him. "So, if you can trespass on private land in the middle of the bleedin' night to do one, where you're not wanted, you can hardly refuse your parishioner who owns that land, can you?"

Then, as Ed was struggling for a reply, amazed at Carver's description of himself as a parishioner, Carver's tone changed.

"Probably you messing about on the mound that caused my problems in the first place, don't think my friend the bishop would be too pleased by you refusing help. Not very bleedin' Christian that, is it?"

So Carver was himself again, but it wasn't the threat that influenced Ed's decision. He was no longer the weak and feeble priest he'd been eighteen months ago, nor was it a sense of compassion. Rather it was his strong and growing sense that whatever was frightening Carver in the Hall was linked to what terrified him.

"Very well, I'll just let my wife know."

"No need, I already told her when I knocked at your house."

Ed followed him out of the now almost fully-dark church, locking the door behind him. Outside the sun was no more than a smudge of red as it sunk beneath the Edge to the west. Without fully knowing what he was doing, Ed found himself quoting:

"Past touch and sight and sound.
Not further to be found.
Now hopeless underground
Falls the remorseful day."

"What's that?" Carver asked.

"Sorry, it's the sunset, I was quoting Housman."

"Never mind bleedin' Housman, it's my house you should be worried about. Come on, get going, it's nearly dark."

He was right, it was. The last rays of sun disappeared beneath the Edge and Ed followed Carver across the graveyard towards the Hall in the gathering gloom. Maybe it was because he was as uncomfortable with Ed's company as Ed was with Carver's that the walk was conducted in total silence, affording Ed time to consider the situation as they trudged down the long, bleak drive to the Hall.

The topic occupying his thoughts was the meaning of one of Carver's remarks – "otherwise it'll be gone again". What was it that would be gone again? What was spooking him so badly? He was no clearer to reaching any conclusion by the time they reached the front door.

Hesitation. For a moment they stood together outside. Inside it seemed every possible light in the Hall was shining, but Carver seemed reluctant to enter. He looked towards Ed as if to say something, but at that moment the door swung open to reveal a thick-necked and shaven-headed man bulging out of a tight T-shirt.

"Thought it were you, Boss."

Carver made no acknowledgement other than to walk in. Ed followed him. Once inside, Carver walked through to a reception room where he proceeded to pour himself a very stiff measure out of a decanter while Ed watched.

"You can have one when you're finished."

"Finished what? You need at least to tell me what I'm looking for."

"I've told you before but you never listened."

"Well, please tell me again."

"Hard to describe, sort of a black shadowy thing that's like not all there, moves about funny, like here and there at the same time."

Ed recognised it, he'd seen it, the presence in the churchyard, the entity that Heatly-Smythe had described as 'Watching'. He felt fear flood into his veins as confidence trickled out. So this was where it was.

"You alright, Joyce? You gone pale."

For the first time, Carver regained a semblance of his aggressive, bullying self.

"Where does this thing manifest itself most strongly?"

"It goes all over but mainly upstairs, seems to like upstairs."

Ed didn't need to ask more. At least he now knew where the thing had gone.

Carver said, as if ordering a servant, "So, get on with it then."

"It's not as simple as that. I'll need to look around, see what I can find. After that I can decide upon the best course of action."

Carver refilled the empty glass.

"Look round then, go where you want, only any locked doors stay locked see?"

"Yes, I see."

"You want Baz to go with you?"

Ed inferred that Baz must be the gorilla who'd opened the door.

"No, it will be more effective if I'm left alone."

"Suit yourself, your funeral, innit?"

So it was that Ed finally came to investigate the interior of Carver's iteration of Skendleby Hall. A most peculiar half an hour it was too. He found nothing specific, but had to admit that a very strange atmosphere pervaded the place. It had changed and changed for the worse since the Davenports decamped.

The building itself was wrong, and the wrong was caused by considerably more than Carver's philistine, celebrity makeover, which was by no means untypical here in the footballer belt of North Cheshire. He was sure, for instance, that 'Castle Rooney', which wasn't far away, wouldn't be infected by such a pall of gloom.

But that's all he found, nothing worse.

Until, that is, he ventured down a final short corridor on the second floor. This was the final section of his inspection and he was pretty sure he wouldn't find anything much amiss. He was trying to work out what he would say to Carver when it hit him. Not a sudden cold feeling or any of the other stuff that ghost stories tell you to expect. Rather it was a sudden wave of depression, a type of morbid pathology, a presentiment of the unimaginable. He seemed incapable of movement and his thoughts reduced to a patch of darkness. Then the image came to him in all its horror as it sidled into his passive brain. Winding sheets, corruption beyond death, and a shapeless shifting. But there was geography to it, he knew it was behind the door directly in front of him.

Behind that door it was gathering itself. He'd found it, found what Carver feared, what he feared, and he knew this as sure as he knew anything. There behind that door, shrouded and Bible-black, it waited. He wanted to move but, as in a nightmare, he couldn't. He might have been screaming, he knew his mouth was wide agape. Then he felt it move.

His bowels turned to water as the door slowly swung open.

Chapter 11: The Dark in the Afternoon

It proved to be the most unusual case conference Anderson had experienced, and he was out of his depth from the start. There was a channel of communication between Viv and Theodrakis that he'd neither expected nor could fathom. Part of him was relieved at this, the part that wanted to steer clear of Skendleby. But there was another part of him, the detective, which felt excluded.

"We need to talk to Margaret Trescothic again," said Theodrakis

"Agreed, but not while the Vanarvi woman is there," Viv replied.

"No, she won't talk if Claire's there."

"She can't prevent it, we are the Law."

Theodrakis didn't reply, just favoured her with a particular expression.

Viv backtracked. "Ok, so it'll have to be when she's not there."

"And how will we arrange that? Claire will know exactly what we're up to."

They were sitting in the glass cubicle that constituted Viv's office. It was late, Anderson was meant to be meeting PC Gemma Dixon in the City Vaults at eight and it was already way past seven. He made his sole contribution to date.

"Get Vanarvi out of the house."

Viv snapped at him. "And how do we do that, Jimmy? Ask her in advance to be out when we call."

Theodrakis cut in. "Not such a bad idea, maybe Giles could find a way to do it."

Anderson saw a faint blush cross Viv's face at the mention of Giles. "No, I don't want to involve Dr Glover."

"Well, Steve Watkins then, he won't have seen her since Samos and they seemed pretty close back then."

****

To his relief, Gemma had waited and was still at the bar when he arrived.

"Took your time, Jimmy, thought you'd stood me up."

He kissed her muttering, "Thanks, I was worried you'd have gone, can't believe what I'm having to do now."

"Ghost Busters?"

She wasn't meant to know about the new unit, but through a combination of pillow talk and in-house deduction, the joke about the new unit was circulating throughout the station building and soon a less-than-pleased chief would have it relayed to him by a lay member of the Police Commission. Anderson, who was guilty of the pillow talk, nodded in reply.

"Skendleby?" she asked.

She must have noticed the anxiety framing his expression, so added, "Look, there's a table come free over there, go and nab it while I buy you a drink."

They'd agreed that she paid half and anyway, she earned more than he did as a consequence of her singing gigs. He waited at the table until she arrived with the drink. Placing a pint on the table in front of him, she demanded, "Go on, tell, you know I'll get it out of you in the end. Better get it out of the way now, you're going to be a very busy boy later."

"Yeah, it's Skendleby, but apparently there may be other things we have to look into. It's doing my head in and there's another level that Zorba and her are on that I just don't get."

"Don't get or don't believe?"

"Don't know, you choose."

"Come on, Jimmy, have to do better than that."

"I don't know, I just don't like it, you know what it's doing to me. You're the one who wakes me up from the nightmares."

"The one about them weird trees and stuff?"

"Amongst other things, yeah. I don't know, Gemma, I hate being there, makes me feel funny, messes with my head. It's like they're trying to make me do something."

He paused to take a drink and collect his thoughts.

"And it's not only me, take a good look at the boss, see how much weight she's losing, and as for Zorba…he's already strange enough, but he's seen more of it than anyone and he lives on fear. I need to get out of this."

Gemma decided he needed to get stuff off his chest so stayed silent.

"Remember how you felt after that Skendleby incident you got the commendation for?"

She nodded.

"Well, I'm up to my head in that shit every day and I'm beginning to feel I'm being…"

"How do, Sarge; Gemma, mind if we join you?"

PCs Wolfie Smith and Slim Slater squeezed onto their table so Anderson wasn't able to tell her.

****

Giles's exasperation showed in his voice, "You're kidding me?"

"You know I would not do that, Giles, why do you ask?"

"Because Steve asked me the same thing. I thought you hadn't talked to him since he got back."

"I haven't, please tell me what you mean by Steve saying the same thing."

"He wants to see Claire, asked me to fix it up for him."

"And?"

"And I told him it was a bad idea."

"Well, I'd like you to go ahead and do it."

"I thought your advice was to keep away from her."

"In general, yes, but these are special circumstances."

"He's too fragile, it's too risky. Come and see him, Alexis, he'd love to see you and then you'd understand."

"Let me explain why he needs to see her, Giles."

It took longer to convince Giles than Theodrakis expected, and by the end he was himself worried by what he was asking of Steve. The image of the broken man he'd last seen on Samos still haunted both his dreams and his conscience and he was more frightened of Claire than he cared to admit, even to himself. Well not of Claire per se, rather of whatever had got inside her. This guilt wasn't alleviated when that night he called at Giles's house.

Steve was stretched out on the grubby, cord sofa. He looked exhausted. There seemed hardly anything left of him other than an etiolated, emaciated shell of his former self. Steve briefly raised his hand in a limp salute.

"Good to see you, Alexis, I never really got the chance to thank you for what you did back there. Giles says there's something you want to ask me."

Giles had quit the room, washed his hands of it, and left them to it. Theodrakis lowered himself gingerly into the non-too-clean armchair facing the sofa.

"Yes, and I won't even pretend it wasn't my idea or that it won't be bad for you."

"And?"

"When I asked Giles he told me you'd asked the same thing yourself about meeting Claire. May I enquire why?"

"You mean after what she did to me? The way she destroyed the only thing I ever loved, destroyed my happiness, my whole fucking life. Look at me, Alexis, just look at me, tell me what you see."

Theodrakis couldn't answer, just sat and stared, watched the track of the single tear trickling down below Steve's left eye. He too felt like crying, not only for Steve, but also for himself. He'd lost his love too, left her in Greece, a place he knew he'd never see again. Like Steve, he was changed beyond restoration and the sudden feeling of loss incapacitated him. So he sat silent and desolate, not knowing how to proceed.

Steve said softly. "It's Ok, Alexis, I'll do it, I need to see her. See if all the things I've been thinking are real. I need to do it for Alekka, for you, for Giles, for what I once was. Just tell me what you need from it."

Theodrakis couldn't, he was crying now, alone in a cold land, on a dirty chair with only the comfort of strangers to look to. He put his face in his hands. He felt a gentle pressure on his back and taking his hands from his face saw Steve had left the sofa and was standing above him gently massaging his shoulders.

"Take your time, tell me what you want."

He turned his head towards the kitchen and shouted, "Giles, bring the brandy bottle."

Moments later, Theodrakis felt a glass being pushed into his hand and took a gulp of the rough burning liquid. It brought him sufficiently to himself to stammer, "I'm sorry, so undignified, I'm sorry."

"Doesn't matter, you're with people who understand, with friends, isn't he, Gi?"

Giles nodded.

"Yeah, it's Ok, Alexis, you've joined the league of broken archaeologists. I'm sending out for pizza, you stay here, eat with us, you look like you need something. I'll go open a couple of bottles of red."

This was exactly the type of offer that would previously have nauseated his fastidious tastes, now it felt more like being home, sharing the brotherhood of the damned. Later they agreed a plan of action. Giles would fix a meeting for Steve and Claire in a public place. Then, with the wine finished, Theodrakis, overcome by exhaustion, curled up in the armchair and slept.

****

Pulling up in the grounds of the house, Viv asked Theodrakis, "You're certain she isn't here?"

"Certain. Giles texted me, he dropped Steve off at the place. She was there."

"Ok, let's go in. Jimmy, you better stay in the car and warn us if we're going to be interrupted."

Anderson nodded. Viv and Theodrakis left the car and headed for the front door. A thin, grey drizzle was seeping from the clouds. After sufficient time to become damp, the door was opened by a young woman with a mass of coarse, black hair. She appeared surprised to see them.

"DI Campbell and Colonel Theodrakis of Greater Manchester Police to see Margaret Trescothic."

"Margaret? No one of that name lives here."

"Nevertheless, we'll come in and check for ourselves."

There was no reply but the woman moved aside so they were able to walk inside. The place was filthy, neglected and smelt rank. Both found themselves wondering how the beautiful house they'd last seen had deteriorated so rapidly. Avoiding the broken glass, empty bottles and other refuse strewn across the stained carpet, they made their way to the room they remembered as the 'Gathering' room.

Here the neglect intensified. Half pulled curtains and greasy windows served to obscure much of the light. Viv sensed more than saw a small rodent scuttle across the floor. Neither she nor Theodrakis wanted to touch, let alone sit on, any of the furniture. It was like entering a space deserted for decades, and the desolation poured off it in waves. They stood close together in a small patch of grey light, bemused and wondering what to do next.

After some moments spent staring out of smeary windows into the unrelenting drizzle, there came the sound of footsteps and an instant later a stooped and greying woman shuffled into the room. Neither Theodrakis nor Viv recognised Margaret Trescothic.

"I thought I sensed a different presence in the house."

"Mrs Trescothic?"

The apparition nodded assent.

"It's DI Campbell and Colonel..."

"I know who you are, I remember. It's almost a pleasure to see you. I can see from your faces you're shocked at what you see, thank God."

"Thank God?"

"Yes, you see what I see, so I'm not mad, not alone anymore."

She began to weep. Viv, moved by her plight, reached out to take her arm. "What happened here?"

"Never mind that, there's no time, she'll be back soon."

"You mean Claire? No, she's in a meeting, and she'll be away for a couple of hours."

"You don't understand her, you need to leave here while you can, tell Olga, please tell her..."

"Tell her what, Margaret?"

The voice came from the doorway behind them. Viv and Theodrakis turned towards the sound, Margaret Trescothic fell to her knees. Claire giggled. "Viv, honey, and little Theodrakis, do you like the changes I've made? So pleased there's someone else to appreciate them. Only Margaret and I can fully admire the real nature of the place following my little makeover."

Margaret was shuffling on her knees towards the shadows in the far corner of the room, Claire pointed towards her and laughed.

"Do you like what I've done with her? She's of no further use now. I think the only reason I let her live is that she brings out the artist in me; consider her a work in progress. Still, can't be too compassionate."

She snapped her fingers. "Go back to your room, old woman, and stay there."

Margaret headed for the door. Theodrakis managed to croak, "What are you doing?"

"I'm teaching you about reality, isn't it fun?"

"Fun?"

"I wouldn't have thought you'd be surprised, you saw what Vassilis wrought every day on Samos."

"But that was illusion, a beautiful illusion, but this, this is..."

"This?"

The sound was vicious, sibilant and terrifying.

"This is reality, my reality, this is entropy. Wherever we go the law of entropy accelerates, it is our nature.

Whereas with Vassilis – that cheap, fairground huckster – that, as you said, was just illusion. Pathetic, weak illusion to confuse children. I can do that quite easily; look, I'll show you what my followers in this house see."

The room reverted to its former glory, the beautiful house Margaret and Olga had created, complete with subtle odours of spice and incense.

"I don't think you are quite ready for this, are you?"

Theodrakis took Viv's arm and began to walk her out of the room. "Come on, Viv, we have to get out of here."

"Yes, go, and don't think yourselves lucky to be out of here because what you've seen will eat into your brains. So it should, for this is where you will end up as order disintegrates."

As Theodrakis propelled them from the room, Claire touched Viv on the arm. "Next time, you won't get away so lightly. Honey, you're still part of my plans; try not to think of me when you close your eyes tonight. And you, Theodrakis, clown, puny man, how foolish to think you could trick me."

They stumbled out through the decomposing hall to the car. Anderson looked surprised to see them.

"Help me get her into the car then drive."

Once the car had made it to the road, Theodrakis snapped, "Why didn't you warn us?"

"Warn you about what?"

"Claire coming back, what do you think?"

"No one came back, you were only in there about two minutes, there was nobody else."

In the back seat, Viv was moaning softly to herself.

Anderson asked, "What's up with her, what happened to you in there?"

Theodrakis didn't answer, instead he blurted out a question of his own, "Steve, what has she done to Steve?"

Chapter 12: Things We Didn't Expect

In the time it took the door to open fully he froze and in the flash of that second Ed imagined he saw many things, none of them explicable, all of them mentally dislocating. Downstairs there was a shriek of terror. Carver, he thought, then all his senses concentrated on the horror before his eyes. It was like the watcher in the churchyard, black and shifting, but at a more rapid rate. It was a metamorphosis in progress, flickering across numerous forms.

But, unlike the watcher, this was more than a Hades bobbin in tattered, black, grave dressing. There was something else in it, something younger, something of flesh. It appeared to oscillate wildly for a microsecond, then settled down into a fixed form.

"Hiyaa, Ed, come to join me in the shower?"

Suzzie-Jade in a black, silk kimono. Behind him, Carver was on the stairs, pointing, shouting, "There it is, you see it now, you see it, exercise it exercise it now, make it go away."

With the last words, his voice changed from terror to childish bafflement.

"Where'd it go, where's it gone?"

"Been on the pills again, have we, babes? Better take some downers or your blood pressure will go through the roof."

Ed's eyes were on Suzzie-Jade as she taunted Carver. He understood that, despite her teasing venom, she too was uncertain. Carver turned, went back down the stairs and disappeared into the games room. He was looking so close to tears that Ed pitied him. He felt a hand on his arm. "Come and talk to me, Ed, I'm feelin' all funny."

She fumbled for his hand, located it and led him back down the corridor and into a spacious bedroom with dressing room off it. She sat on the bed. "What just happened?"

"He asked me to come to the Hall and exorcise it, he's..."

"Not him, what happened to me?"

"I don't know, the lighting was rather..."

"I was in the shower, then somewhere else, I was something else, then I'm opening a door and you're there."

Ed couldn't think of anything to offer as an explanation.

"It's me he's scared of, innit? What does he see?"

"I think he sees everything that's frightening him."

"And you, Ed, what did you just see?"

He didn't answer. She hissed at him, "Tell me what you fuckin' saw."

"I don't know, for a second it was like an assortment of black rags, like..."

"Like the thing you see in the churchyard, the thing that frightens you."

"Yes, like that."

"That's what I see too sometimes, when I catch my reflection. That's me, that's what I'm turning into, isn't it?"

He didn't know what to say, she repeated the question. "Isn't it?"

"I don't know, but for a split second I thought that's what you looked like, yes."

"Doesn't last long, but it feels like something's being put into me, makes me feel I've always been here, like I'm part of this place. And I know things. Things I shouldn't know, old things."

"It could be an illusion, look how easy it is for whole audiences to be fooled by magicians. The mind is a very powerful thing."

"You don't really believe that, Ed."

"I don't know what I believe, but I think that what's affecting you is part of the same battle being played out here. Like a mass haunting. There, I've said it, said the thing a modern priest should laugh at."

"Thanks, I'm ok now. You'd better go and see Si. Never exactly dull here, is it?"

She stood up and walked into the dressing room, stripping off the kimono as she went. Ed left the room and trudged downstairs to face Carver. He found him slumped into a vast leather sofa, nursing a large drink.

"It's her who lets it in, innit?"

"I honestly don't know, but I think it's disturbing her as much as you."

"So you admit there is something here then?"

"I don't know, the mind can play funny tricks."

"Never mind your funny tricks, you get across here with all your bits of magic and get rid of it, and if it gets rid of her so much the better. She can go and live in your gaff like what she did at Christmas."

Despite the aggression Carver was trying to build up, Ed felt sorry for him.

"I'll need a day or two but I'll come back in the week and perform a blessing. I don't think it will bother you again before then."

Carver didn't look convinced.

"Listen, I got things to do in town. I'll stay there a couple of days but when I get back I want this sorted. Get it sorted by next weekend cos that's when I'm throwing the planning permission party."

"Planning permission, so soon? I didn't think it had been granted yet."

"Hasn't, but it's in the bag, everyone who matters is onside."

"But what about Devil's Mound?"

"Build round it, then level it when stage three permission comes through."

"But it's a protected site."

"Bollocks. Cause of all the trouble is what it is, and you were part of it."

He stopped and looked round, as if the mention of the mound might bring repercussions to the house, then blurted out, "Not only me thinks that, you should ask that friend of yours who lives in the house with them lezzers."

"Olga?"

"No, not the fat one, the pretty one who helped you cause all that trouble, strange, foreign sounding name."

"Claire Vanarvi?"

"Yeah, that's the one. Bit of a shock for you, is it? That her and me are mates?"

The shock almost made Ed stagger. It threw him out of kilter, even more than what he imagined he'd seen outside Suzzie-Jade's door. For the first time, a smile flickered across Carver's fleshy jowls.

"So, you didn't know, did yer? That shook you, not feelin so bleedin' pleased with yerself now are you, hey? Not so bloody clever now?"

Carver was right, but Ed didn't grace him with a reply. Instead he muttered, "I'll perform the blessing next week."

Then he turned and walked out wishing, not for the first time, that he had it in him to be a man of violence. A feeling reinforced by hearing Carver and his minder sniggering as he left the room.

Outside it was grey with a persistent drizzle which soaked him through as he walked back to the rectory. He was shivering but whether from nerves or the damp he couldn't be sure. All he knew was that whatever was haunting Skendleby was hurrying things towards a climax, a feeling reinforced by the expression on the face of Mary who was waiting at the door.

"Ed, you look so worn down, come in and sit with me."

It was just what he needed but then she added, "I've just had a long chat with Olga and she's agreed that we need to have a frank discussion."

This, after his experience in the Hall, was too much as his face must have shown. Mary said, "Oh, Ed, don't look so shocked, surely you never imagined you could hide anything from me."

He began to blurt out the precursor of an apology but she stopped him.

"Come and sit down. I've poured a sherry which, from the look of you, is much needed."

He followed her into the large drawing room and sunk into one of the threadbare armchairs as she handed him the drink.

"Drink that, it'll steady you. I've just got to take something out of the oven and open a bottle of wine. Then pour yourself another and one for me."

She glided out of the room. He finished the sherry in one gulp and refilled the glass. What was happening to his world, what did Mary suspect? She'd lit the fire; he sat staring into the flames sipping sherry, his mind numbed by anxiety. Mary came back in and he saw she was wearing the slinky dress she usually reserved for her drama society's last night parties. He couldn't hold back the question.

"You say you've spoken to Olga?"

"Yes, she's so much common sense, we found ourselves in complete agreement."

"Agreement of what?"

The question didn't come out the way he'd intended it to, he sounded like a petulant child. He took a large swallow, emptying the glass.

"That she should accompany you to France."

Whatever else had battered him that day faded into insignificance compared to this. He managed not to splutter out the mouthful of sherry, but that was the full extent of his self-control.

"But, how do you know?"

She cut across him. "Know? About you and Olga, or you and France?"

He had no response and put his head in his hands. Mary laughed. "Oh, Ed, don't be so silly, it's not a problem. I trust you completely and I don't suspect what you think I do. Well, the Olga part isn't a problem, it's the France part that scares me."

"But how did you...?"

"What? How did I find out you mean? Well, for a start, you are hopeless at hiding things and I've a pretty good intuition. The rest I don't know, it just came to me out of nowhere. I guess you can't live in this house and not pick up what's going on. Since you had the experience with those birds in the Davenport crypt, things seem to seep into me."

"But I never told you about the birds."

"Not when you were awake you didn't, but you talk about them in your sleep."

"And my meetings with Olga?"

"I've known about those from the very beginning. I understand why you do it and that you try to shelter me from things."

He felt a tsunami of relief sweep over him.

"Thank God."

"Now there are no secrets at least one of your anxieties can disappear. Come on, let's eat."

She walked into the kitchen and he followed. She'd set the ancient farmhouse oak table, which had probably stood there since the 17th century when the house was built, and lit candles. A bottle of red burgundy stood open, he filled two glasses.

"I'm going to talk while I serve the meal, Ed. It makes it easier for me. I don't want to look at your face or be interrupted while I tell what I must."

Ed, remembering his experience in the Chop House, wondered if every meal with wine would be like this. What he heard next did nothing to detach him from this opinion.

"I know Olga has a role, you need help, that's why she must go with you to France."

"But she doesn't know about France."

"She does now and she's agreed to go with you."

"But I've not told her about it."

"No, I have."

"How did you know?"

"That's the strange thing, Ed, the frightening thing. I don't know how I know, only that I do know."

She placed a steaming earthenware pot of coq au vin on the table between their places and then returned to the Aga, saying, "Before you go you need to talk to Davenport. There's something he needs to do."

"But he's so frail."

"He's enough strength left for one last task. He'll live long enough to pay the debt he owes."

"Debt? What are you talking about, Mary?"

"This is down to him. He deserted his post, he let Carver in. He can't run away from that, there's a reckoning to be paid."

There was something numinous in the words and the timbre of her voice that iced the very air in kitchen. In the ensuing still silence, Ed sensed a presence beside theirs in the room.

"Tell him, you tell him, Ed, he's to watch Carver. He will understand when the time is right and when the time is right he will know what he must do."

"But he's so frail, anything stressful will kill him."

"I'm sure it will. But it's his one chance of expiation."

"But he's done nothing wrong."

At this she turned to face him, her kindly faced transformed as if by some terrifying ancient mask. Harsh-voiced, she snapped, "Done nothing wrong? He's done everything wrong. He fled the field, opened the way for Carver and brought this down on us. He can pay for it now or pay worse after he's dead."

This frightened him more than anything he'd experienced at the Hall, but he managed to retain sufficient self-control to ask, "Mary, what are you saying, what do you know that makes you talk like this?"

Then, as if a spell were broken, whatever fearful thing had been in the kitchen with them moved on. The numinous chill of otherness faded and the temperature normalised. Mary slumped down into the chair opposite him, her face dead white. He laid his hands on her shoulders and shook her very gently.

"Mary, are you all right? What just happened? Please speak to me."

"I don't know, it comes to me in waves, small epiphanies then, thank God, it goes, like your depressive fits but shorter. I only get through by knowing it will eventually end. Tomorrow I hope I'll wake up remembering nothing of this."

They sat in silence for some time, the comforting features of their kitchen rearranging themselves back into a pattern of unthreatening normality. Mary put a salad and some crisp bread on the table and Ed served the coq au vin. They ate in silence, drinking the wine quickly. When both the wine and food were finished she said, "What's coming will be a test for you, Ed, perhaps the final test. There are things you need to learn. Now open another bottle of Burgundy and tell me what you learnt from those documents."

He did as she asked, leaving nothing out. It felt like confession. When he stumbled to a close she stood up, reaching out her hand. He took it and stood, tipsy and unsteady on his feet. She leant towards him and whispered in his ear, "There's something else. I don't know where this message comes from either, particularly after the night we've had, but…"

"But?"

"But I know this is the moment. Come to bed, bring the wine."

Carrying the two full glasses of wine he followed her up the stairs.

Chapter 13: 'There is Always Another One Walking Beside You'

Giles dropped him off at the lights and he walked the short distance to the coffee house. He felt nervous, not because of meeting Claire, but because he was having to relearn the skills of everyday social intercourse. He'd never liked coffee houses and particularly those in the posher end of Skendleby.

The place was only half full and there was no sign of her. He ordered an Americano and a toasted sandwich, even though he had no appetite for food these days. He placed this particular order because that's what the man served before him had asked for and he wanted to blend in.

He picked up a tatty copy of the local paper which had been abandoned and scanned it without much attention. The events of the world, global and local, were devoid of interest for him. The only article to catch his eye was a piece on the local effects of global warming, which featured a picture of the strange and rapid-growing white saplings he'd encountered on the Moss and which he knew were entirely unrelated to climate change.

Dropping the paper back onto the table he sniffed at the soggy, reheated sandwich. It did nothing to rekindle his lost appetite. Looking around him didn't help much as, since his return to the modern world, he was unsure of what was and what was not real.

The previous night he'd had a strange dream about Ed Joyce's wife, a woman he'd only seen on a couple of occasions. She'd sounded like Vassilis and was telling him what he had to do before he could leave this world. But he couldn't understand her and everything began to shift and slide towards chaos and anarchy. He woke up terrified.

Then Claire was here. He hadn't observed her entrance but sensed it. A couple of heads turned, but that was because she was a remarkably beautiful women, not because of the shimmering and sliding aura that surrounded her and which only he could see. Neither, he was sure, would they see the real nature of the horrific necklace clutching and flexing around her throat.

But even though he knew about it the sight of her pregnant, and heavily pregnant, still came as a shock and he wondered what manner of horror her gravid condition would produce. And produce before very long by the look of her, she must be several months gone.

A vestigial, atavistic reaction impelled him to stand as an act of everyday courtesy, but halfway to his feet he remembered what they both were now and why they were here. He sank back onto his chair aware that Claire noted his confusion.

She flashed him a smile of pure malice then slid into the chair across the table and he felt his guts swell with fear, a sensation he hadn't encountered since Samos.

"Steve, you look terrible, however did you manage to survive?"

He didn't know how to respond, he needn't have worried, she answered for him.

"But I suppose you haven't really survived, have you? At least not in the way these primitives in here would recognise. And look, you're pretending to eat, just like you were one of them, oh bless, how sweet. Your imbecility never ceases to amaze, things must be bad if they've had to resort to utilising the likes of you."

The honeyed enmity in her voice turned his mind back to the afternoon on Samos, when she'd tricked him into betraying Alekka, the only love of his life. Despite the changes he'd undergone he still feared her, but now he hated her too. He tried to avoid looking into her eyes – he knew the danger of that. While this was going round his head she opened proceedings.

"You're here because you need to see me, aren't you, Steve? But now you've seen me you can't take it, can you? Can't take it anymore than that weak, opinionated little slut, Alekka. Did you know she chose to kill herself rather than look at me? She wet herself in terror then threw herself off the rock into the sea? So much for the strength of her love and her supposed powers. I lured her in, used her, and all the silly little trollop could manage in reply was to kill herself, so droll."

Steve was surprised at the wave of grief that flowed through him, he thought he'd lost the capacity for this. Claire hadn't finished.

"Not that she had much longer. I'd intended to use her body, quite a good one Vassilis conjured for her, have a bit of fun then pitch her, or what remained of her, into the sea. I suppose in that sense she saved me the bother, but it would have been amusing to taunt you with an account of her ecstasy and agony. Still, as they say here, you can't have everything. Although, as with all their other acquired wisdoms, they've got that wrong too as I will shortly demonstrate."

He stayed silent.

"Oh, and you can stop trying to avoid eye contact, Steve, I'm not going to deconstruct you in here in front of all these people. Although it would be rather fun to see their reaction."

He sat up and looked back at her. Then something strange happened. As he struggled to meet her gaze he remembered the old Claire behind the implacable horror of the eyes staring him out. So instead of fear, to his surprise, he felt sympathy, a feeling of love for the original, sweet Claire who had sacrificed everything in an attempt to save them.

He looked into her eyes and something changed, like the fragmentation of a computer program, a glitch in a machine. The eyes lost their focus, blinked, went blank, flickered back then for an instant it was the original Claire he saw, the self sacrificing, loving young woman. Only a fleeting glimpse, but he saw it, saw her and heard a whispered voice from somewhere distant.

"Oh, Steve, tell him, tell Giles..."

But it faded. The eyes reverted to a burst of disordered, mechanical failure before snapping back to their original terrifying intensity. He found himself again in the presence of the demonic. But for an instance, he'd seen it lose control, temporarily give way to another force and this gave him comfort. What came next didn't, the malicious smile returned.

"Well done, Stevie, seems I underestimated you, didn't know you had that trick in you, you always seemed so weak."

"What do you want?"

"You wouldn't even begin to understand if I told you, and despite the little bit of promise you displayed you haven't the time to learn as I will have to terminate you shortly. It seems you may be more dangerous than you look."

He braced himself for what would come next, as the rest of the coffee shop customers continued with their uneventful break, unaware that anything even slightly sinister was occurring right next to them.

"So, why did you agree to meet me, Claire?"

"Well, one of the things about inhabiting these primitive life forms is you have to accept all the synaptic baggage, so let's just say I was curious."

"And the baby? It's Giles's baby, isn't it?"

"Only in the sense that self-replicating hasn't been developed here yet and I needed a sperm donor."

"So why have it?"

"Don't be so disingenuous, Steve, I think you've already worked out why I need it, it's the only means of cultivation that works down here."

"So it's a normal baby?"

"Hard to answer that, Steve."

"In terms of genetics?"

"DNA will be human so physically you could say so, but I think, as you will discover, it will possess some rather special characteristics."

She smiled her bloodcurdling smile. Steve hung on for one more question.

"What have you done with Claire?"

"But you already know, Steve. You saw."

As she spoke she flashed him a smile, not the demonic one, but Claire's old smile.

"There you are, a glimpse of what you once knew. Happy now? I certainly am. She's the last of these imperfect vessels I'll have to carry around in me. All over soon, well for us, if not for you."

For a moment he thought she was about to leave, but she checked herself.

"One thing Claire did get right though was her belief in ghosts. You live surrounded by them and never see them. You never see them because you don't know where to look or even what you're looking for. You believe in all the wrong things, ghosts are not what you think they are. Remember what that clown Vassilis told you: 'The dead travel fast'? And you should know because after all, they blighted your life. Byeee."

Then she was gone without him noticing her go. He picked up his coffee, it was hot, the sandwich was still warm, everyone in the cafe was in the same place. Yet the encounter had seemed to last for ages. He glanced at his watch, it was less than ninety seconds since he'd been served. She'd been right. The dead travel fast.

****

He had more time than he'd counted on and, as it wasn't raining, he decided he'd walk the back lanes to Lindow. Gentle walk though it was, he was out of breath and unsteady on his feet by the time he arrived.

Jan greeted him with a smile, steered him between the saplings, which, sensing his presence, began a low-pitched hissing, and helped him sit down at the edge of the trench. Working with her again wasn't a problem, she had more serious demons to face.

He didn't want to look at Giles, didn't want to answer any questions about Claire or the baby. What could he say that would be less than devastating? He comforted himself with Giles's ability to move on from one relationship to another, and he knew Giles was seeing another woman from his furtive evasion of certain questions.

He didn't have long to wait. Giles uncoiled himself from the trench and sat on the bank facing him. He said, "Almost finished here, be glad to get away."

He followed a few seconds later with, "How did your meeting with Claire go?"

"I only saw her for a few seconds, the rest of the time I was speaking with something else."

"Must have been quick, you've hardly been away."

"It didn't feel quick."

"And?"

"And I don't know what to tell you, Gi, other than not to think about it, not about her or the baby."

"Bad then."

Steve nodded, changed the subject. "Nothing to be gained here, Giles, not for us, not for the police. This is all confusion, just like Samos. Once things have moved on, the Moss will settle back down to protecting its real dead."

Giles didn't reply, didn't look up to it.

Jan answered for him. "So, what are we doing here?"

"Wasting our time. I think you two should forget all this and go back to investigating requests for planning permission that might damage archaeological evidence in the real world."

She fished out a pack of cigarettes and offered him one.

"No thanks, I've found they don't do anything for me anymore."

Giles slipped back into the trench to carry on, Jan lit up, then said, "A while ago, at the house, Claire asked me, Leonie and Rose to conduct a search of the cellar area beneath the house, she wanted us to find something buried down there."

"And?"

"I didn't want to, I knew things were going wrong in the house, I could see things the others, except for Olga, couldn't. Instead I got out. Just like me, isn't it? Soon as it gets difficult I run."

Her chin began to wobble, the precursor to tears.

Steve ignored this, asking, "I meant, 'and did they find anything?'"

"I think so but they never said a word to me. Whatever they found can only be bad. Leonie looks like she's going to pieces and both of them are off work again. Maybe you should try and talk to Leonie."

"Perhaps. Be good to know what it was they found."

"Olga says Ed has an idea. He thinks the place was visited by some type of magician back in the 17th century, she said one of her ancestors was mixed up in it."

The clouds were growing heavier and miles away over the tree line there was a distant flash of lightening followed some time later by a dull rumble of thunder. Being out on the Moss sifting through a charnel house of ancient bones didn't seem a good place to be. Around them the white saplings were swaying to an interior rhythm. Steve shouted to Giles who was down on his hands and knees in the trench.

"Come on, Gi, time to pack up."

Giles turned his head but remained crouched then, mumbled, "Under a juniper tree the bones sang, scattered and shiny."

"What are you talking about?"

"It's a quote from Eliot, it never made sense before."

"Forget poetry, there's a storm coming."

"You're right, we're wasting our time, we may..."

His words were drowned out by a thunderous roar above them, almost in sync with a dazzling flash. The storm reached them at a frightening pace and the first fat, heavy raindrops were splattering onto the earth. Giles scrambled out. "Get the tools packed up; leave the excavation as it is, we're not achieving anything."

They collected the tools and scrambled into the van in time to see a fork of lightening strike a field just beyond the Moss. The sound of rain on the metal roof was so intense they couldn't hear the bleating of Giles's mobile.

"Forget it, Giles, concentrate on driving or we'll get bogged down before we can get off this ground".

Already the saplings were lost to visibility in the downpour as the van bumped, slid and rattled across the Moss onto the track leading to the road. Whoever had been trying to contact Giles was persistent and the mobile rang and was ignored several times before Giles, having reached the track, pulled up to answer it.

"Hello."

"…Ok, Norman, what's up?"

"…You're joking?"

"…What now, yeah, yeah, understood. Ok, tell them I'm coming."

He rang off and turned his head so both Steve and Jan could hear.

"Police want me, they've closed down the site, Norman was saying something about the metro link shutting down, wasn't making much sense but it seems there's an emergency and our excavation's causing it."

Behind them on the Moss the rain stopped, the clouds having vanished. Over the scar of the excavated trench a watery rainbow arched over the rhythmically swaying saplings.

Chapter 14: Bell, Book and Candle

Ed found that the best way he could function was to compartmentalise and the way he managed this was by making lists. Lists of things he could actually do. This cut the impossible up into bite-sized chunks and kept him busy. When he wasn't busy his mind wandered into desolate, frightening territory and the internal crow became agitated.

This methodology was currently particularly important to him, and Mary's behaviour, which over a short period of time had swerved from being terrifying to erotically charged, had added considerably to his preoccupations. Whereas he felt he coped adequately with the latter mode, the former was doubly disconcerting. She had always been the epitome of sense and security, and as such provided an antidote to the demonic, so her insistence on him taking Olga with him on a French quest stunned him, to such an extent that he'd put it to the bottom of his 'to do' list, with his visit to Davenport not very far above it. These were the reasons why he found himself walking down the drive of Skendleby Hall with the equipment he needed for a service of blessing to which he had appended certain adaptations.

It certainly deviated from Anglian guidelines for a blessing, leaning, as it did, upon the Antiochian branch of Greek Orthodoxy. For reasons he couldn't elucidate, Ed felt the constant repetitions of the Antiochian cannon lent heft to the casting out of demons. He had brought along the equipment that had accompanied him on his only previous attempt at exorcism: a censor, a holy wafer, holy water and a large wooden crucifix. Stuff he'd hoped never to have the need to employ again in this capacity.

He didn't have to remind himself of the last occasion he'd attempted to employ this self-help ceremony and its accompanying kit. It had been for the blessing he'd attempted on the Skendleby Mound, which had gone spectacularly wrong. The catastrophic psychic reverberations of this last attempt to divert evil lay all around.

The portents couldn't be considered auspicious, at least those from the weather gods. The day before had been characterised by unexpected storms and today the sky was filled in by black cloud from which intermittent blasts of hail emanated. Ed caught himself muttering, "The skies of doom."

Like his previous attempt at dispersing the powers of the dark, this one hadn't started particularly well either. Mrs Carver – "I told you, call me Suzzie-Jade," – had rung this morning to inform him she intended to be present in the capacity of a participant. She'd even told him she'd be wearing an outfit customised for the ceremony. Being familiar with her fashion style, Ed found it difficult to reconcile this with a blessing.

He liked her well enough, but their last interaction had been deeply troubling and if it hadn't been for Mary's behaviour he would probably have brooded on it. Then there was Carver's, admittedly ignorant and inaccurate, expectation of a full-blown exorcism.

Ed believed in spiritual power when properly channelled, he'd seen it work, but there was a huge gap between that and the type of TV-show cleansing expected by Carver. A TV exorcism brought his mind back to Suzzie-Jade, and if anyone fitted that particular bill as a participant, it was her. Fortunately, there was scant time for further conjecture; he was almost at the house.

As he moved his hand towards the doorbell the door swung open and Suzzie-Jade stood before him. He took a step backwards, she took him by surprise, he'd never seen her like this, certainly never imagined her like this. It was like confronting an entirely separate entity.

"You ready for this, Ed?"

He didn't answer, her appearance knocked him off kilter. Perhaps he'd never really seen her before. Her face was scrubbed dead white, all the orange perma-tan scraped off, the change was almost shocking. So much so it almost masked the equally striking change of couture.

Gone was the body-hugging Lycra emphasising the cleavage, long legs and erogenous zones. In its place a simple, shapeless floor length dress that appeared fashioned out of an ancient blackout curtain left over from the blitz.

"Ed, did you hear?"

"Sorry, I wasn't listening, you took me by surprise."

"Thought I might. Now listen before Si gets here."

But he was still too shaken by her metamorphosis, couldn't decide if she looked otherworldly or corpse-like.

"Ed, concentrate."

Through the open door he glimpsed the shadow of an approaching figure, Carver.

"Ed, when you do this make certain you don't cast out the wrong one, the one we need to remain here, the one who mustn't be disturbed."

He had no time to understand this piece of Gnosticism, let alone respond to it as, within seconds, Carver was upon them. It seemed Suzzie-Jade's appearance was as much of a shock to him as it had been to Ed.

"Bloody hell, what you done to yourself?"

It was the first time Ed ever experienced fellow feeling with Carver, but it wasn't destined to last. Carver wasn't in the mood to reciprocate, he snapped at his wife. "S'not a bloody pantomime, get them rags off, this is serious."

Suzzie-Jade turned towards him and made a brief utterance so softly pitched Ed couldn't catch it. Carver obviously could, his face turned as pale as hers and he quickly took a couple of backward steps.

For a moment husband and wife stood facing each other, locked in a deadly stare. Carver's face was a picture of terror, Ed couldn't see hers as it was turned away from him. The three stood frozen outside the Hall door like a triptych from the brush of Hans Memling.

The silence was so palpable Ed felt it stifling him. Then from the high trees at the estate boundary there came the harsh carking of crows. As if released from a spell, Carver turned and hurried back into the Hall. Suzzie-Jade turned to face Ed, the whiteness of her face had acquired a luminous quality. Her eyes glowed yellow. "Remember, Ed, any time I tell you to stop, then you stop."

She followed Carver inside and Ed stumbled after her, feeling denuded of any semblance of the confidence he'd previously managed to muster. Inside, the Hall felt its usual forbidding self that Carver's most strenuous efforts to replace with a modern celebrity feel had failed to touch. But there was something else, a strange feeling of expectancy.

Ed caught it within a few paces of entering, it felt as if he was expected, that something knew him and was awaiting him. This feeling was so strong that he was hardly aware of Carver's hectoring tone.

"Listen, I want it done proper this time, you owe me that for all the trouble you've caused."

It appeared that whatever it was he felt threatening him had changed him from an unthinking type of atheist into a type of fearful believer. Ed wasn't surprised, his own experience of Skendleby had wrought a similar, if more cerebral and spiritual, change in him.

Behind him the sound of the front door shutting and Suzzie-Jade's footsteps in the echoing hall.

"The house is empty apart from us; I've sent the servants and Si's minders away for the day."

Carver, red in the face, snapped peevishly at her, "What you done that for, who said you could?"

She turned her face towards him and he shut up. Ed could see sweat trickling down his face and the patches at his armpits. She spoke one sentence, hushed but chilling in tone.

"Why don't you go into the gym and play with your muscles, Si? You just leave this to me and the vicar."

It wasn't really a question, it allowed no alternative and Carver understood this. Ed watched expressions of petulance followed by alarm cross his suddenly vulnerable face. For a time it appeared he was about to reply. But he didn't. He shot her an expression containing both loathing and terror then stalked off.

"Just you and me then, Ed, go on, get started."

"I thought I'd make a circuit of all the rooms, offering prayers, and then..."

He trailed to a stop, what was he doing here? She stood waiting for him to continue, watching him. He was beginning to feel rather afraid of her. The white face reminded him of something haunting his dreams. He began to wonder if he was actually still asleep and that this was the worst type of dream. But it wasn't, instead it was part of what he'd heard the Greek detective Theodrakis describe as "walking through Hell".

"Then, if I felt anything peculiar in a particular area, I'd conduct a blessing."

"Well, it's a big house, better get started. This is the only chance you'll get, the house doesn't like being messed around with."

If he hadn't been so flustered he'd probably spend time thinking about this peculiar utterance and question how she knew and what she knew. She hadn't finished.

"And after this is all over I'll make sure no one ever messes with it again."

There wasn't anything else to say. He unpacked the tools of his trade, the agents of exorcism, and wriggled into the adapted cassock he'd last worn on Devil's mound.

Skendleby Hall, although modest by Restoration standards, was still large enough to make the task of praying in every room an exhausting enterprise. However, although tiring and edgy, it presented Ed with no terrors, just the feeling of a house built for a different age that never became a home. The final section, excluding the cellars, which he'd deliberately left till last, comprised the small suite of rooms belonging to Suzzie-Jade.

He'd been aware of her presence during the process but not seen her. It was as if she was watching him. She'd made no attempt to participate so why the elaborate make over? Then it occurred to him – it was because she'd wanted Carver kept away and, although he couldn't think why, she was also trying to intimidate him.

She didn't want the house purged of whatever it was that terrified Carver, in fact, she wanted it preserved. This was a chilling revelation but he'd no time to dwell on it, he'd reached the door to her boudoir.

He opened it and walked in; she was there standing in the centre of the room like a statue, drinking in the light from the window. How'd she got in here before him? He'd been sure she'd been behind him, dogging his footsteps. Now he felt it, nothing like a poltergeist or an unhappy spirit, something very different, numinous and unknowable. He'd been wasting his time, wasting Carver's time, this was nothing you could exorcise.

She slowly turned her head. Now he saw the white face and glinting yellow eyes. For a moment their glances held, then she smiled. "Finished, Ed?"

The spell was broken but he'd seen what he saw and felt it too. She returned her gaze toward the window and, as if magnetised, his glance followed it. Followed it straight across the fields towards where Devil's Mound lay glittering in the sunlight. The room was created to watch over the mound, which she would see last thing at night and first thing on waking.

He was finished, had seen all he wanted to see.

She asked, "Felt the need to exorcise anything, Ed?"

"Not in the house perhaps, but at least I've said prayers in all the rooms except yours."

"You're quite welcome to bless my rooms if you like."

"Would it do any good?"

"Not really."

"But I've not been in the cellars…"

She wasn't listening; she walked past him towards the stairs, calling back over her shoulder to him. "You wanna see what haunts Si? Watch this."

He repacked his bag and set out after her, it was easy to find her by following the noise of shouting. It was Carver's voice, coming from outside the games room.

"What you been doing? It's here, it's here, you gone and woke it up, you gone and bleedin' woke it up, look, look."

Ed rushed down the corridor to find a red faced Carver shouting in terror and pointing towards an ill-lit corner of the passageway.

"There, it's there, it come down the stairs, exercise it, exercise the bleedin' thing."

Ed looked, could see nothing, but he felt a wave of sympathy for Carver. He tried to calm him.

"I've prayed all over the house, I felt no evil presence. I think you are becoming overwrought, perhaps we could pray together, it may help."

But Carver didn't hear him; his eyes were fixed on the poorly lit corner in the angle of the passage. Ed peered myopically in the same direction and, to his surprise, detected movement and saw Suzzie-Jade appear to detach herself from the shadows of the passage and emerge into full view.

"Upsetting yourself again are you, babes?"

Ed couldn't quite work out what was happening, couldn't understand how it was happening. It felt unreal. Carver turned to him.

"I get it, you're in it together, aren't yer? No one makes a fool of Si Carver."

Then he stopped. It seemed to Ed he was lost, like a child in the dark. A moment's silence then Carver pushed past him, heading for the front door. Once he reached it he turned and shouted back, "You'll regret this."

Ed wasn't sure who this was aimed at but suspected it was him. The door slammed, followed shortly after by the sound of the Range Rover accelerating down the drive.

"Told you, Ed." She looked amused. "Now you've finished, I'll make you a cup of tea."

"I haven't been down to the cellars."

"I wouldn't go down there if I were you."

"I promised Mr Carver."

"Si's gone, no need now."

"All the same, I promised."

"He needn't know."

"But I would."

"Suit yourself, but you won't enjoy it."

"I suspect you're right, but I must."

She shrugged and led the way to the heavy, locked door, behind which lay the stairs that descended to the most ancient part of the house. She pulled back the locks, tugged open the door and began the descent; he followed. The light was poor down here and there was an odour of damp and mouldering earth. Down here it felt unlike any other part of the house he'd visited, down here he was frightened.

"Told you you wouldn't like it, want to go back up?"

"No, I'm going to finish what I started."

"Let me stop you there, Ed. I told you there were things you shouldn't meddle with and this is where they live. You can look but I don't think you'll want to do much praying."

By this time they'd reached a large open area with several shut doors leading off. It was lit by a series of ceiling lamps, all of which looked expensive and new. But there was a contrast between the appearance of the fixtures and the light they produced. For all the good they did the space might as well have been lit by a single, swinging forty-watt bulb. Swinging because the light was constantly shifting in a slowed-down strobe effect. This made it difficult to focus on anything, as everything was in constant motion. Ed understood why Carver was afraid.

"Seen enough?"

He couldn't reply. She walked towards the periphery of clear visibility into the zone where the light distorted reality.

"Si won't come down here anymore."

He tried to focus on her, all he could see was the dead-white face, but in the flickering gloom it wouldn't stay steady, in fact, it appeared to have multiplied. He was watching a pattern of mutating black and white, constantly shifting, slithering shadows.

Then she was back by his side.

"Strange that, innit, I can't take it for too long; it's like a mix between a massive high and dying, now you see me, now you don't. Had enough?"

He had. They walked quickly back up the stairs where she led him to the kitchen and made him a tea, he sat at the table in shock. She left the room. It was some time before he took his first sip, the tea had cooled to tepid. Carver had been right, the house did need exorcising, but it was the task of a magnitude way beyond his limits. Then she was back.

The white face and funeral black were gone, replaced by the customary lycra and orange tan. He was both pleased and relieved with the change.

"Now do you understand, Ed?"

"I saw things down there, things that shouldn't..."

"That's why it's best not to go down there. Here, have some more tea."

She picked up the pot and poured them both a cup before adding, "Strange how people always miss what's right under their noses, innit?"

Chapter 15: An Unexpected Gathering

"Now, I'd like to introduce you to Mr Choatmann..."

The chief's preamble to the meeting faltered to a halt at this point and they turned their eyes towards the slight figure with the goatee beard who'd sat silent up to this point watching them through sharp, bird-like eyes.

"Mr Choatmann is from, he's from, that is, he's been sent, like..."

"Perhaps I should introduce myself, Chief Constable. I'm here to assist, I represent an organisation that has a direct interest in matters of this nature. In terms of my status, let's say that's on a need to know basis. On that need-to-know basis, you now know all you need to. I'm sure you will appreciate that everything that follows is highly confidential. Perhaps I should add that any breach of that confidentiality would be immediately apparent and treated with severity."

He concluded by treating all present with a sardonic smile. They'd been called into the meeting at very short notice, just Viv and Theodrakis, not Jimmy, that had been specific, so Viv was doubly surprised to see Giles at the table.

Not as surprised as he was. A car had been dispatched to bring him to the police headquarters where they now were, not a police car and certainly not a police driver, an upmarket four by four with dark-tinted windows. The ride had been unsettling so he was much relieved to see Viv and Theodrakis. He suspected something bad was about to unfold, he'd become pretty good at sensing these things and he knew at once that whatever Choatmann was here for, it wouldn't be comforting.

Choatmann consulted his tablet and then looked up. His long, greying hair was scraped back from his forehead into a ponytail extending a fair way down his back. His was a most disconcerting presence, mild and slight at first glance, like a millionaire technology nerd from Silicon Valley, but once he opened his mouth to speak he became far more chilling.

"Allow me to indulge myself by beginning with a quote, as I think Eliot sums up the way you need to regard me rather well: '*He who has seen what has happened and who sees what is to happen.*'"

He paused, presumably for effect, and Giles studied the faces of the others for their reactions. Viv looked strained, Theodrakis impassive, while the chief's expression oscillated between bewilderment and disgust. Giles had waded through so much frightening shit in the past eighteen months that he felt Choatmann would have to produce something pretty impressive to disconcert him. He didn't have to wait long.

"To be brief, we've been monitoring what we term an 'episode'. We are aware of others, not many, although they do appear to be becoming more frequent and it's far from impossible that calamitous events throughout history emanated from the same source. However, these episodes are difficult to identify and much harder to interpret. The one you encounter here, it seems, is more protracted than any of the others and for the first time we have established a link between two such episodes."

He removed his spectacles and polished them with a crisply-folded handkerchief while regarding his audience in the manner of one who takes satisfaction from his work.

"And the reason for my presence today is that the link, or rather the links, are currently sitting round this table."

He followed the delivery of this line with a little chuckle, and Giles began to see where this was leading.

"Because you, Syntagmatarchis Theodrakis, and you, Doctor Glover, were both on Samos during the episode, there as well as being involved with the current one in Skendleby. In fact, Doctor Glover, having observed you over the past eighteen months, it would seem that wherever you apply the blade of your trowel, an episode springs out."

Giles, who had taken a visceral dislike to everything about Choatmann, was sufficiently wound up to foolishly say, "So, if these things are so common, how come there's no mention of them on the news media or the web?"

"Because, for reasons I won't disclose to you, we do not wish them to be known, although it is possible that somewhere deep in the darker layers of the web there may be coded speculative references. However, these are being monitored, so to all intents and purposes, our news blackout has been effective. Until, of course, the current little pantomime you are staging."

"This is no pantomime and there's much you're not telling us."

To Giles's surprise, it was Viv who challenged Choatmann. He smiled condescendingly at her, replying, "Obviously your second point is correct."

"We don't even know who you are or who you represent."

"Correct again, fortunately for you, and believe me, for your peace of mind you must hope it stays that way. But this is wasting time; as your chief will corroborate, I carry a level of authority that far outranks any other authority in this city."

The chief nodded his corroboration and Choatmann turned to Giles.

"I need some information from you, Doctor Glover, and don't be foolish enough to try and obfuscate, we already know far more than you can possibly imagine."

Giles nodded, avoided Choatmann's stare then said, "Ok, but give me some idea how you know all this and what you want from us."

"All I'm prepared to say is that our knowledge came from a surprising coalescence of security monitoring and scientific research data. As for what we want, well I won't know that until I've heard what you've got to say. So, over to you, tell us what's happening beneath the surface of this city; expatiate."

"I've not been conducting the excavation, but it seems we have an unexpected gathering of the dead under the Metro link development."

"Unexpected?"

"Yes, in that it's undocumented, not linked to any recorded burial site, covering an almost impossible span of time and of a magnitude greater than the city at the various times could support. There's too many who just shouldn't be there. And..."

"And?"

"And they keep moving about. Take your eye off them and their disposition changes. It's like turning up to excavate a different site every day, whatever was there when you packed up the night before has been reordered."

"Have you seen anything like this before?"

"Something similar perhaps."

"Where?"

"Skendleby and Samos."

"Any connection?"

"I've not had time to analyse..."

"Bullshit."

Choatmann crashed his fist onto the table with surprising force, everyone jumped.

"Don't play games with me, Glover, not if you know what's good for you. When I ask a question, you answer it, that's how the game works. A sad fact, which, if you don't tell me what I need to know, you will soon discover. Now cooperate."

While Giles was thinking what to say, Theodrakis interceded, "Perhaps I might be able to clarify matters."

Choatmann turned to him and nodded assent. Theodrakis said, "There is a connection in the modus operandi of both episodes and I suspect also here in central Manchester. First, an obvious disturbance of the archaeological evidence that creates an illogical distortion to the record and contradicts what is possible. Second, a series of senseless, violent crimes with no evidence and no motive. We haven't reached that state in the city yet. The next stage, on Samos, although not England, was a breakdown of law and order and a concomitant descent into anarchy."

"But you solved it on Samos?"

"Rather there was a cessation of the pattern of events."

"I hope you are not being disingenuous, Syntagmatarchis."

"Far from it. I'm giving you what happened, nothing was solved, the events were brought to a halt and we were left with an explanation, including suspects, that enabled the case to be concluded in an apparently acceptable manner."

"What did you mean by the 'events were brought to a halt?'"

"I don't know, but that's how it appeared to me. Something halted the carnage and left us with an answer to give to the public and our superiors."

"So, what was it that made it stop?"

"Something else."

"And in Skendleby?"

"In Skendleby, I suspect we may be moving in a different way and at a slower pace towards a similar conclusion."

"So, you believe that whatever set these events in motion was terminated by something else? Not by you or your colleagues."

"Yes."

"But you took certain actions and on the face of it these actions were successful?"

"Yes."

"What led you to the actions you took?"

"That's what I could never understand. We, or rather I, was fed suggestions by other agents."

"Such as?"

"You won't believe me."

"I suspect that, rather terrifying as it might be, I may well. Who prompted you?"

For a moment, Giles thought Theodrakis wouldn't reply. He prayed that would be the case, but, "A madman, the decomposing corpse of a colleague, a haunted academic, a hedge witch and, most of all, a man who I'm not sure even existed."

For the first time, Choatmann displayed a vestige of sympathy. He smiled at Theodrakis. "Thank you, Syntagmatarchis, I know that's the truth as you see it. Why couldn't you have done that, Glover?"

Giles knew the question was rhetorical.

Choatmann asked Theodrakis, "And the man who didn't exist?"

"He was called Vassilis, Steve Watkins knew him better than I did."

"Ah, the elusive Doctor Watkins who managed to disappear completely from our radar but has mysteriously reappeared and is living, if I'm not mistaken, with you, Glover."

Giles nodded.

"And would you agree with Syntagmatarchis Theodrakis's analysis of events on Samos?"

Giles nodded, then added quietly, "Alexis was much closer to events than I was, but that's how I remember it."

"And your ex-partner, Ms Vanarvi, was there too I think?"

"Yes."

"And her take on this?"

"You'd have to ask her."

"I don't think that would be a good idea, do you?"

"No."

"Good, at last we're making some progress."

Choatmann turned back to Theodrakis. "And these agents who aided you on Samos; are there any equivalents in Skendleby?"

"I'm not sure, I think there may be, but they're in a state of transition. Sorry, that's all the sense I can make of things."

"So, you have reached the stage where you can begin to speculate?"

"More that I've reached the stage where I'm opening myself up to the possibility that something's maybe going to happen upon which I may speculate."

Had he been less immersed in this questioning, Theodrakis might have seen the amazed stares his two police colleagues were directing at him.

Choatmann said almost compassionately, "Almost there now, Syntagmatarchis. One last question. Have you any idea how you might in some way speed this process up?"

"I'm working on it."

"Is there any point in me pressing you further?"

"No."

"No, I think you're right, thank you."

He turned towards Giles. "Next time I ask you something, Glover, that's how I expect you to perform."

He directed a watery smile towards Viv and the chief. "Strange how little our two senior police colleagues managed to contribute to proceedings, don't you think?"

For a moment, Giles felt the chief might erupt, but he didn't, just sat silent. Choatmann transferred his tablet and papers into a monogrammed and expensive-looking leather satchel, cleared his throat and brought the meeting to its conclusion.

"Be advised, nothing we have discussed leaves this room. Say nothing to Sgt Anderson, he has a part to play and when the time comes I'll speak to him. Other than that, believe me, I'm truly sorry for you. None of you deserves to have gotten mixed up in this, but sadly you are. Even sadder is the fact that you'll be seeing me again, although I don't know when."

Now the chief did erupt. "Who the fucking hell are you? Who sent you, who fucking sent you?"

Giles was surprised at Choatmann's response.

"All I can do is repeat that you have my sympathy, not that it will help you."

He chuckled to himself like one making a joke, then added, "Now, this is what you must do. Remember Theodrakis found a way to calm things on Samos and you, Glover, with your friends, some of whom are sadly no longer with us, slowed things down in Skendleby. If necessary, to the exclusion of everything else, find a way to prevent this from escalating to the next level. Deal with the symptoms and give us time to understand the cause."

The chief asked, "How can we contact you?"

"You can't."

Choatmann slung the satchel over his shoulder, walked to the door and slipped out.

Chapter 16: Sky Bar

He hadn't felt this good in ages. Despite the Skendleby development being ahead of schedule, he'd felt nothing but a constant undertow of fear. Now he saw the way out, saw how he'd get his own back, make them pay. Best of all, it came from such an unexpected source.

"It makes such a nice change being out with a real man like you, Si. You don't mind me calling you Si, do you?"

She giggled girlishly as she said this. Si felt a warm glow of satisfaction, this was how women should behave, with respect, not like that slut Suzzie-Ja...He managed to stop himself just in time. Mustn't think of her, it'd start off the horrors again. She'd have to be dealt with but he'd have someone else do that, he didn't want to ever see her again. It would be too difficult to get her out of the house using lawyers so she'd have to disappear.

Making her disappear was more of a problem than he'd ever imagined. With the others, when they'd started taking liberties, it had been easy: a bit of a threat and a payment, and that was it. If he was honest with himself, most of them had been relieved to go – they'd never become comfortable with satisfying Si's mood swings or his occasional needs.

It was different this time round, he'd married her. Why had he done that? Why had she accepted? He was pretty certain she didn't want to go, the more he wanted rid of her the more she dug in. And now, now she was beginning to really get to him, beginning to get under his skin, disrupt his confidence, even frighten…

He stopped himself, couldn't afford to go there, remember what he thought he saw, call to mind how she seemed to be able to change. Change into something that was like 'here and there at the same time,' all in black and shifting. The smell of old earth rotting and then it was gone and the bitch was back in her lycra, taunting him. No one got away with that, no one taunted Si Carver; except that wasn't true now, was it?

He mustn't think like this, must be the drugs getting to him. He'd pay someone really heavy to deal with her. It would cost a packet but it'd be worth it in the end. He pulled himself up out of the deep pool of black thoughts and into the present.

They were sitting in the Sky Bar near the top of the new tower and could see right across the city and out beyond Skendleby. Si owned a couple of the ones advertised as 'Lower Penthouse', which were maintained by his housekeeper, Jason.

They were properties he used for the type of hospitality it would be awkward to host at home. He also used them as boltholes when he needed to escape Skendleby, which these days was becoming more frequent.

The Hall had been a very bad mistake, for which he blamed Davenport. He blamed most things on other people, but Davenport was currently running Suzzie-Jade a very close second as malefactor-in-chief.

In fact, he'd been sitting in the lower penthouse brooding on this when the call had come. It was from a number he didn't know so he wasn't going to answer, which was his default position. Then, without knowing why or how, he discovered he was embroiled in a conversation.

"Mr Carver, how lovely to be able to speak to you after such a long time."

He thought he had a vague memory of the voice, but that came as a secondary reaction. His primary reaction had been to think what a nice voice it was and how its owner obviously had respect and affection for him, and these commodities were in very short supply at Skendleby Hall. So he replied in the least graceless of the inflections he commonly used.

"All right, who is it I'm speaking to?"

"Oh, sorry, how silly of me, I should have said, it's Claire, Claire Vanarvi."

He remembered talking to her around Christmas and she'd suggested they might have a common interest in Devil's Mound that she could help him with, but he'd heard nothing since. He was sure he hadn't given her his mobile number, but she had it and here she was organising him.

"Hope you don't mind this at such short notice, Si, but do you mind if I pop up to see you?"

Pop up? How did she know he was here? He mumbled, "Where are you?"

"Downstairs, in the lobby. I'll meet you in the Sky Bar in five minutes."

The phone went dead, he tried to check details of the last caller but not only were there no details, there was also no record of the call. Then he found himself at the entrance to the Sky Bar, which was surprisingly empty, so he had no difficulty in seeing her occupying a banquette in the prime position, the glass wall facing south across the city and Skendleby towards the Derbyshire hills.

He had a few moments to study her as he crossed to the table. Slight, dark haired, beautiful, if you liked that sort of thing, and obviously pregnant, but it wasn't these details drawing his eyes. He didn't know what compelled him to want to be with her, but it overrode everything. Maybe he should have considered how this meeting came about.

"I've ordered cranberry juice, Si, have to take care of two of us now, but I know you like something a bit stronger so they're bringing your favourite single malt. Now, sit down next to me, we've so much to catch up on."

He slumped down next to her. It was like being back at school, except there he never did what he was told and here he was a model of obedience.

"Now, I know it's none of my business, but I feel I owe it to you as a friend to say that I think you need to be a bit careful about Suzzie-Jade."

He was so startled at this he blurted out, "You're telling me. How do you know?"

"I know a lot of things, Si, and I'm looking out for your interests, and having her in the Hall is not in your interest. Please do tell me to mind my own business if you think I'm intruding."

He didn't think she was intruding. Someone else seeing what that slut was like, it was manna from heaven to Si.

"Tell me about it, but what can I do?"

"Get rid of her, of course?"

"How? You don't know what she's like."

"I know full well what she's like, Simon."

No one called him Simon, he never called himself Simon. The only one who did had been the head teacher at primary school, she'd been the only teacher who could control him. The one who frightened him with her quiet, clever way of speaking, and her cruelty. A cruelty that at the time far surpassed his own embryonic capacity for that skill set.

"I don't think you know what she's like, what she can do."

He faltered, felt himself becoming upset, like his younger schoolboy-self had been when the headmistress had done those things to him. He felt Claire take his hand, he looked up at her.

"I know exactly what she's like, more than that, I know what she is, or what she's becoming."

"Well, if you know what she's like then you can..."

She finished the sentence for him. "Get rid of her? That's what you want, isn't it?"

"Yeah, yeah."

"Consider it done, it will be a pleasure and a very simple one."

"Honest?"

"Yes, I'll rid you of Suzzie-Jade. I would have needed to get around to it sooner or later anyway."

Then something strange happened that ran counter to the safe and comforting feeling that being with Claire was creating for him. Behind her shoulder, beyond the glass wall, a series of black shapes materialised, blocking the sunlight and shedding a flickering penumbra of shadow over their table.

Crows! What were they bleedin' doin here? They didn't live here, they lived in the country in trees, but there weren't any trees down this end of Deansgate. They seemed to hover in the air, suspended, wings spread wide but motionless. It seemed to Si like time and gravity had stopped. He looked round; everything in the bar was still, silent, suspended.

The crows hung motionless on the other side of the glass, wings spread, heads stretching towards him. Set deep in those sharp-beaked, glossy black heads, the dark piercing eyes. Eyes fixed on him and on Claire. Eyes radiating malice and hate penetrating his very soul.

He sat transfixed, unable to move, knowing he was the only person in the Sky Bar who could see them. They'd come for him and he knew these were the same crows who haunted him in the Hall.

How long he sat fixed by their stare he didn't know, but it seemed like it would never end. But, as if in a dream, he saw the expression on Claire's face change, saw her turn her head. She saw them, he knew she did, as for a moment a spasm of surprise distorted her face muscles. Then her face jerked towards the glass, her jaws made a snapping motion and the crows were gone in a flurry of black feathers and the noise of the bar enveloped him again.

After this the mood of the afternoon changed, the ambience of mutual admiration and comfort replaced by edge and anxiety.

"Can you remember the Hall being infested by crows when you first saw it, Simon?"

"Don't think so."

"Were they there when you first moved in?"

"Dunno, don't think so."

"But I bet they were there after Suzzie-Jade moved in."

He cast his mind back, he couldn't be sure, and he'd no clear memory of the sequence. He thought they'd first appeared when the archaeologists started to mess about with the mound. He was about to say this but Claire got in first.

"I bet you can't remember a time since she moved in when they haven't been there."

"I dunno, maybe you're right, I think she moved in about the same time as the archaeologists started messing with the mound. Yeah, that's right because Richardson had come round to warn me that the archaeologists pushing their noses in around there could cause trouble for the development. We was outside looking over the wall at the mound when the van with her stuff came down the drive."

"And can you remember the crows being there then?"

"Don't think so."

"But that's when you started to notice them, isn't it?"

"Suppose."

"Don't you find it strange, Simon, that the archaeologists, the crows and Suzzie-Jade all arrived together and after that everything began to go wrong? That's a bit too much of a coincidence, don't you think?"

Now that she'd said it he realised how much sense it made. He wasn't sure where all this was going, but he didn't have to wait long.

"You hadn't known her that long before you moved to Skendleby, had you, Simon. How did you meet?"

He cast his mind back. He'd been feeling a bit exposed since his last girlfriend had been paid off and a mover and shaker like him needed a bit of eye candy on his arm when he moved up socially into the Hall. A wife would come in handy for entertaining and all that society stuff.

Then he'd run into her at one of his clubs, she'd been dating a minor league footballer. They'd had a drink and she'd made it clear she wanted to move on up as well. No one knew much about her and the rumour was she might have been a high-end escort girl. They'd got on, she'd seemed level headed enough to accept the transaction for what it was and they'd got together. It had seemed a good idea at the time.

"Did you know much about her when you met, Simon?"

"Well, a bit."

"Enough to know what type of entity you were inviting into your home?"

"Entity?"

"Haven't you noticed anything strange about her?"

"Like what?"

"Well, let's begin with personality swings and move on to shape shifting. Does she frighten you, Simon, I think she does. Tell me I'm right."

How could she know this? Had she been watching him? He gulped down the last of the single malt, it went down the wrong way, burning his windpipe. He began to cough and splutter. He felt the touch of her arm across his shoulder, he felt a wave of comfort flowing through him.

"You mustn't worry, Simon, there's a solution to all this, but you must understand what's happening in Skendleby. The archaeologists, Suzzie-Jade and that old fool Davenport are all in it together. And do you know why?"

He'd finished choking now and his head felt clearer. She was right, she'd sussed it all out, he asked, "So, what do I need to do?"

Without knowing why he trusted her and felt a warm glow when she replied. "It's what we need to do, Simon, you're not alone anymore."

And she was right, of course, he was a big player. No one messed with Si Carver.

"So, how do we fix it?"

"We start by understanding the heart of the problem: Devil's Mound. That's what's delaying your project, that's the source of the other problems too. Solve that and I promise you the rest will disappear."

The waiter materialised with fresh drinks. Claire acknowledged him with a slight nod and he withdrew, thanking her. Showed real class that did, Si was well impressed. She was the type of woman he needed, pregnant too and having kids was trending heavily these days, proper status symbol kids were, and this one being ready made would save all the bother of the stuff he didn't particularly like that went into knocking kids out.

He was beginning to feel better than he had in months and was fantasising about the future when she said, "So, now you can see what's happening, Simon, it shouldn't take long for a man like you to sort it out."

His look must have shown this wasn't the case.

"Think about it. There are things being done in Skendleby to intimidate you, to drive you out. Are you going to let that happen? A man like you, a winner, a fighter?"

No, he wasn't, and he told her so.

"You go back to the Hall and level that mound."

"Yeah, I'll get my people onto it."

In a colder, almost threatening tone, she snapped, "No, Simon; no people, just you. You have to do this, you have to destroy the mound, every bit of it, along with everything under it. Everything, you understand?"

He didn't fully but looking at her he didn't want to argue.

"You have to trust me. I know a lot more about this business than you do. But you've seen more than enough of it, haven't you? It's scared you out of your house, a tough man like you scared away. You've seen things you don't believe in, haven't you, things that terrify you?

"You don't want to end up like Richardson or Gifford, do you? That's why you're here, skulking in this tower. How long do you think you'll last when people get to know that?"

He didn't know what to say except that she was right. As if she could read his inner thoughts, her tone softened.

"It must seem difficult for you but, believe me, your problems are over. Once the mound has gone then so will Suzzie-Jade. She needs the mound, she feeds off it."

"What do you mean, she feeds off it? What does that mean?"

"Do you really want to know, Simon? Do you really?"

He didn't, so he just shook his head.

"Very sensible, I don't think you'd have enjoyed the answer. But don't worry too much about her, she hasn't got the power to destroy you." There was a pause before she added, "Yet."

This wasn't the way he wanted things to go and it was about to get worse.

"There's only one person you should fear and do you know who that is?"

He looked into her eyes and he knew.

"Fortunately for you, we're on the same side. I'm your friend and you better ensure it stays that way."

He nodded, he recognised real, total evil when he saw it.

"So, what do…"

She didn't wait until he finished.

"Just do what I say when the time is right. When you've done that I'll dispose of Suzzie-Jade and, after that, it's all behind you. I'll be in touch."

He nodded, it was all he felt able to do.

"There's a good boy. Well, it's been great fun, Ciao."

He didn't see her leave. In fact, what happened next was a bit of a blur, but when he got up to leave the Sky Bar it was empty and dark. The lights had been turned off so what light there was came through the windows. In the distance were the hills and below them, Skendleby.

Chapter 17: Watching Brief

Spits and spats of rain drifted down out of a grey sky and these, supplemented by drops descending from the low-hanging leaves he brushed against on his walk down the drive, ensured it was a fairly wet Ed Joyce who arrived at Davenport's front door. His progress must have been monitored as the door opened before he managed to ring the bell.

"Come in, come in, good of you to visit on such a day, Joyce."

"Thank you, Sir Nigel, most inclement weather."

This was how they now addressed each other after an early flirtation with the quotidian of abbreviated first names. This had never quite felt comfortable. Joyce and Sir Nigel seemed more natural. The formality, however, masked a deep and emotional relationship that standing together against the dark forces in Skendleby had engendered.

Ed was gratified to observe that Davenport, dressed in his traditional garb of a sports jacket worn over a yellow sweater, check shirt and green tie, was looking better than he'd seemed in weeks. He'd been accompanied to the door by one of the old dogs that never left his side. As Ed followed him through to the living room, the other dog, prone by the fire, twitched its tail and made a feeble but unsuccessful effort to rise.

Davenport said, "Poor old girl's not too good, finds it difficult to move these days."

The perambulating hound gave its immobile partner a sympathetic sniff then resettled itself next to her by the fire.

"We're growing old together."

Ed nodded and then agreed to take a cup of the tea that Davenport offered. This appeared almost immediately, accompanied by cake brought in by Debo. She laid the tray on a table, shook Ed's hand – mangling his fingers – gave the fire a poke and exited.

"Should I assume this is more than just a social visit, Joyce? Things are stirring again, aren't they? I can sense it growing."

"Sadly, yes."

However, as always before getting down to business, there were proprieties to be observed, so Ed spooned sugar into his cup and accepted a large wedge of Victoria sponge, a cake of which he was particularly fond, and Debo's was renowned in the locality, always selling out quickly in the church's fund raising activities. But the shadows couldn't be ignored indefinitely, so wiping the crumbs from his mouth, Ed began. "I'm going to be taking a short trip, Sir Nigel."

"Oh yes, and where would that be to?"

"France."

Davenport nodded. "Well, I daresay you could do with a break."

"Not exactly a break."

"If not a pleasure trip then I assume you're following up your research, but I don't imagine it'll bring you much joy."

"No, not a pleasure trip, but interesting places all the same: Cluny, Laon and Quarrie Les Tombes."

Ed may have imagined it, but he thought he saw Davenport grimace before replying, "Those are some strange, if interesting, places. I know them quite well. Laon in particular, standing gaunt and threatening on that crag. I'll bet you didn't know it's the place that horror writer fellow, Blackwood, used as the setting for 'Ancient Sorceries', and as for Quarrie!"

This time there was a definite shudder as Davenport spoke the final word, so Ed waited for what he was sure would follow.

"I've been there, can't say I liked it. The summer before going up to Sandhurst I went with friends on a walking tour in the Morvan, it wasn't a national park back then. We camped near Quarrie for a stopover and walked in at night to eat. Strange place for Burgundy; high up, remote, felt alien, the church in particular; it's surrounded by hundreds of medieval stone coffins, just lying there on the ground. Place gave me the shivers."

Ed felt himself growing cold at the description. He said, "Yes, I'm aware of the reputation, but we won't be staying there long."

"We? Don't tell me you're involving Mary in this business?"

"No, not Mary."

"One of the archaeologists then?"

"No, actually I'm going with Olga Hickman."

Davenport favoured him with an 'old-fashioned' look, which Ed attempted to ignore saying, "One of her ancestors got mixed up with Skendleby at the close of the 16th century."

Davenport continued to eye him suspiciously and following a brief silence, Ed betrayed his feeling of guilt by blurting out, "Anyway, it's Mary who insisted she accompanies me, apparently the two of them have discussed it."

Davenport didn't appear particularly mollified by this revelation, so Ed hurried on to the real reason for his visit.

"Anyway, Sir Nigel, that's not the reason for my visit, there's something I need to ask of you."

"Be my guest, fire away."

Ed faltered, he wasn't quite sure how to handle this; he wasn't even sure what it was he needed to say. To give himself time to think, he reached for the teapot and poured a second cup for both himself and Davenport. Apart from the crackle of the fire and the ticking of the clock, the room was silent, both dogs having drifted into sleep.

A torpor of tranquillity that Ed knew he was about to disturb. However, it wasn't only his reluctance to disturb the atmosphere that held him back. He was troubled by an emotionally raw intuition that this was the last time they would sit together in companionable silence enjoying tea and cake by the fire while the dogs dozed and dreamed in its warmth. This vestige of old England would soon be swept away and never recovered. They might have sat together in silence for some time had Davenport not demanded, "Come on then, Joyce, out with it, ask me whatever it is that's disturbing you."

But Ed faltered. He'd brought all this trouble down on Davenport through his meddling with things he should have left alone.

"Joyce?"

A softer inflection but no less insistent. Ed finally got to the purpose of his visit.

"I think while I'm away something is going to happen that must be prevented at all costs."

"Then why go?"

"Because I have to. Because I'm being led towards something."

"Who's doing the leading?"

"I'm not quite sure. At first I thought it was my research, but it wasn't. Something was leading me to the evidence."

"Something?"

"Yes, it's the only way I can describe it."

"Well, how do you know it's for the good? That it's not something trying to harm you?"

"Don't know. Can't be sure but it's gone to a considerable amount of trouble, it's shown me all the clues that others before us had gathered and, as we know, they all failed."

"You may fail."

"I admit that's highly possible but I must try."

"Why France? Why Quarrie les Tombes?"

"Because that's where the trail leads. I think there's something hidden there, something we need to know. Something none of our predecessors managed to find."

"And the Hickman women?"

"Her involvement in this goes back almost as far as yours does I think, and there's something else."

This was left hanging in the air. Davenport said nothing and Ed thought this was motivated by more than just a sense of delicacy or good manners. On the rug by the fire the elderly bitch twitched and whimpered in her sleep.

"I think her role is to either test me or afford some measure of protection. I can't be sure which"

Davenport snorted but said nothing.

"I know what it sounds like but it's a gut feeling and I've come to believe that instinct and emotion are our best defence. We've travelled far beyond the a priori, so logic doesn't count anymore."

"So, what do you want me to do?"

"I want you to keep watch."

"Like my ancestors did and our motto dictates?"

"Yes."

"What for?"

"I'm not sure, but you'll know it when you see it."

"And when I see it?"

"I think you'll know what to do, I think it's what you've managed to stay alive for."

Ed didn't know where this last bit came from but he knew it was right and he felt a wave of melancholic sympathy for the old man.

"I'm sorry that came out the way it did, I didn't..."

Davenport held up a hand to silence him.

"Don't apologise, I feel that too. Strange how one can never escape a sense of duty."

They sat for a while watching the dogs, then Ed said, "Watch Carver, whatever's happening in the Hall is working on him. He had me try to exorcise it. There is something in there but I'm not sure it's anything threatening to us. It felt more like..."

Ed hesitated, not knowing how to say the next bit. But he didn't need to, Davenport supplied the denouement.

"The ghosts of the Davenports. That's what you were going to say, wasn't it?"

"Something like that."

"Well, I'll watch while you're away, I promise."

"There's something that might help you."

"That will be a comfort."

"No, I mean it, but the help will come from a source you won't expect."

"Now I am intrigued, come on, out with it, man."

"Well, if Mrs Carver contacts you listen carefully to what she says."

Davenport spluttered. "What, that trollop?"

"Listen, please, I can't really say more because I don't really know, but she's not what she seems. If she asks you to do something please at least consider it."

"And what's she likely to ask me to do?"

"I don't know, but if it happens, do it, do what she asks."

Davenport sat back in his chair and stared at him. Ed held his gaze until Davenport suddenly smiled, saying, "Look at how you've grown, Joyce. See the man you've become and be proud of it. When we first met you were a frightened little busybody."

He laughed, looked genuinely pleased.

"How things change. Now it's you giving the orders. Orders which I will obey regarding Mrs Carver. It will be interesting to see how she gets on with Debo if she turns up here."

"Well, she could always offer her a piece of cake."

The conversation had ended; both men sensed it and got to their feet. Davenport looked tired. Then, as they moved to shake hands, something curious happened – Davenport said, "As you know, we never managed to produce an heir so I'm the last of my line. But, if I'd had a son, I'd have been proud if he'd been like you."

So, instead of shaking hands, they essayed a brief, but deeply felt half embrace, after which Davenport concluded, "Goodbye, Joyce, take care in France."

"Goodbye, Sir Nigel, I'll see myself out."

Davenport lowered himself gratefully back into the armchair and Ed made his way towards the door. He turned back and Davenport gave him a brief wave. He looked frail and Ed knew he'd never see him again. On the short walk back to the rectory in the drizzling rain he experienced a deep sense of loss and wished he'd thanked Davenport for the compliment. Wished he'd replied that he'd never really had a father, at least one who'd cared, and that Davenport was the nearest thing to that in his life.

****

The crow shook some of the water from its feathers without taking its eyes off the mound. All day it had perched there on a stump of tree by the estate boundary. It had replaced one of its brothers who had watched through the night. Later he, in turn, would be replaced.

He watched the mound and watched the pale white travesty of a tree that twisted and turned in the windless sky above it. Watched so intently that it ignored the tiny woodland creatures that therefore passed in safety below him. The crow smelt death in the tree, death in the mound. Not healthy death, carcass death that can be torn, ripped and eaten. Something worse, something outside nature and its laws.

The mound and tree weren't of nature, weren't of crow world with its rules. They smelt of things that would not rot the way nature intended, they smelt of a death that had never lived. Never lived but was now moving. The crow sensed this movement, stirring in the mound beneath the twitching root bole of the un-tree.

Soon it would begin.

Chapter 18: Necropolis

"Giles."

The shout echoed along the narrow tunnel leading down to the dark excavation chamber.

"Gi, come here, quick."

He scrambled up from the map table and picked his way gingerly towards the sound of the voice. Before he reached the epicentre of the excavation, eerily lit by arc lamps, Steve was shouting again.

"I think it's making sense, I think I'm getting it."

They were digging several metres below street level adjacent to the Metro extension workings: a zone where the concrete and the metaphysical seemed, in some strange way, to coincide. It was the fifth day on site.

Above, at street level, the weather was surprisingly clement for Manchester, but down here in the damp dark of clay and rubble the benefits were lost apart from an oblique glimpse of blue sky from the lip of the outermost working.

A tunnel led from this working into a substantial subterranean space the size of a football stadium, on the other side of which lay cellars of pre-existing 18th century buildings. This was the space that had freaked Norman and, subsequently, the police.

It was filled with the dead, a charnel house that ought not to exist. However, this necropolis did, at least when compared to the shifting evidence of Lindow Moss, make an element of sense.

Not the bones of course, they made no sense, shifting constantly in a horizontal dance of death. But they'd found something else, something that didn't shift. A structure that fascinated them as archaeologists and which they were pretty sure would, when they got round to reporting it to the police, fascinate them too.

They told themselves they'd delayed reporting this structure to give it a chance to commence behaving in the same irrational manner as the Lindow site and avoid wasting police time but that wasn't their true reason. The true reason was that this was different and they needed to examine it without interruption.

Structure was probably the wrong term for it, burial would be more accurate. It had certainly been constructed in a fashion that pointed to the methodology and ritual of Neolithic antecedents. Not that this would have interested the police. However, its occupant would interest them greatly.

Whereas the fashioning of the tomb itself was prehistoric, its incumbent was distinctly modern. A corpse, a fairly recent one, partly decomposed but still replete with tissue and hair clinging to the complete skeletal core. A far cry from the Neolithic, both in terms of practice and dating. This definitely was, as Steve had said after examining it, "a crime scene, but not like the ones we know, Jim.'"

The early Star Trek-inflected humour was neither particularly original nor funny, but humour, as anyone who has ever faced life-threatening situations will attest, is the best antidote to fear.

Giles joined Steve, who was perched above the body, where, against all excavation and health and safety regulations, he lit a cigarette. He offered one to Steve who refused.

"You need to listen carefully to me, Gi. We got it very wrong in Skendleby, maybe this will help us put things right."

Giles nodded and three different shadows of his magnified, helmeted head projected by the arc lights nodded in agreement on the dark underground walls flanking this gruesome space.

"I'm pretty certain I know what this is, which I'll get to in a minute, but more than that I've been forming an idea of what it's trying to say. You ready for this?"

The four heads of Giles once again nodded.

"It's a message, in fact, I think it's one of several messages, but this is the first we've managed to recognise. I don't think this is the meaningless stuff we saw on Samos. I think this is to help us, to warn us..."

He stopped and looked at Giles, looked at him to see if he'd protest or laugh. Giles did neither, they'd both come too far for that, what he did do was get to his feet.

"Can you tell me this outside, Steve? Be easier."

"No, has to be in here, by this thing, we don't know how long it'll last. Smoke another, clear your mind and listen, listen for what I miss."

"Ok."

He sat back down. Steve's voice seemed to be coming from far away, and the clash of artificial light and underground dark distorted his vision. His head felt fuzzy, like he was about to faint or go into a trance. He shook his head to clear it, fought down a wave of panic. He lit another smoke, felt it burning its way through his dry lips and the smoke stinging his eyes. Curiously, this real physical discomfort seemed to help. He settled down to listen.

"It's always been about archaeology, right from the start. Archaeology is about decoding meaning from the physical past, because everything made in the past had a purpose. Identify the artefact and work towards its purpose. The artefact doesn't lose its meaning when it's lost or buried, does it? It still retains its original meaning."

"So?"

"So, we're archaeologists, we interpret the evidence and build the picture."

"And?"

"And what if this is a form of communication, what if it's being put here so we can infer what it means?"

"Why?"

"Why? Because it's our fucking job, it's what we do is why. How better to communicate something to archaeologists?"

"But who's communicating and why not just tell us?"

"Grow up, Giles, haven't you learned anything? I don't know why and I don't know where from, but I do know there's something in this meant for us. These assemblages have meaning, they've been deliberately chosen and constructed of stuff we understand the significance of. We've just failed to see what's right under our noses. But with this, this atrocity, I think they've got through."

They sat in silence for a while.

"Everything here in its own way is real, earthbound and real, all these things are clues, a series of assemblages, using the tools of our trade, thrown out one after the other until we get one we recognise."

"But who's doing it?"

"No idea, but it's here and it's all we've got and I think I can read it."

Once more silence. Steve tried again.

"Jodrell Bank, the radio telescope near Skendleby, spends all day and night looking for messages from the stars that come in the form of radio waves. We either don't get them or fail to recognise them. Maybe there are other channels that we don't even consider and therefore wouldn't recognise either."

"What, like this?"

"Why not? You got a better idea?"

"No."

"So, we have a series of impossible archaeological assemblages all without context which constantly change. Now we have one I think I can interpret and it's stabilised."

"What, you mean like trial and error?"

"Yeah. When two people without a shared language try to communicate that's how it works until gradually you experience growing familiarity and recognition."

"How does it help?"

"Well, for a start, if I'm right and we begin to understand the message, then all these archaeological chimeras and crime scenes will cease. You said that was the main objective the police gave you."

Giles looked unconvinced.

"Gi, this was what I've been sent back for. I'm beginning to understand now. We have to follow this, and follow it quickly, because I don't think I've much time left."

"Ok, tell me what this means then."

"I don't want to have to do this twice. Call the police in, might as well kill two birds with one stone."

Giles made the call, they didn't have long to wait. After an indeterminate but probably short time sitting in the sepulchral silence, they heard footsteps descending from the world of light above their heads. Giles was surprised and then pleased to see Viv followed by Theodrakis. More so when Viv helped him to his feet, kissing him gently on the cheek. Perhaps they had become an item.

She favoured Steve with a distant nod, a distance she maintained. It occurred to Giles she was loath to go near him and, more than that, she feared him. Steve seemed to understand and accept this. He remained sitting on the far lip of the excavation, merely raising his voice to say, "The corpse is modern, a young woman I think, who has been positioned with great care – that must be significant. Otherwise I've no observations..."

She cut him off. "How long have you had this? This is evidence, you should have reported it immediately. I could charge you."

Her gaze at Steve was angry, but when she turned to Giles she looked hurt.

Steve remained calm. "But you won't. Think about it, it could have been unreal like the others. We had to make sure and during the wait I've come up with some useful stuff."

"So you're a detective now, are you?"

"No, as I was about to say, I've no observations on the body, I've not touched it, that's your province, but I'll bet the death wasn't a consequence of natural causes."

"And how would you know that?"

"Because I've come across similar examples in a prehistoric context."

"Ok, what have you got?"

"I'll tell you but hear me out before you get mad."

She nodded and he began. "Since we found this corpse, which was partially exposed, as if someone wanted us to find it, I've spent a couple of very long days filtering the stuff surrounding it. It's been carefully put together in a series of layers with carefully separated objects in each; fetish objects, I'm certain. This whole burial is encoded with a ritual we need to understand."

"And?"

"And it's not a one off. I've worked on two similar inhumations. One on Crete, one in Turkey, and it's very similar to a recent find in Israel. In fact, I think that's the one this attempts to replicate." He paused, there was no interruption.

"It was a major find, even made the news. Grosman, who led the Hebrew University excavation team, uncovered a particularly unusual burial from the late Natufian period about twelve thousand years ago. What he found surprised him enough to conclude it was probably a shamanic burial. Look, I can show you some of the stuff."

Viv walked across to him and he pointed to carefully marked fragments of bone, stone and shell along with some crude carvings of animals and what looked like models of human limbs.

"There are masses more of this stuff which we've not had time to examine. Since we've found it and started serious work it's remained stable, no change like the Lindow stuff. There has to be a reason for that."

"And?"

"And I don't think you'll believe me."

"I might, I've seen something like this before."

This came as a surprise, but there was no time to unpack it. Steve carried on. "I think it's remained stable because whatever put it here knows we've recognised it and that we may now figure out the code."

"Code?"

"It's a type of message. There have been others but this is the first we've understood as such."

"So, you think we're dealing with some power that communicates only through archaeologists? The chief will love this."

The sarcasm was bitter. Theodrakis said gently, "Well, that wouldn't be the strangest thing we've encountered, would it?"

Viv considered this, "So, what's the message?"

"I don't know yet, I need time for that, but the nearest I can get is that it's showing us either something we need to find or something we need to do. But whatever else, the care taken over the burial of this young woman is central to it. If there is a message then it's the ritual regarding the body we need to focus on if we're going to decode it."

Viv nodded. "Leave it to us now, this is a crime scene but I'll need a full briefing on this, including your ideas about a message."

She began to make calls and they grabbed their stuff and left. There was no farewell kiss for Giles. Outside, the daylight temporarily dazzled them so Giles couldn't be quite sure, but as they passed the side of Central Library, he thought he caught a glimpse of a figure standing in its shadow watching the entrance to the police investigation. More of a silhouette really, a silhouette of a slight, bearded man with long hair and a pony-tail, a satchel hanging from his shoulder. Choatmann!

****

By eight that evening, they were sitting in the Royal Oak, drinking. Too fraught to go home, and Giles in particular needed something to loosen him up. The last time they'd sat together in this old Didsbury pub had been the night

Steve was attacked on Devil's Mound, a fact Giles was careful not to mention.

The drink didn't loosen them much. Steve could hardly drink anyway these days and as they no longer shared the capacity for small talk and banter they ended up discussing the very thing they'd come to the pub to avoid. It was while listening to Steve talk about encoding the message from the site that the idea came to Giles.

"It's not just the stuff, Steve, it's the place too."

"What?"

"Remember Marcus Fox? He said it was places that were haunted, not people. Certain places retain a residue of extreme events, which they keep replaying like a tape. The landscape is essential to the haunting and some places attract it. You know, some places have a special feel, a genius loci."

"Your point being?"

"That Skendleby attracts these things like a kind of magnet. I think somewhere deep down I've felt this ever since I was at school and they unearthed the Celtic sacrificial victim buried under the peat at Lindow."

He noticed Steve wasn't listening. "You all right, Steve?"

"You don't see them, you don't, but I see them, they're hunting me down, I have to keep moving."

"What?"

"I'm trying to explain how I feel and Aeschylus does it better than me."

"Aeschylus?"

"Yeah, if anyone was haunted he was: ghosts of the dead he'd fought beside, ghosts of those he created to expiate his own guilt."

"Not really making much sense, Steve."

"Aeschylus fought for Athens, tried to escape into his plays but couldn't. Had to get away from Athens. That's like me. I'll hang on to do what I have to, but after that, if I'm still even half alive like now, I'll have to run and the Furies will follow."

Giles recognised the despair but had no idea what to say. In the event, he was saved having to try.

A woman's voice interrupted them. "I know more about the Furies than either of you ever will."

They turned their heads and found themselves staring at the pale, diminutive figure of Lisa Richardson.

Chapter 19: The Quest, Part One

It hadn't started well and Ed had plenty of time to reflect on this while sitting trapped in the gridlocked snake of traffic five miles from Dover. Following the breakdown of the 'Border Control' talks with the French government, such queues were apparently the norm. Consequently, they would arrive in France too late to make their hotel reservation in Laon and would have to try and find somewhere in Calais. Olga was working on this but the signal to her mobile was, at best, intermittent.

Mary had been strange and distant this morning when he left. He felt guilty, but she'd been the one pushing this venture. The strained farewell depressed his spirits and made him lonely and anxious as he drove to pick Olga up. He considered turning back but then realised that, without quite knowing how he'd got there, he'd arrived at the flat.

Olga was waiting for him outside the front door with a small holdall. She was wearing the tight-fitting skirt she'd worn when they'd first met for a drink and he felt his guilt merge with a feeling of vague sexual arousal – not a good start. Since then everything that could had gone wrong: the M6 and M1 were their normal sluggish stop-go selves and the approach road to Dover was little more than a car park. So he had plenty of time to brood, and one of the things he brooded on was the call from Mary.

Apparently, shortly after he'd left, an invitation had arrived to a memorial service for Gwen. There was no name attached to it, just a schedule to meet at Shrewsbury Crematorium at 2pm Monday to view a plaque and rosebush and then attend a short service at St Eata's church. The anonymity of this leant it a slightly unsettling air and it had certainly unsettled Mary when he suggested she might go in his stead.

"I won't. There was something peculiar about her death, and why this delay and who has organised it? Who won't leave a name?"

"It is a little odd, I admit, but I think someone should attend bearing in mind what we went through together."

"Well, it's not going to be me."

Ed cast about for an alternative. Marcus Fox was dead, Davenport too ill, Steve too damaged and, for reasons he didn't care to articulate to himself, he didn't want to consider Claire.

"Mary, would you pass it on to Giles? He liked her and I think he is the most suitable candidate."

"All right, but I'm not sure he'll thank you for it."

There was a pause, causing Ed to think there had been a break in the signal, but after a few seconds she added, "Ed, take care over there, be very careful."

Then there was a break in the signal and the conversation terminated. When he tried to call back later there was no answer.

After a long wait at border control, it was dark when they finally drove through the drizzle onto the back of the crowded ferry. It was darker still when they drove off, feeling wet and cold. Having failed to find anywhere in the centre to stay, a kind hotelier, having made enquiries on their behalf, directed them towards a cheap hotel on the beach: the 'Residence du Golf'.

On the winding drive they passed several groups of men hanging about on corners who did not look to be local. The hotel had one room left, which the night porter described as a family room. It was, in fact, a small double room looking out over the beach, with a small windowless space just inside the door by the bathroom containing two bunks. Ed opted for this.

Adjacent to 'Residence du Golf' was an empty restaurant about to close for the night where they managed to persuade, or rather bribe, a reluctant waiter to let them quickly drink a bottle of wine and eat a plate of bread and cheese. Through the window they watched the ferries drift in and out of the port and vague groups of figures moving on the dark beach.

Shortly after he'd settled into the cramped upper bunk, the door to the bedroom opened and Ed saw a backlit Olga, wearing only a small T-shirt, in the doorway.

"Wouldn't you be more comfortable in here with me, Ed?"

"Thanks very much, but I'm fine here, thanks."

He spent the remainder of the night tossing and turning in the fetid darkness tormented by loneliness, anxiety and lust.

Next day, under a lowering sky, without breakfast, they drove silently out of Calais through the shut-down businesses, shuttered shops and graffiti, skirting a couple of wretched overspill migrant camps. It rained all the way to Laon, but at least the autoroute was fluid. The town, standing high on its plug of rock, was visible for miles and, as they drove up the steep, winding road, the sun broke through the drizzle and a rainbow arched across the great cathedral.

The hotel was situated right at the top in the bend of a narrow street, and Ed had some difficulty manoeuvring the car through an archway into the narrow courtyard. After a longish wait in the gloomy reception hall, which led them to imagine the place was closed, a small man in a cardigan appeared and asked, "A double room?"

Olga looked at him and Ed hurriedly gabbled, "No, two singles if you have them, please."

"Of course, you are our only guests. Will you want dinner? The restaurant is well respected."

He didn't want dinner but felt sorry for the man and said, "Yes, that would be lovely."

"Good, be here at eight."

The keys were handed over and they made their way across sloping floors through winding passages to a couple of adjacent second floor rooms overlooking the courtyard. After a wash they set out to explore Laon.

If Calais had seemed empty, Laon was emptier and wore a melancholic air of neglect. They set out for the cathedral, where Ed hoped to pick up the trail of the 12th century cleric and historian Robert de Torigny, prior of Bec, or at least the missing sections of his history.

On the way through twisting streets they saw no one save a party of French girl guides in uniform marching along singing a traditional song. They looked as if they might belong to a different age. The massive cathedral towered above them, beautiful and strange, and they entered into its cool and peaceful interior.

They found nothing, neither there nor in the Templar chapel, nor in any of the other 12th and 13th century ecclesiastical buildings grouped around the ancient town core.

Sitting outside a bar opposite the cathedral a tired and irritated Olga asked, "Didn't you have any plan for when we got here, Ed? My feet are killing me and these shoes are too tight for all this walking."

"Well, in Manchester the documents found me. I thought it would be the same here."

"Brilliant."

She called into the bar for two more shots of pastis, which they drank in a rather disagreeable silence broken only when Olga finished her drink, threw some euros onto the table and muttered, as much to herself as to Ed, "Better hope that dinner is more than Ok."

She got up and began to limp back towards the hotel and Ed, after a last glance at the bizarre statuary on the cathedral front, followed.

After a brief shower and an unsuccessful attempt to ring Mary, he joined Olga in the dining room. It had obviously seen better days and a pall of silence hung over it, not helped by the rather frosty silence between them. Ed was reflecting they'd probably feel better after a good night's sleep and was about to go and search for a menu when the man in the cardigan brought a couple of aperitifs over to their table.

"May we see the menu?"

"No menu tonight, with only four, perhaps five, guests. Dinner's a set menu with wine."

It was too late to find anywhere else so they decided to make the best of it. The aperitif, followed by a plentiful supply of wine, loosened their tongues and reignited a sense of amity. The other two diners were a pair of exceedingly ancient women in rather dilapidated fur coats. They sat in the far corner, said nothing, picked at their food and refused even the slightest acknowledgement of Ed and Olga.

The food, however, was excellent, if simple, and they had reached the main course of bavette in a red wine sauce accompanied with potato dauphinoise, green beans and a type of shallot confit, when a third diner entered the room. It was obviously raining outside as he brushed water droplets from his trench coat and fedora before hanging them on a hook. He looked around and they saw a long, thin face adorned with a pointed beard, rather like a portrait by Van Eyck.

He saw them watching and made directly for their table, where he pulled out one of the surplus chairs and seated himself.

"Sorry to keep you waiting, I was held up by some rather unpleasant complications."

Ed was about to make a mild remark about mistaken identity when Olga said, rather rudely he felt, "Who are you? We didn't invite you to join us."

"Oh, I rather think you did. In fact, you've been looking for me all day. I saw you but couldn't join you. You are the Reverend Edmund Joyce and the redoubtable, and sometimes to be feared, Olga Hickman, and you need what I can give you."

Olga closed her mouth and Ed enquired, "You knew we were coming?"

"Yes, you've been expected for rather a long time, still, better late than never. Eat as we talk, don't let the bavette go cold, it's rather good here, don't you think?"

There seemed to be no alternative so Ed said, "Perhaps you'd like to join us? The waiter indicated that there may be a fifth diner."

The man chuckled. "What? Join you to eat? Well, that would prove interesting for you. But no thank you, I won't be here any longer than it takes me to tell you a little historical story and when it's done I think you will be glad I refused your most generous offer."

He smiled as he said this, but there was little mirth in that smile or warmth in his eyes. The waiter at this moment entered the room, but on seeing the third member of their party turned and went back out.

"Many years ago, before the building of the cathedral that so interested you, a young cleric travelled to Laon from the priory at Bec. He carried with him something he was desperate to be rid of, something that created a pall of darkness that covered him, drenching his spirit. He took it to the church that stood where the cathedral stands now.

"Within the dark of that church he came across a presence cloaked in black who took the thing he carried. As he handed it over a crash of thunder shook the church and the presence uncovered its features. The young man fled in fear for his soul. He only just got out in time, a lightning storm hit the church and in the course of that night fire destroyed it utterly.

"The architectural history books date the destruction of the church to 1111, but that is a deliberate obfuscation. The actual date was 1135, the year Henry I was murdered by witchcraft, although in the history books this is disguised as a chronic attack of indigestion brought on by a 'Surfeit of Lampreys,' a gluttonous gorging on fish, or rather, a type of eel. So prosaic and so believable."

He paused and considered his audience before asking, "That's what you came to hear, is it not?"

Ed didn't know what to say, he nodded. Their guest took the wine bottle and shared the contents between their two glasses.

"I think you need that. Almost finished. Do you know who the young man in the story was, can you guess?"

There was no response.

"No? I didn't think so. Then I'll tell you. He was your historian, Robert de Torigny, and he fled back to Bec as if the very devils from Hell were at his back, which, in a sense, of course, they were. He was foolish enough to write this and much else in his original journal, which is why so much of it had to be removed. But of course you know that much already. He went beyond his allotted task and meddled, something with which I think both of you are familiar. Do not meddle, I repeat, do not meddle. You have been allocated a vital task. Stick to it."

The expression on his face as he said this was so curious it made Ed feel quite sick, so much so that he thought he was about to faint. A face of shadows in a room grown suddenly dark.

"But to accomplish your task you must look in the right place. This is what I have to tell you, after which our time together is done. Tomorrow, early – at first light – go to the other end of town, to the Eglise Saint-Martin close by the Porte de Soissons. You will find it is open. Look at the wooden carvings on the misericordes of the choir stalls near the altar. When the light shines directly through the window, you will see what you need."

He got up and walked to the door, where in one swift movement he replaced his hat and cloak. He turned back to them. "Be on time, do not fail otherwise you will see me again and, believe me, that you should dread."

Then he was gone; the light slowly regained its brightness. They looked around them and the place was empty, the old ladies in fur had gone. They had no appetite for cheese or dessert, which was as well, as none were offered. They were the only two people left in the hotel. That night they slept in the same room with the door locked and there was no thought of lust in either of them.

At first light they dressed hurriedly and left the hotel, making their way towards the Porte de Soissons. Walking in this direction they had a better view of the dereliction the recent years had brought to Laon: shabby doors, shut up shops and graffiti scrawled across any available surface. All the same, when they saw it, Eglise Saint-Martin was possessed of a certain grandeur standing grey and massive above the valley.

The main door was locked but a brief circumnavigation discovered a side door, which was not only unlocked but standing open, as if awaiting them. They entered and allowed their eyes to become accustomed to the grey light. The scale of the church was emphasised by its scant furnishing. It had an uncared for and desolate feel, very different from the strange richness of the cathedral.

As they stood gazing about themselves, the rising sun made its appearance at the east window, sending a slant of sunlight across the nave and directly illuminating the choir stalls. There was a faint echo, a type of skittering sound, then silence.

They picked their way across the dusty stone floor of the silent, empty church towards their objective. In front of the altar, Ed fell to his knees and prayed. Olga stood and watched. Then they began their search. On all fours, they fell to scrabbling at the back of the seats to examine the misericordes for clues. They were uncertain of what to expect and the wooden ledges proffered little help, being either plain or carved with very simple patterns. Ed was beginning to suspect they had misheard their instructions when he heard Olga's voice emanating from the occluded gloom of the rear row of stalls.

"Ed, this one's different."

He joined her, crouching to his knees in the musty space beneath the seats. It was too deep in the shadows to see anything clearly.

"Use the torch app on your phone."

He scrambled for his phone and shone the beam.

"It is different, not only the carving, but the wood itself, this looks to be far older than the rest, this one doesn't belong here."

And she was right, positioned in darkest and most inaccessible part of the stall was a misericorde of darker, deeply worn wood. Ed didn't want to touch it, he found it strangely repellent.

"Go on, Ed, check it out, you're the expert in these things."

Reluctantly, he squirmed his way down onto his back and directed the torch beam. On the ancient wood there were three crude carvings, which, viewing from left to right, showed: a baby in a cradle, a cloaked figure appearing to sever one of the infant's fingers with a blade and, finally, something resembling a necklace made of tiny fingers.

He dropped the phone and the space returned to darkness. Eventually, having recovered the phone, he regained sufficient presence of mind to photograph the gruesome artefact. Then, with beating hearts, they fled the church as fast as their legs could carry them.

"Let's get a coffee at the hotel then get away from here."

But this too was fated not to go to plan. As they turned, out of breath and shaken, through the arch into the hotel courtyard, they saw their bags had been packed and left beside the car. As for the hotel, it looked like it hadn't been open for years.

Chapter 20: Ceremony

He was screaming, trying to claw his way out of the nightmare.

"Wake up, it's only a dream."

He came round. Where was he? Who was he? What was happening? A moment of panic then the face before him slid slowly into recognition. He gasped, relieved, she cradled him like a child.

"It's all right, just a dream, you're safe now, Giles."

But he knew this last bit was untrue, he'd never feel safe again. This was no longer a world where anyone could be safe. He sat up, drawing in deep gasps of air and trying to drive the images from his mind. He knew where he was now, the bedroom of Viv's flat. She turned on the bedside light. He sat looking at the walls trying to banish the vision.

He'd been wandering lost on a high moor. Somewhere in front of him was a version of Skendleby Mound, somewhere behind him, not far, was Lisa. The surface of the moor was seeded with teeth sticking up through the tussocks of course grass. Sharp white teeth.

"I'll make us a cup of tea."

"Yeah, that'll keep the demons at bay."

It was meant as a joke, but it didn't come out sounding like one.

"I'll be back soon."

And she was. They drank the tea and Giles wondered if Steve was similarly afflicted in whatever type of sleep it was that he currently enjoyed. His thoughts turned to Lisa again and what she'd said in the pub. He didn't want to think of that, certainly didn't want to talk about it and, to deflect the possibility, he asked, "When we were under the city looking at that body you said 'I've seen something like this before.' How could you have done that?"

"When I was working on the witchcraft murders in London I had a dream where a lot of the research and the evidence came together. What you found was exactly what I dreamt. That's why I think I'm here. That's why I feel like I'm being watched."

Now he tried to comfort her. "That's just a symptom of the strain you're under."

She rolled her eyes dismissively. "You don't believe that. It's not just the things I see round here. You saw it too. You saw him by the library: Choatmann, that loathsome creature watching us, looking for something, telling us nothing. What does he want? The chief's scared of him, and nothing frightens the chief."

Then she let it all out, all the accumulated fear and self-loathing. Let it out in one long, tearful and barely articulate stream of grief ending with a repeated coda of, "I'm such a fraud, such a fraud."

This last statement was something that he could comment on.

"No, Viv, you're not a fraud, it's only the uncertain and afraid who can deal with this stuff, only those who've peeped over the edge of the abyss and held its gaze. The egos, those with too much to lose, are the ones who can't cope, they're the frauds. Not you, you're here for a purpose. The tea's gone cold, I'll make some more."

He brought fresh mugs back to bed.

"What did you mean, 'I'm here for a purpose?'"

"It was Ed who said that."

"Tell me about him."

She snuggled up to him and Giles began to talk. They were still engaged in this when the first rays of sunlight came spilling through the blinds. Still talking when the alarm made its unnecessary wake up call as Giles was concluding,

"And, despite appearances, I think Ed's the strongest of all of us."

He was interrupted by a whistle from his mobile announcing the arrival of a text.

"There's a coincidence, a text from Mary. It's a bit early in the day for that."

"What is it?"

"An invitation to attend a memorial service for Gwen."

"The suicide?"

"Yeah, but I still find that hard to believe. Mary says Ed wants me to go, it's in Shrewsbury. Too short notice, it's this afternoon."

"Maybe you should go, do you good to get away from this for a day. "

And that was how it was decided.

****

By noon he was en route for Shrewsbury. It felt odd driving there alone. In the past he'd always gone with Claire, but that was something he didn't want to think about. There'd been no sign of Steve either in the archaeological unit's office that morning or at the house when he returned to change.

He'd been wondering what to wear for the ceremony, thought of a black tie, but then thought that was more for funerals and he wasn't sure this was a funeral, surely she'd have already been buried by now. This set him to thinking about why Claire hadn't gone to the funeral, whenever it had taken place. In the end he'd settled for his one good suit, which was darkish and, to his surprise, too big for him. Apparently he'd lost a great deal of weight since he'd last worn it.

Reflecting on the reasons for the weight loss took him to thinking about Skendleby, and it was a short mental distance from that to Lisa. Her appearance in the pub had dissolved the night into panic and chaos. To Giles it was like moving from listening to Steve talking about Aeschylus's plays to actually being in one. Steve certainly acted as if the Furies were after him.

He'd jumped up from the table, spilling his and Giles's beers, and stood, pale-faced, staring at her, staring at her like she was fresh from Hell itself.

She'd tried to speak to him. "Steve, we need to talk..."

That was all she'd managed before he turned and bolted from the pub. Giles hadn't seen or heard from him since.

Lisa had looked at Giles.

"There's things he needs to know, things I'll have to tell you instead."

People were staring at them, one of the bar staff arrived at the table with a cloth to mop up the spilt beer.

Giles needed a little time. "I'm replacing my drink, do you want one?"

"What do you think?"

He'd taken that as a no and made his way to the bar, where he'd tried to gather his thoughts before returning to the newly-mopped table with a pint. Lisa was sitting in Steve's place and started to talk as soon as Giles sat down.

"I thought he was changed, didn't think he'd react like that, didn't mean to scare him, especially after last time."

Giles said nothing, sat and watched her, tried to work out what it was he was looking at.

"I've been trying to understand what's been happening to me since Skendleby. I know I'm not right in the head and never will be, but I've finally figured something out."

She paused, Giles felt pity for her. "When she was lured into attempting that suicidal exorcism..."

"She?"

"Claire. When she, Claire, was fooled into offering herself as a host for that parasite from Hell it should have taken the demon out of me and into her. I should have been emptied, set free. But I wasn't. It was like when you get something stuck in your throat and can't cough the last little bit up, so you keep on coughing because you can still feel it there. You understand?"

He nodded.

"Not the entire demon managed to jump bodies, a fragment was left behind, and that bit is still in me, not much, but enough to leave it incomplete and me damned. That's why I'm like I am."

Giles's face must have looked as baffled as he intellectually was.

"Listen, Giles, a portion of the demon didn't get out, it's still there inside me and that's why these thoughts still come to me, not in full, just fragments."

She paused for breath. "I think Steve recognised those fragments, and that's why he ran."

Giles felt the hairs on his arms and the back of his neck standing up with the impending horror.

"Soon it will happen. I don't know what, I only get fragments, confused flashes, but this is almost finished. Whatever it is that you fear is almost upon you and you should fear it. Fear it with all your soul."

She stopped again, sat in her chair, slight and pale. She didn't look real, he wanted to leave, and he finished the beer in two large swallows.

"Sit down, I've not finished."

He hadn't realised he was halfway to his feet. He slumped back into his chair. The pub had ceased to exist, what was this which was coming? Lisa leant across the table towards him. He could smell her sour breath, see the sharp, badly-cleaned teeth as she opened her mouth.

"So, part of me is still missing, that's why I'll never be right. I've tried to be quiet, not draw attention to myself, fade into the background, you know, 'poor little Lisa'. But now I understand things better, see them differently, I can't do that anymore."

He waited, holding his breath.

"Because if part of the demon is still in me..."

Here it was, the thing that was coming, the thought he dreaded.

"Then there's room inside the thing it left me for but couldn't quite fill. I think there's a bit of Claire left in there, slowing it down."

"Jesus!"

It was his first contribution to the conversation.

"Then there's the baby. Think of the baby, what is its purpose ? Your baby, Giles, you put it in there."

She sat back, sweat on her forehead; her stomach made a gurgling sound, her eyes held his. "That's for you to think about, Giles. What nature of baby will it be? I think I've finished now, you can leave, don't try to find me, I've said what I had to.

She got up and walked away from the table and out of the pub. He'd sat for a second then rushed to the gents, where he was violently sick. Sometime later, when he felt safe to come out, he rang Viv and asked to stay the night at her flat.

****

He stopped the car. His thoughts had taken him so deep that he neither knew where he was nor how he'd got there. But he'd come to the end of the M56 and gone way past his turn off, and so would be too late to make the crematorium component of the afternoon.

It took longer than he thought it would to re-orientate himself sufficiently to resume the journey, about fifteen minutes before he was mentally stable enough to drive and find an alternate route to St Eata's church.

The church, when he finally managed to locate it, was by the side of the river, set back behind a large pub which doubled as a hotel. The hotel component was currently hosting a conference and large numbers of suited individuals were drinking and smoking in the gardens. There was no sign of an available parking space so he ended up parking a five-minute walk away.

The walk gave him space to calm down and also time to appreciate the church itself, as he approached it. Beautiful in proportion, it was also an archaeologist's dream, made of sandstone blocks that had been dressed for another location and another purpose. He was looking at a 12th century church that had been built with stone robbed from a Roman site, which he guessed must be the town of Viroconium only a few miles away.

It was while he was admiring this and the carved heads on the church walls that he heard the sound of music from inside. The ceremony had started. He was late. He gently opened the door and slipped inside, where he gave his eyes a moment to adjust to the muted light of candles. He caught the words "celebration of the life of our dear friend, Gwen" and realised things had just got going.

The pews were almost all full and sitting beneath a ruggedly attractive timber ceiling sat a mind-blowingly bizarre congregation. This was no ordinary service.

Most of the celebrants looked to be over sixty, but there was a good smattering of the young. Some were dressed formally, he noted a couple of morning suits, but there were also a great deal of brightly coloured, hippyish garments that would not have looked out of place at Woodstock or the Isle of Wight circa 1970.

The main celebrants were sitting at the front on a row of chairs facing the congregation. He'd never seen a more diverse grouping dressed in outfits that scaled the spectrum from high Anglican to Druidical pagan. Gwen had obviously had a full life and there was much about her he'd never suspected. He was glad. He'd liked her, she'd been wise, kind and slow to judge. You couldn't ask for more than that.

She deserved a happier end, or at least someone with her when it arrived. Another Skendleby victim. He was drawn out of this reverie by the realisation that someone was speaking to him. In the second pew from the back, just in front of him, an elderly lady was gesturing. "I've got a seat for you here, dear, come on, it's going to be so lovely."

Not having other options, he shuffled towards her and she rose to take his arm and guide him towards the space.

It was while she was doing this he saw that she was dressed as some type of fairy in loosely flowing robes with a chiffon scarf headband, the ties of which mingled with her long, grey hair.

"Come on, dear, you don't want to miss anything. The mind trance music we started with was wonderful and it's levitation by spirit next, and then some memories and funny stories from her old Oxford friends before the pagan blessing. What a lovely turn out, don't you think?"

Looking around he couldn't help but agree with her, so he settled into the pew and watched and listened. It was an emotionally rich brew and he began to feel glad he'd made the effort. Also, to his surprise, he felt at one with the rest of the congregation. There was an inescapable feeling of good will and communion.

Periodically, his fairy friend would tug at his arm and point someone out or explain one of the references or blessings. When a group of strikingly-dressed pagans, some carrying wands and wearing ornamental metallic skull caps, rose to give a blessing, he felt her tug at his arm. He turned expecting a warm smile and further elucidation. But instead she'd become agitated, shaking mumbling.

"Oh no. Not now, not now, it's not right, not fair."

Before he could enquire what was wrong she turned her gaze full upon him. "I'm so sorry, dear, you need to be strong, you must be strong."

"Sorry?"

"She's coming, you see, I feel her born on an ill wind, almost here."

Before he could respond, in an attempt to clarify the situation, a sharp blast of wind flowed down the aisle as the door was flung open behind him. It then slammed shut with a crash. He turned to look.

Claire.

Chapter 21: What Manner of Succubus?

Their morning didn't get any better. They spent ages trying to find somewhere with a decent restroom where they could grab coffee and a croissant. This took them the best part of an hour and they ended up in exactly the type of autoroute stop-over they'd hoped to avoid.

The coffee was poor, the croissant stale and the restrooms were closed for cleaning, a process that seemed to take ages and result in little evidence of cleanliness when finally completed. It was only then that they let themselves mention the grizzly misericordes from Laon.

First, Ed checked the photos in order to confirm he hadn't made a mistake. He hadn't. Illuminated by the light of the flash, the carvings were even worse. Other than identifying a terrible instance of twelfth century child abuse, they made no progress and decided to postpone thinking about it until safely ensconced in a hotel that night.

Laon left them feeling tainted and the whole French trip was pressing down on them like some shadow-wreathed nightmare. They decided to drive past Beaune to Cluny, complete their task as quickly as possible and then return to Beaune and check into the most modern hotel they could find. They'd had their fill of ancient churches and atmospheres haunted by the past. The more brightly lit and twinkly the hotel, the better.

Looking at the map, the route to Cluny seemed straightforward, which is why what followed was so disturbing.

The problems started with Beaune, or rather, what Ed thought was the Beaune exit. It couldn't have been, however, as the further from the exit they drove the more isolated the countryside became. They paused in a gap by a field gate to consult the map. It didn't help.

How could they be lost only fifteen minutes away from the autoroute? Ed tried his phone for directions but there was no signal. He switched it off but must have hit the wrong button because the photos of the misericorde appeared and would not be dispelled. They hadn't wanted to discuss it previously, now it was hard to avoid.

"That last picture reminds me of something, Ed, something terrible just out of reach."

"Sadly, I remember all too well what they remind me of, something I'll carry with me until my dying day. It's the bone I removed from the mound and buried under the church after the exorcism and Claire's..."

He got no further.

"That's it, Claire, that's where I've seen it."

"Seen what?"

"The necklace. It's a necklace of bones, she was wearing it."

"But..."

"Don't stop me, it might fade. At the house before I left, why I left. During a gathering, Claire turned her gaze on me. It was like a time lapse, the others thought she was still speaking to them, making jokes, they were laughing. But she wasn't, she was taunting me and I saw the necklace she was wearing wasn't what they saw. It wasn't new and shiny ivory, it looked like bone, old bones."

She was considerably upset. Ed knew better than to interrupt.

"There was a link missing."

He knew no prompting was required and, in any case, he didn't really want to hear what would follow.

"Ed, what if what we saw in Laon is the last link, what would that mean?"

He managed to shut down the phone, restart the car and drive off. For a while, neither of them spoke. After an hour of seeming to drive around in circles, they picked up a signpost for Charolles. They shouldn't have been anywhere near Charolles but could, at least, locate it in the road atlas. Ed decided it was better to be sure of their position, even if it meant wasting more time, and that meant heading for Charolles.

It took far longer to get there than the distance on the signpost indicated, and they stopped for a late lunch in a slow-serving truck stop restaurant. It shouldn't have been slow, there were no trucks, and in fact they were the only customers. The food was good but it was after three when they finally paid the bill.

At the car, Ed couldn't find the keys and it took a further twenty-five minutes before the waiter located them in the courtyard at the back of the kitchens. This was odd – the toilets were inside, so neither of them had been out there.

They got to Charolles quickly and managed to negotiate it without difficulty. It seemed deserted, particularly the area around the station, generating an impression of deep melancholy exaggerated by the heavy, low-lying cloud that thickened as the day wore on.

Shortly after re-crossing the rail track, there was a diversion sign redirecting them onto a minor road. So, sometime between five and six, several hours behind schedule, they entered Cluny from the wrong direction. The brightly lit and twinkly motel in Beaune was no longer an option so they settled for finding somewhere in or abutting Cluny.

Rather, it was Ed who settled for this. Olga had not spoken since the stop for lunch. She'd sat slumped and morose in the passenger seat, and Ed thought she was perhaps ill.

At the third attempt he struck lucky. A small roadside hotel a couple of miles outside town set in fields inhabited by a herd of white Charolais cattle. Ed considered this a belated slice of luck, the first two hotels they'd tried had been closed and full, in that order. This one,' L'Aubegerge de Bourgogne', was empty and they took adjacent double rooms on the top floor, sharing a bathroom on the corridor.

After settling in, he knocked on Olga's door to suggest a reconnaissance of Cluny, to organise the activity there that was now, out of necessity, postponed until tomorrow. No answer to his knock.

"Olga?"

No answer.

"Olga?"

Again, no response. He tried the door, it was locked.

"Olga, I'm driving into town for a look around, do you want to come?"

After a pause he heard a few indistinct words, one of which sounded like Claire.

"Olga, what was that? I'm asking if you want to come into Cluny."

"No."

There was no further communication from behind the door so he set off. Ed, of course, had read a great deal concerning the Benedictine abbey of Cluny and had long wanted to visit it. At first sight, it didn't disappoint. The remains dominated the town, standing gaunt in the Place de l'Abbaye. He thought he saw lights inside but the doors were locked and he experienced similar frustration at the Palace of Pope Gelasius, the Hotel de Ville and the Musee Ochier.

He tried to ring Mary. The phone had a signal but he couldn't make a connection. Rather loathe to return empty handed to the silently morose Olga, he pressed on to Abbey Church which, on inspection, also seemed closed. Just beyond, however, lay a gothic construction he guessed must be Chapelle de Bourbon. The door was ajar. He was about to enter when a voice from the shadowy interior said, "Come back tomorrow at ten."

The door was pushed closed. It began to rain. He retraced his steps to the car and drove back to the hotel. At reception he was greeted by a sentence in French he found difficult to interpret. Taken literally, the proprietor had said, "Just in time, the hour between dog and wolf is upon us."

In fact, he was still trying to make sense of this when the man retreated into the private office behind the desk saying, "Dinner is at eight."

Taken in all, it had been a most unsettling day. He decided to have a shower and not attempt to contact Olga until just before dinner time. The door to his room opened at his first touch, which was unexpected, as he remembered having locked it. However, whatever surprise that engendered was immediately dispersed by what ensued.

His first reaction was he must be in the wrong room, but that wasn't the case – his stuff was strewn all over it. Whatever his next reaction might have been was overtaken by events.

Sprawled across the bed, open legs facing him, was Olga. She was naked and her hands were busy between her thighs. She knew he was there, looked at him, smiled and removed one damp fingered hand to beckon him over. He started to protest but found himself moving towards the bed driven by a spasm of lust, powerful as a seizure. Her arms opened wide to receive him and her legs spread further apart.

He was almost touching when he saw her eyes; open but blank. He turned, rushed out and fled into the bathroom, locking the door. Some brief fumbling relieved the physical discomfort but not the mental. He sat on the toilet seat and tried to compose himself.

After a period of indeterminate length, it might have been an hour or just a few moments, he heard a distinct sound: keening or weeping. Fearing a trap he ignored this but his natural kindness overrode his reluctance and he opened the door and tiptoed down the corridor. His room was empty, the sounds came from behind Olga's door. He wrote a note and slipped it under, "Dinner at eight."

****

"She can still reach us, even here."

Ed poured some more Chablis into her glass. He'd come down to dinner five minutes early and had two bottles opened: a Chablis and a Givry rouge 2009 from a nearby estate, Parize et Fils. Normally a moderate drinker, he reckoned this would be an exceptional night. As yet his only words had been a greeting and an offer of wine. He'd wondered how the dinner would go and it was proving worse than his expectations.

"Claire."

He nodded, encouraging her to continue.

"She knows we're here. I've felt her presence growing all day. What we're doing is too dangerous, Ed, we shouldn't have come."

He topped up his own glass, the Chablis was almost finished.

"I don't know what happened, I couldn't help myself. I don't even know how or when I got into your room."

She swigged back her wine and he poured the last of the Chablis into her empty glass. A waiter, who Ed recognised as the proprietor of the gnostic utterances, arrived with a plate of cold jambon done in the local style with some cornichons, which he silently placed on the table. Ed put a little on each of their plates and began to eat. He was surprisingly hungry.

"I saw her, she was wearing that necklace, stroking it like it was a lover, then I saw Margaret. She looked so sad, so old, shabby and ill."

"You must eat something."

She took a mouthful. "I left Margaret, I left her to Claire, and I thought it was because I was jealous, but looking back she made me go. She orchestrates everything. I think she's driving us, she wants us to do this."

Ed considered this but for the time said nothing.

"Poor Margaret, I loved her...I love her and I left her. Left her to Claire who will destroy her once she's used her up."

There was a period of silence while the plates were cleared away. Ed poured some of the Givry into the larger glasses and took a sip, it was excellent.

"Claire is manipulating us to do her will, Ed. We need to go home, I need to get Margaret out of there, ask her to forgive me."

It was while she was saying this that the thought hovering somewhere in the ether finally percolated Ed's consciousness. It had to rest there a moment as two plates of a heavy, wine-rich beef stew were placed before them.

"I'm not sure, Olga. I think it's more likely that everything we've experienced today has been trying to put us off, particularly that episode in the bedroom. We've been tested."

"Tested?"

"Yes, and look, we're here, eating dinner and talking, so we've come through it. I think we finish what we started: a couple more days then home."

"And Margaret?"

"I think you could be right about her."

They finished the stew and the cheese that followed but declined dessert. The waiter brought each of them a digestif they hadn't ordered, saying, to their surprise, "You've done well today. Remember to be on time for the appointment at ten tomorrow. I'll lock the door as I leave tonight but lock your bedroom doors all the same."

That night they settled down together fully clothed, and despite the sound of something moving around on the gravel beneath their window, they slept surprisingly well.

****

Next morning, after an early breakfast served by an elderly woman they hadn't previously seen, they packed up and drove into Cluny. Parking in the Place de L'Abbaye, there was time for a quick inspection of the beautiful medieval facings of both secular and spiritual buildings.

On the stroke of ten, Ed knocked on the door of the Chapelle de Bourbon. The door was promptly opened by a man who looked familiar but who they could not place. There followed a lengthy exploration of a pretty unremarkable interior accompanied by a rambling exposition of its merits. This was delivered in a rapid and regional French that proved difficult to follow. At the end of which they were invited to examine a granary considered worthy of interest and a rather dilapidated tower.

By eleven-thirty, as the cloud mass hovered low above the spires of Cluny, they were no wiser as to their objective.

"I think we're wasting our time, Ed, you sure this is what we're meant to be looking at?"

"I don't know, I expected our guide to steer us in the right direction."

"Well, perhaps we should push on to Quarre les Tombes."

"Let's grab a coffee first."

They returned to Place De L'Abbaye and entered a bar full of locals. The room was loud with talk, very different from their recent experience. The only two spare chairs were at a table already occupied by a man whose face was hidden behind a newspaper. Olga went in search of the ladies while Ed approached the table. The damp heat of the place caused Ed's spectacles to mist over so he failed to recognise the face of their new companion when he replied to his request to join him.

When the mist cleared he found himself sitting across from their guide of that morning, or possibly their host from last night; out of context it was hard to tell. The man favoured him with an enigmatic smile.

"Disconcertingly peculiar life, isn't it?"

Ed felt the man, whoever it was, was mocking him and felt his temper beginning to rise, but before he could say anything, "I waited for you here so I could speak to you alone. I think your companion has had enough shocks for one day."

Ed had just translated this into English when his interlocutor spoke again. This time there was no need to translate, the man spoke one sentence in an English that was either regionally inflected or from an earlier time.

"From the front of the church at Quarrie, face the square and count your way to the thirty fourth stone coffin, the cracked one, that's where you search."

He stood up and walked away. Ed's specs misted over again so he lost sight of the guide before he reached the door.

Chapter 22: What Manner of Child?

The church doors crashed shut, the sound resounding up and around the tie and collar beams in the timber roof. For a split second the congregation's attention was diverted from the celebration of Gwen's life, then it was as if the doors had never opened.

Except if you were Giles. For Giles, the experience was entirely different. Claire favoured him with a wink, strolled down the centre aisle and picked up the picture of Gwen from the plinth where it lay on an artist's easel. Then she turned it upside down and stood for a moment mocking the congregation, who saw none of this. Giles saw and was held spellbound with horror, wondering at her purpose. She answered the question he'd thought but not asked. "I'm doing it because I can, because I choose to, to relieve the boredom."

He sat motionless, unable to reply and she continued. "Let me show you what this place, your little universe, will look like when my work is done."

As he watched the church disappeared to be replaced by darkness, black and impenetrable, no flicker of light. Had it not been for her voice in his mind he would have been deprived of all sensory feedback.

"This is what your universe will become once entropy accelerates: nothing. No mass, no stars, no light, just some barely detectable background radiation, a ghost of a far away memory."

She put the first finger and thumb of her left hand together. "And it's just this far away."

"You're not Claire."

Giles wasn't the only person not suspended in trance; the voice came from next to him, from his elderly, eldritch companion, the geriatric fairy. He wasn't the only one who was shocked. It seemed to take Claire by surprise. The black absence of being was replaced by the 12th century church.

"You're not the troubled girl who Gwen loved and saved."

Claire stared at her, as if trying to focus.

"Put that picture back the right way, you owe everything to Gwen, she sacrificed for you... "

She got no further. Without seeming to move, Clare was beside them. "You always claimed to have the sight, seems you were more than the mad, old bat I took you for."

"And you seemed such a sweet girl after Gwen reclaimed you, but I knew there was something wrong inside you, a void waiting to be filled."

"Well, a shame you left it too late to do anything about it. I suppose it was you who placed all those crow feathers around her plaque in the crematorium."

"No, there weren't any there when we left, perhaps something other than you is watching."

Claire stared at her, looked as if she was about to speak, but before she could, "Why do that to Gwen? She loved you so much. She never ever harmed anyone."

Claire made a brief gesture, little more than a shrug of the shoulders, and the brave and elderly fairy slumped back into her seat, Giles suspected from a stroke or heart attack. However, he had the distinct impression that the verbal exchange had knocked Claire temporarily out of kilter. It gave him one brief chance to ask the question that had been oppressing him since she'd left him for the women's house.

"The baby, Claire. What about the baby?"

Something stared out at him through eyes he'd never seen the like of. For a moment he feared he was about to receive the same treatment meted out to the fairy. Then, without knowing why, he asked, "How far gone are you?"

Whatever she might have been about to do was paused, instead she sneered, "Bit late to act the concerned parent now you're rutting with that incompetent policewoman who's making such a mess of the investigations."

"But you look about eight months gone and it can't be that long."

She favoured him with a smile that could shrivel apples. "I can never get over your naivety, Giles, never manage to plumb the shallows of your puny intellect."

"It's our baby, Claire."

"Our baby? This lump I'm growing? This primitive life form that detracts from the minimal pleasure that this crude, fleshy form affords. Do you really want me to tell you about that?"

Sitting so close to her, he didn't want that at all. He wished he'd never asked, but it seemed that this was no longer an option.

"The baby, as you so quaintly term it, is merely a necessary artefact. Wasteful and unproductive like everything else on this backward planet where the most evolved life forms are ghosts."

She paused and chuckled. "Except, of course, for humour, which I think is your one and only unique characteristic. How apt that your unique selling point should be something so useless and time wasting, something that enables you to place a veil of unreality between yourselves, your paltry existence and your meagre purpose. Still, I digress."

Horrified as he was, Giles was surprised by this, not at the content but regarding why she should be wasting her time here taunting him in the church. Why bother wasting time on a silly act of malice? It was this reflection that kept him perched on the pew listening.

"You want to know about the baby, I suppose you feel some emotional connection even perhaps responsibility?" She laughed. "Responsibility for an evening in which I subjected you to a couple of hours of abuse, admittedly mildly stimulating for me, and during which I drew the seed out of you so necessary to the project. What a primitive reproduction system you depend on, I can't see much future for it."

Why was she doing this? Was she in control? Was he here for a purpose? The thoughts chased around his mind as he listened to the vindictive monologue.

"This" – she indicated her gravid belly – "growing lump of meat has a purpose. One that can only be realised once it is delivered following the local laws of physics which obtain round here and, as the local laws are close to immutable, must be observed. A particular child is needed so it has to be cultivated. Once that's done and the harvesting has been carried out I can leave and return to something important."

She smiled and Giles was horrified, but fascinated.

"So inefficient growing a complete and organically complex, if mentally primitive, organism when all that is required is one tiny section of bone. What a waste of resource, what a waste of effort. But that's this place all over, wouldn't you agree, Giles?"

He didn't answer, his mind was clogged by the image of the helpless foetus cocooned in its fluid home in her womb. Now horror had been replaced with the urge to cry.

"Just look around you, Giles. This old church, born out of some long-dead impulse, packed full of people blubbering over an old woman who'd exceeded her usefulness. I mean, even more advanced cultures who don't possess a sense of humour would have to laugh."

Giles remembered how kind, brave and decent Gwen had been.

"Still, to get back to the point, it's virtually over now. A couple of minor details to attend to then just the harvesting and it's done and I can leave."

After a pause, perhaps to let the significance of the words sink in, she added, "Not that you and your pathetic, interfering friends will be around when that occurs, Giles. And although I'm sure you won't be able to appreciate it now, it's lucky for you that's how it will go. Kinder that way really, whatever that means. So strange, but once you get to inhabit one of these bodies you can't stop saying stupid things."

He sat, struck dumb by a sudden flood of grief and futility.

Claire stated again,

"And to think all this started with a haunting and..."

It was then that whatever he'd been brought here for happened.

There was a tiny ripple in the material of the dress covering her belly. It was repeated. He saw a change in her posture. She turned her head towards him, her eyes looked different, the unborn child was kicking. Then he did the most instinctive thing he'd ever done in his life. He reached out and gently placed the palm of his hand on her belly.

"Look, it's kicking; its little feet are kicking."

He felt her hand cover his, found himself looking into a confused pair of eyes similar to those of the old Claire.

"Where are we?"

"St Eata's church, a celebration of Gwen's life."

"I've been here before, I remember. I know most of these people?"

She stared wildly around before asking, "Where's Gwen, I don't see her?"

"Gwen's de..."

He felt her hand pull away, she was covering her face, crying. "I remember, I remember. For a moment I thought I'd woken up, thought I was free."

If she hadn't woken up, the church had. Time had restarted, the service was continuing. But not as before, there was a restlessness. People at the front were turning their heads, looking to see what was happening at the back. The speakers seemed to have lost their place, there was an atmosphere of confusion. Giles understood his window of opportunity was brief.

"Claire, Claire, hang on, you have to concentrate."

"I killed her, I did it, didn't I? This thing I'm part of?"

"Tell me, tell me what's happening. I can help, tell me what I need to do."

She began to wail in despair.

"Just listen to me, listen."

He said this but had no idea what he would say or what they should do. Her despair was infectious.

"What have I done? What have I let in? What have I let in?"

She looked wild and lost, terrified like a panicked fawn surprised by a predator at the water hole. The child kicked again, she tried to feel it with her hands. "It's our baby, Giles, our baby kicking inside."

"Hold on to that, Claire, hold on."

"What's happening to me? What's happening?"

They were making too much noise, people were looking, making shushing sounds. Near the altar, a confused celebrant had noticed the picture of Gwen was upside down and moved to turn it the right way up.

Giles decided he had to get her out of the church and away. He started to tug her to her feet. "Come on, quick, let's get out of here."

But it had never really been a possibility, he could feel from her hand she was reverting.

She pulled him back down onto the pew and began to speak, this time more measured and deliberate, as if it was her last chance. "It's too late, Giles, it's almost done, all the preparations have been made, just one little step to take."

He could see a range of changes sweep across her eyes and knew she was being dragged back. She made a final effort. "You don't know what type of actuality this really is, your world is..."

Then her eyes snapped shut and when they opened again it was something else behind them. The hand he was holding was ice cold and he pulled his away. Several members of the congregation were now angrily approaching, then they froze as the spell returned. The pregnant entity beside him said, "Seems only fair to finish off what she was going to say."

Giles waited.

"She was going to tell you that your world is so fragile. It's a slender illusion and, as such, is so easy for us to feed off. That was her final, and make no mistake it was final, message for you. Do I need to spell it out?"

Giles couldn't reply. He thought he was maybe going into a state of shock.

"Well, I will anyway, it's never really possible to overestimate how preternaturally dim you are. What the silly girl was going to say, and for once she got something right, was, 'There is no hope, there never was, it's over.'"

He couldn't see Claire anymore, just heard a malicious chuckling somewhere inside his head and the impression of the words.

"Seems I do have a sense of humour after all. I can't resist leaving you to sort all this out. Look how angry you've made them."

The church was bustling with life, he was surrounded by furious and distorted faces.

"Who are you?"

"How dare you come in here and desecrate Gwen's memory."

People were trying to manhandle him to his feet to the sound of a female voice placing a curse on him. As he was dragged upright he heard one voice out of kilter with the rest and, turning his head, saw the fairy woman who'd invited him to sit with her. She was trying to get a message across to him. He saw her lips moving and read as much as heard her message.

"Remember the child, it's still your child."

She then slumped back across the pew and the people surrounding Giles split into two groups: one trying to revive her and call up the emergency services and the other manhandling Giles towards the door. He was hustled out.

Someone said, "If you ever come here again we will report this to the police."

Then the doors crashed shut behind him. He stumbled towards where he'd left the car. It took some time to find it, his mind was spinning and his limbs were shaking. He wondered what the celebrants of Gwen's service would remember the following day and if his elderly friend would survive, if she had ever existed.

He was still shaking when he eventually found his car in its parking space by the river. He wanted a drink but decided that wouldn't be a good idea in his current state and he'd be better getting as far away from here as he could.

However, he was trembling so much that he found it difficult to place the key in the ignition. He was in no fit state to drive. He sat staring at the key until some crows, who must have just settled in the trees fringing the riverbank, started up with an awful racket of cawing which began to grate on his nerves.

He managed to start the car and manoeuvre it onto the road without accident. He pointed it north towards Skendleby and drove.

He had no idea what he was going to do.

Chapter 23: Crow Fall

He knew it was her speaking, even if there weren't any words as such, even if she wasn't here, it was her and she was inside his head. Or maybe it was the drugs he'd taken at his clubs over the years. Maybe it was them, some type of after effect. But he knew it wasn't, he knew his drugs and knew what effect they had and none of the effects amounted to hearing a very clear and threatening message.

The words weren't threatening, they came out almost as if he was being done a favour and he was 'in luck'. But he wasn't, he was being manipulated by a bully far worse than himself. What he'd heard was,

"If you go and stand by your front door, Mr Carver, you'll see something that I guarantee you will enjoy, you can regard it as a down payment on our little deal."

It was her, the woman from the house who'd messed with his head in the Sky bar – the Vanarvi woman. It was her voice and there was no missing the point in the second part of her message.

"The time for your part of the deal is fast approaching – only a few days to wait – and I know you won't want to let me down, will you?"

He didn't, he wanted all this to stop and to let him get on with enjoying the success of his development. It was now highly visible. The old airfield had gone, so had the fields around it and the road improvements were well underway, snarling up the traffic for miles around. Best of all, the steel bones of the retail and leisure development were now sticking up into the sky.

Soon those wankers who'd protested would see their view of the Pennines to the east or the Edge to the west replaced by his 'Leisure and Living' development. Serve them right that would. Best of all, for some of them the development would be their only view.

So why couldn't he enjoy it the way he should? It seemed so unfair. He was still mulling this over when he realised he'd made his way to the front door without thinking about it. Still, now he was here, he might as well take a look.

Perhaps Vanarvi had arranged for that bitch Suzzie-Jade to be knocked over and killed or something. But that would be too much to hope for, as Vanarvi had called this a down payment. So perhaps she'd only be injured and it would turn terminal later.

He was so engrossed in this fantasy that at first he missed the event he'd come to watch. However, watching wasn't the primary activity as the first indication of anything happening was aural. This was because the first of the events themselves took place beyond the range of vision in the woods by the estate boundary.

Carver stood by his door with growing impatience, his mood oscillating between anxiety and aggression, a particularly unappealing and lethal mixture in someone of his psychological nature. The longer he stood waiting the further the balance swung towards aggression. He was preparing to give up and find someone to work the accumulating anger off on when his aural antennae began to register a type of disturbance.

Not much to register at first and, for Carver, certainly nothing to get excited over: a series of sporadic sounds. Sounds he couldn't identify, but compelling all the same. The closest he could get to placing what he was hearing was the sound of a hammer on wet earth. The sound he actually remembered was of a hammer on soft tissue, but that was something from his past which he now chose to disassociate himself from.

It was, however, this association with his former activity working on his memory that kept him watching long enough to avoid missing the promised down payment. For another couple of minutes, there was nothing to see – just the sound of further periodic soft thumps.

Then something dark fell from a copse of trees on the drive and crashed to earth. It happened so quickly he couldn't be sure what it was. It made no sound as it fell, just a soft thump as it landed and lay still. If this was the down payment it wasn't much to shout about. He began to walk towards it when one, then another, came plummeting down from a tree closer to the house; thump, thump.

Leaving the shelter of the doorway, he was walking to investigate when he heard a sound behind him, up on the roof. It was a different sound, the sound of something sliding down the tiles before catching momentarily on the guttering. He turned just in time to be able to see and avoid a large, black feathery mass hurtling towards him.

He felt a faint brush of feathers against his shoulder as he dodged back inside the door frame from where he watched the extraordinary phenomenon with a horrified fascination.

It was raining crows. They came tumbling down from trees, outbuildings and the house roofs. They made no sound and it was obvious to him that they were dead from the moment they began their fall. After a time, this strange downpour ceased and he stood in shock, looking out over the landscaped front of his estate now covered in the still bodies of black carrion.

There must have been over a hundred of them, and this was without counting the ones at the rear of the house and the ones hidden amongst the trees. If this was a down payment it wasn't making him feel grateful. In fact, what he felt was a terrible sense of contamination. He'd come to hate and fear these birds since moving into Skendleby Hall.

He stood and waited, gripped by a childish fear that they might return to life and perhaps come for him. When to his relief this didn't happen, the fear was replaced by a morbid repulsion at the thought of touching them and wondering who he could get to clear this up quickly.

He had a horror that the crow corpses might decompose and pollute his land. Then an image of what

Suzzie-Jade might look like when dead percolated his consciousness, but even this didn't help as much it should have. Fortunately, help was at hand. He saw the black BMW of one of his club employees turning down the drive.

The car pulled up and a shaven-headed brute wearing dark glasses, despite the dullness of the day, emerged.

"Mornin' boss, got that good stuff you wanted."

"Never mind that, get rid of them."

"What are they?"

"Crows, innit, get 'em cleaned up."

"Been out shootin' boss?"

"How stupid are you? Just get them cleaned up, get them out of my sight."

"How do you get rid of...?"

"Gather them up in sacks and burn them, burn the fucking dirty things."

****

The first concrete evidence something was wrong confronted Suzzie-Jade as she was finishing her morning run. She'd reached the home straight and was heading towards the estate wall when she first smelt the smoke and the other smell it was masking. She knew something was coming. There had been a numinous stillness all morning, as if the wood was holding its breath in anticipation. She could almost taste it in the air.

She sensed something very wrong but didn't know what it was, although the smoke carried the stink of something rancid, roasting. Then she came across the first crow.

It was lying across the path on its back, its head unnaturally twisted to one side. She knew from this it had been dead when it dropped from the tree, its neck broken. She wondered how this could happen and who would want, or be able for that matter, to climb a tree, surprise a crow and twist its head so savagely.

Within seconds she'd stopped considering this as a possible modus operandi because the scatter of crows lying on the ground increased, the closer she drew to the estate wall. They'd all suffered the same fate. Now she thought she knew what the smell in the smoke was. This assessment was quickly confirmed.

Having stepped over the corpses of half a dozen corvids and seen at least twice as many in the woodland fringing the path, she reached the wall and, pulling herself up until she could see over, she looked towards the Hall. Spread-eagled across the lawns at the front of the house, to the right of the drive, was a further scattering of prone, black birds, some of a prodigious size.

The area to the left was almost clear and she could see the figure of one of Si's thugs; Ace, she thought. He was picking up crows and placing them in a sack. The large, reeking bonfire which he then headed towards told its own story.

She had no love for crows, they infested the woods surrounding the Hall and for a period had infested the Hall itself. But since she'd begun to see things differently she realised they were here for a purpose, even though, like her own purpose, she wasn't sure what it was. She was sure, however, that this was connected to Si and that was disturbing.

She followed the wall to the gate and jogged across the grass to the front door, ignoring the greeting of Ace en route. Inside Si was slumped into a sofa in the games room drinking what looked like a very large scotch.

"Bit early for that, innit, babes?"

She mentally kicked herself. She wanted information and baiting him wasn't the way to get it, but she'd cultivated a reaction to it and enjoyed the results. To her relief he didn't react with his usual display of petulant anger.

"Seen them crows, all over the lawn? Came crashing down out of the trees, all together. Didn't know there were so many of them."

She didn't know if this display of reasonableness was a consequence of the drink or shock, but she wasn't about to waste it.

"Did you see what happened, Si?"

"Yeah, I seen it all."

"I've just come through a load more of them in the woods."

He shivered at the thought but didn't answer. She tried a direct question. "Any idea why? You're not behind this, are you, Si?"

"Me, you mean me, and them crows?"

She could tell that he was as surprised as she by the event and considerably more upset by it. Funny that a man like him should be bothered by the death of a few birds, there must be something else.

"Apart from us, have you any idea who would want to do something like this?"

"Not about the crows, innit, part of something else. I didn't like em, now they've gone. That's what she must have mea..."

He realised who he was talking to and what he'd almost said.

"Who's that you've been talking to, Si?"

But he wouldn't say, he staggered over to the bar and poured himself another drink. It was pathetic and if she hadn't known what he was really like she'd have felt sorry for him, maybe tried to make him feel better. But she did know, so she left him to his drink, backed out of the room and left the house.

Looking up from tipping another bag of dead birds onto the fire, Ace saw her running down the drive towards the estate gates. He had mixed emotions watching her, lustful envy of Carver and a dislike bordering on the pathological.

****

Davenport had been feeling the pains in his chest growing worse all morning and knew the end couldn't be far off. It was the end of an era. The old bitch had got to a state of discomfort the day before and he knew he couldn't postpone the moment when he had to put her down. He wouldn't take her to a vet, that's no way to treat family in his book, so he waited until Debo was out then did it himself, weeping afterwards.

He'd buried her in the garden in a shallower grave than he'd have liked but a deeper one would have taken more strength than he possessed. This had plunged her mate into a fit of gloom that seemed to have knocked the stuffing out of it. So it was almost a relief when the doorbell chimed. He hoped it would be Ed, he'd been having premonitions that things were not going well with him.

However, on opening the front door, the surprise of who he found standing there rapidly dispelled any other thoughts. It took him some time to recognise the bizarrely-dressed figure on his doorstep.

"Mrs Carver, I didn't recognise you at first."

She said nothing and, after a pause, good manners overcame his inclinations. "Please, come in."

He ushered her into the lounge where the old dog stumbled to its feet and lumbered towards her to give her hands a lick. This surprised Davenport, as he'd always considered his dogs good judges of character.

"Please, sit down. I must confess I never expected to see you here."

"I never expected to be here but things have changed. I need your help."

He wasn't sure he liked where this was going.

"Where's your other dog?"

"I beg your pardon?"

"You had two."

Davenport was about to answer when she said, "Do you mind if we talk outside, it'll help me think?"

They walked through the kitchen and out through a door in the conservatory into the back garden, with its freshly dug grave. The old dog followed them out and lurched up to the grave where it proceeded to sniff about in a most mournful fashion.

"Now, will you tell me what this visit is about, if you've been sent by your husband, Mrs Carver, then..."

"Call me Suz..." She stopped herself and said, "No, I've not been sent by Si, he'd hate to know I was here. Something's happening in Skendleby, something terrible and I think you know what it is. No, please let me finish. It's like a haunting, but worse, and I think it's using Si, trying to make him do something bad and he is a very bad man."

"Why tell me this?"

"Because it's your fault, it's your land and it's your responsibility he's there."

"He bought the land."

"You had no right to sell it. I don't care about Si but you leaving that land started all this off and you are to blame for what he's going to do."

He felt this like a body blow, she must have noticed.

"You are a good man so you know what I'm talking about. Something bad is coming and Si is going to start it off, he has to be stopped."

"But what?"

"I don't know, only that it won't be long now. You'll know it when you see it. After all, you are the spirit of the land, I think you'll feel it like I do."

He felt like he was talking to a completely different person; her accent and everything except the clothes had changed.

"You say you feel the mood of the land?"

"Yeah, strange, isn't it."

"So, what do I do?"

"You watch, particularly the mound, your family have always done that, I catch glimpses of them sometimes. Then, when you see the thing begin, stop it."

"Why me?"

"Because you are the only one who will recognise the significance of it. Whatever Si tries to do, stop him. That's all I came to say."

He didn't understand but felt she was right, it was almost the same message Ed had given him.

"What did you mean by you saw my family? They're all long dead."

"Yes, but you still believe I see them, don't you?"

He nodded. "Would you like some tea?"

"No, I have to get back."

They walked round to the front drive, where she turned towards him and, to his huge surprise, kissed him on the cheek, saying, "I wish you'd been my Dad, would have made things simpler and better."

Then she walked off. The dog followed her to the gate where it sat and watched her break into a jog back to the Hall.

Davenport tried to collect his thoughts and when he had, he was left with two conclusions. The first was he was being offered a chance to expiate his guilt and this time he wouldn't fail. The second conclusion was a kind of compensation. It came as a growing awareness that perhaps he had at last passed on his guardianship of the land to someone, who, although not a Davenport as far as he was aware, understood the obligations.

He called the dog in and returned to the house. Once inside he unlocked the draw where he kept his old service revolver.

Chapter 24: Les Tombes

A pall of acrid black smoke hung above the gridlocked traffic, something all too familiar throughout the painfully slow morning and afternoon. They were still several kilometres from Calais and during the last couple of hours hadn't moved a metre. The smoke stung their eyes and it didn't make any difference if the windows were open or shut.

The smoke emanated from the French protesters' roadblock of choice: a pile of rubber, truck tyres dumped in the road and ignited. Ed had given up wondering why the gendarmes didn't prevent these toxic bonfires from being built and lit. There seemed to be a particular protocol covering the transaction: the tyres were lit, the traffic stopped and eventually the debris was cleared. Further down the road the procedure would be repeated.

From his uncertain translation of the autoroute radio station broadcasts, Ed had gathered it would be like this all the way to Calais. Not that arriving at the port would make things much better, as there were reports of industrial action at the ferry terminal, the Eurostar line was blocked and the residents of the recently reconstituted migrant camps were making periodic assaults on the perimeter fences.

In fact, now they were within striking distance of Calais, they were able to observe groups of youngish looking men attempting to force an entrance into the backs of the stationary trucks. Sparse, hooded figures emerging from the smoke onto the road gave the scene a hellish and sinister aspect.

Europe appeared to be on the verge of breakdown. Earlier on, Ed had made just this point to Olga but received no response. In fact, she hadn't spoken since they'd left Quarrie, just sat hunched and silent in the passenger seat.

The retreat from Quarrie les Tombes had been a nightmare and not only on account of what they learned there, although this had shaken Ed to the core. There was something else, something terrible destabilising Olga and driving her into her current catatonic state.

****

Like all their journeys in France, the distance from Cluny to Quarrie took far longer than it should have. On this occasion, due to a dense, wet mist they drove into as the minor road snaked its way steeply uphill towards the Morvan national park. However, after seeming to have driven half blind through the opaque and deserted countryside for hours, they were relieved, if surprised, to see a sign bearing the legend Quarrie Les Tombes at a crossroad. Minutes later, they found themselves in the main square.

Both hotels recommended in the guidebook were either closed or refusing to answer the door, but there was a tall and thin dilapidated building just across the street from the damp, stained walls of the church. On one of the ground floor windows hung a sign advertising vacant rooms. They pushed open the gate and followed a narrow path to the door, which was open.

Ed led the way and found himself in a small, dark eating area divided by a partition or screen, the purpose of which he couldn't determine. A small, grey-haired woman in a well-worn apron – who he'd failed to notice at first glance – was sitting in a chair by the entrance to a passage. It looked to Ed that she'd been waiting for them, although that seemed hardly possible. She said, without any greeting, "We have two rooms, one on the third floor and one on the second, but they're not ready. Go to the bar and come back later. You can leave your bags in here."

The bar was easy to find for two reasons: it was the only place lit up and it was very noisy. On entering they were greeted by an effusive bearded man who reminded Ed of the eccentric German who had until recently managed Liverpool Football Club. The day had been so disorientating that Ed was prepared to believe that it could very well have been Jorgen Klopp.

They picked their way between crowded tables to the bar, where a gamine barmaid was simultaneously flirting with several customers and serving drinks. Apart from Olga, she was the only female in the place and obviously one of the bar's main attractions.

Ignoring Ed's order she served them both with half litres of a strong local beer on draught and directed them to a small, vacant table in the far corner. "Try this, it's good, you can have wine later."

Ed was too overwhelmed by the way events were progressing to complain, so they carried the unwanted beers to the table. The beer, however, was good and spread a warm relaxed glow through their systems. After some minutes the barmaid arrived at their table with two more beers and a basket containing cutlery, condiments and napkins for a meal they hadn't ordered.

The ambience of the bar enfolded them and they relapsed into a comfortable silence surrounded by the gentle hum of myriad conversations and snatches of traditional chanson from speakers located somewhere in the ceiling. When the first course, a plate of crudities, arrived, Ed decided not to question but just go with the flow, seeing that everyone else in the bar, including Jorgen Klopp, was eating.

After a dish of chicken in sauce, a plate of cheese and a litre of red they were feeling comfortable and replete. During the dessert, the bearded owner approached the table bearing three strong coffees and three glasses of a strong, if unspecified, digestif. He sat down with them.

The time passed pleasantly although Ed had only a very vague understanding of what was said. In fact, the only thing he distinctly remembered was his host saying, "May as well just enjoy this, recharge your batteries. After all, there's nothing that can be done until tomorrow."

It seemed to make sense at the time. After that everything became a little hazy in a comfortably soporific way. They had no memory of paying or leaving, just a vague experience of crossing the square towards their hotel, but no recollection of any transaction on arrival. Ed remembered sinking down, fully clothed, onto a soft bed.

When he woke it was dark.

Dark and, when he managed to find his watch after fumbling around in the gloom, early in the morning. There was no sound, the hotel was as still as death. He felt like he'd been drugged and Eliot's line, "Like a patient etherised on the table," came to him. It was five-fifteen and he lay for a while trying to remember the previous day and make sense of it. He failed on both counts and was still trying to work out why they hadn't tried to even look at the church and the stone coffins when he drifted back into sleep.

He woke again just before seven, too early to try ringing Mary or go down to breakfast, so he had plenty of time to explore the room, which he hadn't noticed the night before. It was curiously old fashioned, particularly the wiring which he was sure wouldn't pass any safety inspection. The furniture was of dark, heavy wood and there was a bowl and a jug of water on the sideboard. It was like walking onto the set of a film based on the early twentieth century.

He fiddled unsuccessfully with the dials of an old radio then tried his mobile. There was no signal. He decided to give Olga until eight then he'd wake her. In the event, this proved unnecessary, as there was a tap on the door. On opening it, he found himself staring at her unnaturally pale face.

"Ed, I've had the strangest dreams. I'm not sure I'm even awake. What's happening?"

"Don't worry, I think we were both overtired and drank a little too much, I'm sure you'll feel better after breakfast."

He spoke with a certainty he didn't possess and was pretty sure she didn't believe him, but they made their way down to breakfast, where they found a table set for two.

"Look at this place, Ed, it hasn't been touched for years, there's something wrong."

"Nothing happened to us in the night so..."

"Speak for yourself. You didn't dream what I did, we need to get out."

The conversation was fractured at that juncture by the arrival of the grey-haired women in the old apron. As he looked at her, Ed realised that – like the trappings of his bedroom – she too looked like something from a historical film. She set a tray down on the table and left. The breakfast consisted of two large bowls of milky coffee, a still-warm baguette, croissants, butter and jam.

The breakfast actually tasted very good but they weren't in the frame of mind to enjoy it.

"We need to get out, Ed, we need to go now."

"Once we've located the coffin, shouldn't take too long."

"I won't stay a minute longer in this place."

"Well, once we've packed our bags."

"Mine's already done. Give me the keys, I'll wait in the car."

"But I shan't be..."

"I won't stay here. What can't you understand about that?"

He handed her the keys and watched her leave before returning to his room and throwing his stuff into his bag. While he was doing so he realised he was constantly looking over his shoulder. He backed out of the room and scurried downstairs to find the old woman and pay the bill.

There was no sign of her, the place felt empty. Empty in a convincingly final way, empty of more than just people. He took his bag to the car, that too was empty and locked, no sign of Olga.

He began to panic so took some deep breaths to steady himself. She'd probably gone for a walk and would soon be back. The sensible thing to do would be to inspect the stone coffins around the church for whatever he was meant to find there and be ready to leave when she returned.

He walked across the road through the fret of early morning mist to the church. It stood grey and sombre, its base completely surrounded by an unbroken (save at the doors) ring of heavy stone coffins in various states of repair, all heavily weathered. Despite being a man of God, he knew that in whatever present he currently inhabited there was no God in this church who would offer him succour.

He stood at the front facing the square, as he had been instructed, then walked towards the rear, counting the stone sarcophagi until he came to the thirty-fourth. This one had been damaged, the lid was cracked and he could see down into the interior. There was no one around and the sepulchral silence of the square accentuated every sound he made.

He crouched on his hands and knees on the damp earth and, using the torch app on his phone, shone the light into the coffin. It didn't help much – it seemed empty except for a space in the near right-hand corner, which the beam, for reasons he was unwilling to consider, wouldn't illuminate. He couldn't neglect this space so with reluctance pushed his arm down into the aperture and began to feel around.

Stone, some organic detritus and then something soft and rotten, hair covered and moistly warm. He shrieked and jumped back up, banging into someone who must have crept up behind him.

"Forgive me my tardiness, I'd intended to relieve you of that particularly unsavoury operation."

The voice was slightly accented, the soft tones of the educated Levant. He turned and found himself looking at a figure clothed in black. Black what, he couldn't be sure of, maybe it was the mist but the garments seemed weirdly indistinct. The face wasn't. He found himself regarding a sallow complexion, an aquiline nose and jet-black hair swept back from the forehead.

But it was the eyes that fascinated – heavy-lidded and lazily half closed, part concealing the striking green of the iris. Taken aback, Ed could only bluster, "I'm looking for something."

"What you want isn't in there."

"But I was told to look in the coffin."

"Perhaps we have become over fond of metaphor. I am the thing you search and I've waited far too long for you to arrive."

"But I only knew I was coming here a matter of days ago."

"Not waiting for you specifically, you just happen to be the first to successfully follow the trail. My brothers and I have waited through the ages."

"So what is it you want me to see?"

"To see? Nothing, there's nothing to see. Do you think we'd be stupid enough to leave evidence lying around?"

"Then what in God's name am I doing here?"

"You are here to learn and to listen to a short message, after which you will return to Skendleby with all speed. There is little time, the endgame has begun."

"But..."

"Listen, what you suspect about the bones is partially correct. Find and preserve the missing link. Keep safe the last link, the last bone, it mustn't be allowed to complete the 'Throat of Death'. To prevent that you must persuade the entity to return to its lair."

Ed was now angry as well as out of his depth.

"If you think I've come all this way to play some stupid word game you can just..."

His interlocutor raised a hand and he stuttered to a stop.

"Tell me, why do you think your little charade at Skendleby failed to work?"

"I don't know."

"Yes, yes you do. In your mind you know exactly why. What was missing?"

"Missing?"

"Yes, what was missing from the tomb and pit when you resealed them?"

"Nothing, the archaeologists recreated the original setup."

"Did they? Was the ceremony an exact copy of the ancient one?"

"Yes, except obviously for the..."

"There, I told you it was already in your mind."

"Come on, you can't..."

"One thing is of the utmost importance. The Skendleby mound is a portal. It's fragile, lose that and you lose everything. Preserve the mound, you know how to use it. Now go, time is short."

"That's not enough."

"It's all I can give you. Leave here straight away, don't bother with your bill, regard that as being on the house, although it is a house you will not be able to find again. Don't worry if the Quarrie you leave looks different to the one you arrived in."

He turned to go then, as if struck by an afterthought, said, "Give my regards to Steve; tell him I look forward to our being reunited."

Ed had a series of questions but he found he was alone and standing in bright sunshine by the car. In the square, a market was in full swing, part of it appeared to be occupying the site of the building they'd slept in. He saw Olga picking her way through the stalls towards him.

"Olga, I need to talk."

"Get in the car and drive. Something terrible is happening at the house, happening to Margaret. We've been lured here to get us out of the way."

He got in and started the engine. Olga slumped beside him and refused to say another word.

****

The traffic started and began to jerk forwards, then gradually speeded up until Ed was driving at almost twenty miles an hour. He drove past the trees and heavy branches that migrants had placed in the road to slow the heavy trucks and which the police had at last managed to clear. The burning tyres had gone, leaving a greasy haze and foul stench. This time, instead of crawling to a halt, they continued to accelerate – maybe they'd be able to get home after all.

They reached the ferry terminal and joined the queue. As he cut off the engine, Olga said, "We're too late, it's happening."

He looked across the docks towards England. The sky was a dense mass of black churning cloud.

Chapter 25: Submerged

"A message? Yes, that's exactly what it is."

The speaker was Theodrakis, the location a dimly lit pub behind the Roman fort deep in the penumbra of the Castlefield railway viaduct. A location chosen with care for its seediness and unpopularity rather than for any particular merit it possessed.

They were there to discuss matters deemed unsafe to raise at police headquarters. Viv, Theodrakis and at the last moment, on a whim of Viv's, a rather uncomfortable Anderson. Theodrakis was unusually loquacious.

"Consider a moment; we are bombarded with unnatural phenomena, none believable and none that lasts more than a few days. Changing, ephemeral and largely unrelated, as if eventually one will make sense to us, make a connection."

The answer didn't satisfy the questioner, Anderson; he put his pint glass down onto the battered and sticky wood surface of the old table, where it made a louder noise in the quiet pub than he'd intended.

"Come on, Sir, you can't expect us to buy that."

"Remember how that tree on the mound made you feel, Jimmy? Made sense of the things at Lindow, have you?"

Anderson said nothing, just picked his beer back up off the table. He didn't like anything about Skendleby, it creeped him out, but this, the stuff Theodrakis was spouting, made it worse. He stole a quick glance at Viv's face, she was hanging onto Theodrakis's every word. She believed. He sat back to listen.

"Consider also the nature of the crime scene under the city. A young woman, missing for some weeks, dies. Maybe of natural causes, we don't know. We do know she'd recently given birth." He looked at Anderson before saying, "We can all agree on that I think?"

Anderson nodded.

"Good. Well, let's look at the circumstances of her interment, shall we? Buried with deliberate and lavish care, surrounded with a series of fetish objects that presumably have individual and collective significance. Everything in its place, everything fixed, unlike the bones and other detritus that seem to swirl and shift. The contrast was intentional, we were meant..."

Anderson couldn't keep silent. "You can't assume that. Look at the stuff at Lindow, all of that was shifting, where was the contrast there? Where was the message?"

"We missed it, whatever was fixed there we didn't see. Whatever we were meant to pick up there we overlooked, which is why we've been presented with this assemblage. Perhaps there have been a series of signs we were meant to recognise and interpret but which we failed to, that's the way things worked on Samos."

Anderson wasn't prepared to concede. "But it wasn't just us who missed it. The archaeologists, Glover and Watkins, missed it; they couldn't make any sense of Lindow."

"But they've interpreted this, haven't they?"

They sat in silence for a moment, then Viv made her first contribution since they'd sat down. "Giles agrees with Theodrakis. He and Watkins say the way the body was treated has archaeological parallels in fairly recent excavations: a shamanic burial or something. The meaning of the stuff under the metro link is much clearer, if we try we may be able to decode it."

"What, like this is some form of communication? Something aimed specifically at us, something that we're meant to read and then act on. Get real."

Apart from the last two words this was exactly the point that Theodrakis was trying to make, but having it spelt out coldly by Anderson emphasised the implications of the assertion. Logic and reality were overturned. Theodrakis must have understood the need for a break. He wasn't a drinking man, but he made his way to the bar for another round.

In his absence Viv said, "I know how this sounds, Jimmy, but remember what he saw on Samos."

"Yeah, him and the archaeologists, they all had the same bad experience and it's affected them all the same."

"It's more than that, Jimmy. I've experienced things here too. I know working with cults and stuff affects us emotionally, but there's something about this that won't be solved by normal procedure. None of this is normal."

He started to protest but she cut him off.

"Ok, ok, if you don't believe me, talk to Gemma. Ask her about what she experienced that night at Skendleby when she won her bravery award. Ask her about Lisa Richardson and the events following that night."

"You've been talking to Gemma behind my back."

"I've been talking to one of my subordinates, Sergeant, which is my job."

Further acrimony was averted by the arrival of Theodrakis with the drinks. If he was aware of the barely suppressed anger he gave no sign of it. Instead he asked Anderson a direct question. "Do you know what actually happened at Skendleby eighteen months ago?"

"Course I do, I investigated there."

"And?"

"There were a series of attacks, carried out by one or more disturbed persons, which then ceased."

"Any idea why they ceased?"

"No, but that's not particularly unusual, happens all the time, look at the unsolved crimes record."

"That wasn't the reason."

Anderson stared at him quizzically.

Theodrakis stared at the yellow-stained ceiling as if deciding something, then, "On the night of the winter solstice eighteen months ago, Giles, Steve and the Rev Joyce, along with Sir Nigel Davenport, believing that they'd let something escape from the Skendleby mound, attempted to put it back."

Anderson looked at Viv. "What? Is this true Ma'am?"
She nodded.

"Then why didn't I know? Who did know?"

He couldn't keep the rising inflections of hurt and anger from his voice.

"No one; they kept it to themselves. Then Watkins told Colonel Theodrakis during the troubles on Samos, and, when he began to figure out what this mock burial was meant to represent, he told me. I then questioned Giles and he admitted it happened. I've only known for a couple of days. It was kept secret."

"The chief?"

"He still doesn't know as far as I'm aware, but recently we discovered that it seems there is knowledge of these events outside Skendleby."

"What?"

"Sorry, Jimmy, that's all I can say."

"So, just the two of you. Why?"

"And Giles."

"Glover, but not the chief, what's going on?"

Theodrakis pushed a pint across the table towards him. "That's what we're trying to explain, Jimmy. We've been through strange times and we need to stick together. Just hear me out to the end, regard it as me thinking aloud, we need your help."

Anderson said nothing. He picked up his pint and began to drink.

Theodrakis interpreted this as a signal of assent. "Whatever they tried at Skendleby didn't work, it made things worse and now two of the original group are dead and one, Claire Vanarvi, is changed utterly; possessed is probably a mild term. What if this dreadful thing we've been investigating beneath the city streets is some type of blueprint for what we need to do, for what they should have done, for what they must try next time?"

"You expect me to believe any of this? It's mad, that's what it is, madness. I have to tell the chief, I have to, can't stay here any longer."

He pushed his pint glass back across the table towards Theodrakis then scrambled to his feet, upsetting the light wooden chair he'd occupied. It tottered on its axis for a moment then fell crashing onto the floor, the noise echoing that of the door Anderson slammed behind him on his way out.

Viv looked at Theodrakis. "I know how he feels, I can barely make myself sit here any longer."

"But unlike him, you've no way out."

"No, I've been brought here for a purpose, everything's been arranged and there's something watching me, haunting my flat."

"It might be watching out for you."

She ignored this. "At my worst, I even suspect my relationship with Giles has been arranged, something else locking the both of us in. I don't know what's real anymore, I can't differentiate between superstitious hysteria and rational thought."

"Don't allow your relationship with Giles to be polluted by this; it's real enough, he's a good man and you need each other."

"And what about Claire? What about the child?"

"I think sorting that out is why you're here, Viv."

She saw he believed this, saw the compassion in his eyes. It made her want to cry because it was what she was coming to believe; there was no way out of this for her. She reached out for Jimmy's three-quarter-full pint glass and began to drink.

****

Anderson's head was spinning, he must have walked for some time without noticing where he was. Without looking he stepped out onto the road; a car horn, loud and angry, and the sound of swerving tyres. He jumped back and inhaled a few deep breaths while taking in his surroundings.

Visibility was poor and the streets were draped in a thickly wet early summer fog. It was unseasonably warm and this uncomfortable combination with the opaque coils of hanging, brownish air made it difficult to breathe. Peering around, he saw he was at the edge of the Castlefield canal basin near the old Hacienda, an area packed at night, when all the clubs and bars opened, but sparsely populated and strangely desolate during the day.

This wasn't a comfortable place to be and, despite his courage and all the things he'd had to deal with in his career, he began to walk quickly. He had no idea what to do and was considering whether he ought to go back to the pub when his phone whistled to him that he'd received a text.

"At the locks by the Keeper's Cottage, come now."

He had no idea who it was from and, strangely, it left no number. The location was very close and, were it not for the fog, would be visible from his current position. After considering the logic of attending a rendezvous of such uncertain provenance in an isolated location, by a canal that on a regular basis yielded the bodies of sundry unfortunates, he found himself walking down the steep gradient towards the tow path.

At water level the fog was thicker, rising in a miasma from the litter-cluttered dirty brown water. He paused under a bridge from which droplets dripped down onto him. He felt very alone, but he wasn't.

A slight, grey figure detached itself from the fog and moved towards him, its features gaining a measure of clarity as it approached. The figure of a wispily-bearded man in a dark-coloured fedora from which a pony tail dangled at the back. He had a satchel hanging by a strap from his left shoulder. Anderson had a hazy recollection of seeing him somewhere before.

"Sergeant Anderson, so good of you to get here so promptly."

"But you knew where I was?"

"Of course. I'm just observing the proprieties. Trying to put you at ease as it were."

"Who are you?"

"That doesn't really concern you, but this will satisfy you as to what I am."

He showed him an identity card that left Anderson in little doubt as to what he was dealing with.

"Good. Now that we both understand our relative positions, the rules of engagement become clear, do they not?"

Anderson nodded.

"Splendid. Now you can begin by telling me about the nature of the conversation you have just enjoyed with Syntagmatarchis Theodrakis and Detective Inspector Campbell, and please don't delude yourself with petit-bourgeois notions of loyalty. We both know you have no choice."

Anderson delivered an accurate, if brief, account of what had transpired.

"Excellent, progress at last."

Of all the events in a disturbing day, Anderson found this response the most baffling and was still puzzling on it when his interlocutor continued.

"Jimmy, you don't mind if I call you Jimmy do you? It makes us seem closer, wouldn't you agree?"

Jimmy wouldn't but recognised the question was rhetorical and that the man was amusing himself.

"Now, Jimmy, I'm afraid I have to tell you that our little conversation is going to change your life and not, initially at least, in a good way. Although, circumstances permitting, further down the track, assuming of course you make it that far, there may be certain compensations."

Anderson again made no response, as far as he could work out there didn't seem to be one.

"Now, following a little briefing which I'm sure you will have no difficulty remembering, I'm going to give you an instruction. An instruction you will carry out when you recognise the appropriate circumstances, which, believe me, you will."

Anderson listened in dread and amazement, almost missing the concluding sentence.

"And I'm afraid after that, everything will be very different for you."

And missing entirely the wistfully delivered final cadence. "Perhaps too different."

Then he was alone with the fog and the sullen, slow murmur of water washing up against the residual ooze and mud.

He had no recollection of seeing the man slip away. Perhaps it had all been a dream from which he'd awake. But he knew it wasn't and he'd never felt so alone in his life. He needed to see Gemma, who, as had been made explicit in the briefing, would become a victim of Skendleby if he failed to comply with his orders.

He followed the deserted canal as far as the lights of the bars on Canal Street, where he rejoined the road and what seemed to be the land of the living.

Some minutes later and out of breath, he crashed through the front door of the police headquarters. But here again, events overtook him. Before he had a chance to look for Gemma, the duty Sergeant called across to him.

"That's great timing, Jimmy, couldn't raise the DI or Zorba. Just had a strange call from Skendleby. There seems to be some trouble. Reports of vandalism and shots, maybe a killing. You'd better get over there straight away."

Chapter 26: So It Begins

Si Carver was having a good day; a visit to the first phase of his vast and risky development project. To be honest there'd been times when he thought he'd overstretched himself, bent too many rules, greased too many palms, overextended his credit, but it looked like he'd come out a winner.

Even better than that, it was ahead of schedule and, as phase one contained the prestige homes, the ones that would really rake in the profit, his liquidity problems were rapidly vanishing. Walking across the ruins of the Skendleby 'Green Belt' torn apart by diggers and bulldozers, he couldn't resist a quiet smile of satisfaction.

After all, this formerly had only been a waste of space: fields and hedgerows, with, according to the archaeologists, traces of earthworks and field patterns from the Middle Ages, or some such bollocks. But now, down to him and his ambition, it was all transformed, it had purpose. It had, through the alchemy of his business methodology, metamorphosed into money.

The starter homes and all the other do-gooder crap would have to wait until later, and only then if his lawyers couldn't find wriggle room in the small print of the contract to remove the commitment to social housing. Anyway, he'd worry about that later as the next phase was the 'Si Carver Retail Park and Leisure Development'.

So, it seemed things hadn't worked out too badly after all. Course, there'd been things he wouldn't have chosen, shocks and the like, but when you thought about it, even the death of Richardson had been a result. If he'd still been around he'd have been a liability, could have caused trouble. And it would have been real trouble because Richardson knew too much.

Si had always known that he'd have to settle with him at some stage, but now with him being dead there were no more skeletons in the cupboard. Except Richardson's of course. Chuckling at his own joke, Si looked contentedly across the acres of trenches and mud stretching out toward the Pennines.

A scene littered with diggers, trucks and men in hard hats. None of this would be here but for him; he'd created it, no one had been able to stop him. Then he looked back at the half finished executive mansions with their tiny garden plots squeezed as close up to each other as was possible. Amazing the amount of money the mugs who brought them would squander in a vain attempt to achieve status through acquisition.

He allowed himself a further congratulatory smile. After all, this was his achievement, this was his legacy for Skendleby. It would never be the same, he'd dragged it into the twenty first century, now it would look just like all the other greenbelt developments, only bigger.

Not that he'd get any gratitude for his contribution and not that this mattered to him, because with the fortune he'd netted he'd sell off Skendleby Hall and flit down to London. That's where the real class and money was.

But it wasn't just the physical reality of his dream project making him feel so good, there was something else, and for this he owed Claire Vanarvi. She may be mad and frightening, and Carver reckoned she was both, but she didn't half get things done. He'd seen the result this morning and it was this, even more than the success of his development, which was enabling him to feel genuinely happy for the first time in about a year.

He'd caught the first inkling of it that morning at breakfast. When he'd come down with a bit of a hangover, shouldn't have drunk so much on top of the coke he'd snorted – there was a different atmosphere. He couldn't put his finger on it but there'd been a change. He managed a decent breakfast for the first time in ages.

He was just finishing when she came into the room and he knew it must be working: the things Claire had promised. The dead crows and stuff had been good for starters, but this was the real deal – he'd never seen Suzzie-Jade like this.

She was pale, confused and looked like she didn't know where she was – like a punch drunk fighter clinging to the ropes. All the sneering and bitchiness had been knocked out of her. She wouldn't be in a hurry to mock him and his sexual performance again. Magic.

Best of all she'd been crying. Something had got through to her vicious little heart to make her cry and, even better, she wanted his help. Help from him! How much more fucking stupid could she possibly get? He wasn't a man to cross; Si Carver never forgave.

She'd peered timidly round the kitchen like she was looking for a trap, then crept uncertainly towards him. "Something's in the house, you need to come and look."

Same mardy tone of voice though. He felt his anger rising, this was more like it. "That's strange, when I said something was in the house you just laughed."

She flinched and changed the tone, sounded plaintive. "Please come and look, I can't think straight, I'm seeing things."

He got up and followed her out of the kitchen and up the stairs leading towards her suite of rooms. He couldn't ever remember her asking him for help before; asking for money, yes, she was always asking for that.

He could feel his anger growing, something that her uncertain progress up the stairs fuelled. He was anticipating how he'd get his own back on her when he realised they'd reached the door to her bedroom.

She stood back to let him go in, not her usual style. At first he wasn't sure what he was looking for, then she pointed to an open draw in the dressing table. He walked across and looked. Inside, skewered to the base of the draw with a masonry nail, was a large crow lying on its back. From the smell and decomposition it had been dead for some time.

A week ago this would have freaked him, given him palpitations, not now. Now he knew what caused it. It had been done for him, his power was back. He laughed, couldn't help himself. How the tables had turned. He saw she was looking at the bed and he followed her gaze.

On the expensive counterpane, by the pillows, the cuddly toys, which he hated, had been replaced. In their stead lay a circle formed of black feathers, at the centre of which was a geometric design comprised of beaks.

Si was lost in admiration at the ingenuity of this. Who could have thought of such a thing? Come to that, how did they manage to get the beaks out of the heads? Brilliant that was. He saw from the bits of stuffing and synthetic fur that the cuddly toys had been savagely ripped apart and shoved under the bed. This was his moment.

"See this? Take a good look cos this is just for starters, see? You try and mess with me and this is what you get. I told you I knew people, powerful people, bet you never thought I had a friend who could manage this. Well, now you know."

There was no reply. Well, what could she say to that? He'd been thinking this was the time to get rid of her, make her pack her bags and leave there and then. But he was enjoying this; it had been laid on for him so he might as well have a bit of fun. Break her down a bit more and then, when she was really broken, he'd slap her around a bit then maybe make her do those things she hated, that'd pay her back for laughing at him.

"Now, you can just stay in here a while and wait to see what else my friend's going to bring along for you. Should be some great surprises to look forward to. Perhaps I'll look in on you tonight, see how you're getting along."

He moved towards the door. She must have gathered what he intended because she lurched after him. But Si was quicker. He'd removed the key from the inside of the door, left the room and slammed it behind him. He could hear her scrabbling at the handle as he turned the key in the lock.

"Enjoy yourself, should get really interesting in there when it goes dark."

He could hear the sobs and screams as he walked down the corridor towards the stairs. By the time he was on the stairs he was thinking about her replacement.

Perhaps someone a bit older, the type who'd want to look after him, you know, mother him a bit, and classier. Much classier, the type who'd like watching Downton Abbey or something. They'd stay at home and never complain, but would behave and look good in public. He'd begin to ask around for someone suitable.

Downstairs, Tegan, a 'hostess' from his 'Elite Night Club' was taking her turn as housekeeper, not that she was any good at it.

"Listen, I'm going out. Don't go upstairs whatever you hear, understand?"

Tegan nodded. She'd never intended going upstairs anyway and was just relieved he was going out. She watched his Range Rover recede down the drive then lit a cigarette and sat down to while away the hours with her IPhone, ignoring the noise from upstairs, which sounded like some birds must have got into the house.

****

He'd just finished his 'on site' meeting when Claire called. Not called exactly, but he was aware she wanted to see him. Without quite knowing how, he found himself parking up on the gravel drive of a secluded, large old house that had obviously seen better days. He walked up to the front door which was literally hanging open and, after shouting a couple of times, walked inside.

What he found was a nasty shock even for a man like him. A group of three women were laughing at something. At first he thought it must be a TV hidden from view, but it wasn't. They were sitting staring at nothing but acting like they were being told a really funny story. But that wasn't the shocking part.

The place was filthy, damp, mildewed and dilapidated, but they were worse. Clothed in rags, faces red and blotchy, malnutrition and scurvy stamped all across them. What had he walked into? He was staring fascinated when he heard a peal of laughter behind him.

"Isn't it a hoot, the poor dears, and they think they're so happy. I still can't resist jokes like this. I think a sense of humour's the one thing I'll miss when I move on."

His good mood evaporated. He stared at her in horror.

"Oh, come on, Simon, you have to laugh, surely, if you can't appreciate the pure joy of cruelty then who can?"

Si wasn't quite sure if this was intended as a compliment but did understand no answer was required.

"I'll quite miss them when I dispose of them after the birth. I'd offer you a drink but the law of entropy has accelerated so quickly here recently that I doubt you'd enjoy it very much."

She looked far more pregnant than when he'd seen her a few days ago; ready to give birth. Something was accelerating rapidly in her as well. He managed to stammer, "What do you want?"

"That's not very grateful for all the lovely surprises I've given Mrs Carver recently."

He was really scared now, his tongue dry in his mouth, but he needed to know what was happening. He stammered again, "What do you want?"

"I want you to destroy the mound, I want you to level it with one of your diggers and I want it done tonight, well before midnight."

"I can't, I've already tried, and it's too dangerous."

"Are you disobeying me, Simon?"

She seemed to change as she said this, sort of go fuzzy at the edges and begin to slip into an entirely different shape. One he didn't want to see, even the beginning of. The initial suggestion of the transformation having already turned his bowels to water. He squealed, "Stop, I'll do it."

"Now, there's a clever boy. You understand how much more frightening I am than anything else you can imagine. Isn't that right?"

He nodded, behind him the three decaying women began to laugh louder.

"There, they think I've told them a particularly funny joke. I think I'll give you a little of what they've got, help you carry out the task."

"Why can't you do it? You've got the power, why me?"

"Because I can't, the local laws of physics prevent it and it would damage me too much. So it has to be you."

"What about me, won't it damage me?"

"Probably, who cares?"

The next thing he remembered was waking up in the driver's seat of his car outside his own front door. He couldn't remember going to sleep, couldn't remember driving home, but he could remember the dream and what was expected of him. Strangely it didn't frighten him any more. In fact, he almost looked forward to it. He was feeling good again.

****

Tegan was surprised he was back so soon and even more surprised to see him in such a good mood.

"Anything happen while I was out?"

"Just some noise upstairs."

"So, what did you do?"

"Nuffin."

She wasn't daft, she understood the way things were between Carver and Suzzie-Jade, who she resented for her wealth and high-handed manner. Also she knew better than to cross Carver.

"Won't need you tonight, Teegs, so you can go." He fished a fifty-pound note out of his wallet. "Here, get a taxi, get it now and you can keep the change."

She couldn't believe her luck. No point wasting fifty quid so she waited till Carver left the room then phoned her current boyfriend, a mixed martial arts fighter, to collect her.

Once she'd gone he changed into some jeans and went to look at the digger that had been left round the back of the Hall since the strange, but well deserved death of Gifford on Lindow Moss. It was in good order and started at the first touch. Funny that, he'd expected the battery to have gone flat.

He decided to wait until dusk to bulldoze the mound as the roads would be quiet then. He almost regretted having to wait, he was looking forward to the job. Why hadn't he thought about doing this himself ages ago? He whiled away the hours in his games room. At least he thought he did, even though he had no memory of what games he'd been on.

Then it was dusk, time to destroy Devil's Mound, time to put an end to his problems. Just as he was pulling on a hoodie, the idea came to him that someone ought to know what he was about to do. He discovered, to his surprise, that he remembered Jim Gibson's mobile number.

Strange that, he didn't think he'd ever used it before. Even stranger was the fact that he considered advertising the act a good idea. But in his mood of hyper optimism he didn't question the discrepancy between action and logic. Then he found himself putting the mobile back in his pocket. Time seemed to be slipping.

Next thing he was aware of was his first glimpse of the mound through the trees. It looked small, insignificant. What had he been so worried about? The gate was open, lucky that, he wouldn't have to stop the digger to open it. He surged forward, surprised the digger had so much speed.

He was vaguely aware of the branches of the strange, white tree whipping round ferociously and a mass of crows circling the mound. But they didn't matter, it was all arranged. He had an image of the Vanarvi woman smiling at him, she was pleased with him. It was going to be easy, the digger seemed to acquire another gear, must be doing about thirty now.

A shaft of late sunlight out of a grey sky hit the mound, illuminating it, picking out the target. He saw he'd raised the massive shovel, didn't remember doing that or even how you did it. There was something coming out of the tree-line by the church. A figure, black and capering, on course to intersect with his trajectory just before he'd hit the mound. This wasn't part of the plan, surely?

But then he saw it was part of her plan, the most brilliant part. He mustn't have seen it properly. As the figure got closer he saw it for what it was. Davenport, the old fool himself. Vanarvi had given him everything in one go.

He'd finish them both together, the mound and Davenport. It would look like an accident; why should he be expected to find anyone on his land?

The old man must be trying to stop him like he always did. Well, not this time he wouldn't. This time Si would finish him off proper. He slowed the digger slightly; give Davenport time to reach him, time to get in front of the digger. If he managed to make it that far, pace he was going should give an old boy like him a heart attack.

It was going like a dream, the old fool was right in front of the digger. At the last minute he lowered the shovel and hit the accelerator pedal. The digger surged forwards, as if sensing the kill.

Gotcha!!!

Chapter 27: On the Mound

Jim felt on edge all day, no particular reason, just 'by the pricking of his thumb'. So when the phone rang he knew it wouldn't be good news. However, he hadn't expected this.

For a few seconds, it sounded like there was no one there at all, unless it was an unwanted selling call from some distant part of the world preceded by a time lapse.

"Hello, Jim Gibson here."

Nothing, he was about to end the call when, "Gibson, it's Si Carver."

Didn't sound like Carver, the voice was distracted, unreal and what's more, seemed disinclined to say anything else. Jim decided it was a hoax but to be on the safe side would give it one final try.

"Mr Carver, what can I do for you? Please speak up, the sound quality is very poor."

"What, who's there?"

"Jim Gibson, editor of the journal, what do you want?"

"What do I want?"

"Yes, you rang me, what do you want?"

There was another pause and Jim decided to terminate the call. However, before his finger managed to hit the 'end call' symbol, a message was delivered and, strangely, delivered in a different voice to Carver's confused tones.

"Go to Skendleby Mound if you want a front page story."

The line went dead, he tried to ring back but it appeared the number no longer existed. He didn't want to re-engage with Skendleby, his first encounter had been enough to scare him off and he'd subsequently seen sufficient damage inflicted on others to realise his judgement had been correct. He turned the sound on the TV back up.

But he couldn't settle. He'd had a feeling something was about to happen and now it had. He got up and, after shouting a message to his wife that he had to go out and wouldn't be long, he picked up his car keys and left the house. It was humid and close outside, with towers of black cloud building over the Pennines.

The roads were clear and the journey took a matter of minutes, but he was sweating by the time he pulled the old Shogun off the road and onto the track leading to Devil's Mound before parking up. He didn't want to drive too close and have to turn the car round in the narrow parking space at the end of the lane. He wanted to be able to make a quick exit.

By the time he was close to the gate leading onto estate land, the sweat patches under his armpits were growing and he could feel moisture trickling down his back. The air hung oppressive, sullen and still, he could feel it pressing down on him. Over the hills to the east, flashes of lightening betokened the arrival of a storm. Then he heard the sound, thought it was thunder, but it wasn't.

He managed to jump clear as a digger, driven at an improbable velocity, hurtled passed. Behind the wheel he caught a glimpse of Si Carver. Carver looked out of control, like the digger was driving him. Jim's eyes followed its trajectory and saw Devil's Mound bathed in sulphurous light.

He'd been about to shout at Carver to stop, but the mound took his breath away. He'd not seen it for over a year and back then it hadn't been surmounted by that white thing of horror; the nightmare parody of a tree. How had it sprung up like that?

Reaching up into the bruised sky, its unnatural, thin bare branches were whipping through the air towards the mass of crows circling just beyond reach. How could the branches thresh about like that when the air hung humid and close?

In those seconds of paralysing horror, during which Jim stared at the unnatural abomination, he lost any capacity to delay or halt what was to follow. He managed to open his mouth to shout a futile warning when two things distracted him utterly.

A crash of thunder split the air directly above the mound while a sturdy figure staggered uncertainly into the path of the digger.

Davenport.

****

All day the pains in his chest had been flickering on and off, around late afternoon they intensified. He knew he was running out of time. The old dog sensed it too, it hadn't taken its eyes off him all day. Davenport had previously thought the dog would fade first, but now he realised he'd beat it to the post, although probably not by much.

He was resigned to death but felt guilty he would predecease any chance to make amends for his stewardship of Skendleby. He sat in his chair and stared out of the window watching the storm over the hills roll towards him. Then, he didn't know how, he sensed Ed, who he knew was stuck across the Channel in the seemingly permanent gridlocked port of Calais, and Mrs Carver. Sensed them reaching out to him.

They were telling him it was time, the last throw of the dice. He rose from the chair with difficulty, put on his waxed jacket with the loaded service revolver in the pocket, then shouted to Debo, "I'm just popping out for some air."

She hurried into the room. "Look at the weather, you'll catch your de..."

"I have to go."

"Have we reached the end?"

"I believe we have, yes."

"It wasn't such a bad innings, was it?"

For the first time he saw teardrops forming in her eyes.

"No, it wasn't a bad innings at all, I've been very lucky."

"As have I." She helped him zip up his coat and kissed him. "Go well, my love, go with God."

The old dog, seeing the coat, tried to struggle to its feet and failed. It began to whimper. Davenport said, "Tell Ed and Mrs Carver that at the end I did my duty."

Outside the air hung oppressive, seeming to cling to him and prevent breathing. He staggered down his drive and set off towards the church. At the lych gate he had to stop and catch his breath. The route he would now follow was a path he had walked almost every day of his life and it seemed strange that this was the last time his feet would tread it.

He didn't reflect further, the growing pressure in his chest wouldn't allow it, pain and determination left no room for anything else. Past the church, across the churchyard where his family lay beneath the ground, then through the gate in the estate wall.

He was bathed in sweat and unsteady on his feet. Before him he saw the hellish tree waving its branches at the crows and beneath, cradled in its roots, nestled Devil's Mound. He was glad to see the crows, he knew their link with Ed and they made him feel less alone.

He joined the track to the mound, wondering what was expected of him. Then halfway towards it he saw the digger burst through the gate and race across the field, shovel raised in anticipation. It would be a close run thing if he could beat it to its target. He forced himself to quicken his pace.

Gasping for breath and wracked with chest pain, he stumbled onto the foot of the mound then turned towards the digger, only twenty yards away. Carver in the cab, manic either singing or shouting – a man possessed. Carver saw him. Davenport watched him steer the digger so it would plough over him, crushing him into the mound and burying him in it.

He steadied himself and drew the revolver from his pocket. His memory carried him back to Aden, when he'd last done this as an officer in the Guards. He'd shot an insurgent through the head before he was shot himself. In his dreams he still saw the man's bemused expression as the bullet shattered his skull.

Ten yards now, the digger almost on him. Carver was screaming something. He spread his feet and steadied the revolver with his other hand, took careful aim at Carver's shiny shaved head. The shovel came down, it would cut him in half. It covered the cab, protecting Carver who disappeared from view.

Five yards, death was his companion. A blinding flash and a deafening crash of thunder, the shovel swept down below cab level, Carver's head reappeared. No time to think, one quick action then oblivion. He squeezed the trigger.

Jim had to blink to clear his eyes, so bright was the lightening, the whole area surrounding the mound dazzling white. In the unnatural light he saw the tractor slew violently around before jolting to a sudden halt on the far side of the mound. Then light departed and darkness regained dominion, the boom of the thunder so loud and near he was knocked off his feet.

He stumbled through darkness towards where he had last seen the figure of Davenport and almost at once tripped over on the irregular ground, falling to his hands and knees. In this position he remained until his eyes became re-accustomed to the gloom. Then he climbed slowly back to his feet and began to pick his way carefully towards the mound.

Something was very wrong, there was no movement ahead of him. The branches of the white tree hung motionless, the crows vanished and the tractor was standing still and silent. Of Davenport and Carver there was no sign. He had stepped outside of himself and beyond reality.

Then he saw a figure slumped in the slight ditch surrounding the mound and he forced himself to press on. Davenport was still alive when he reached him and appeared untouched by the tractor. Jim was kneeling to help him when the old man said quite clearly, "Gibson, isn't it? What are you doing here? Check the digger, check I've stopped him."

Jim reached down to feel if Davenport had been injured.

"Do it now, man, time to bother about me later."

The authentic voice of command. Jim got back onto his feet and lurched towards the silent digger. He understood the unnatural silence as soon as he reached it. Davenport's shot had done its work.

Carver was sprawled back in the driver's seat, a circular hole drilled through his forehead from which dribbled a tiny trail of blood. He was stone dead, his face fixed in its final expression, which, to Jim's surprise, appeared to be one of relief.

Jim had no desire to look further, in fact he wanted to be sick but forced himself to return to Davenport.

"Is he dead?"

"Yes, what the Hell is goi...?"

"No time for that, tell Ed and Mrs Carver the time has come, they must act now."

He slumped back and Jim dropped to his knees to feel for a pulse. "Hang on, Sir Nigel, I'll phone for help."

"Don't bother, I'm finished. Strange I should end up here, where I found the archaeologist on that winter's night. I'm the last of my line, no one to follow me."

He was rambling. Jim called an ambulance, but before there was an answer he heard, "Tell Ed I did my duty at the end, tell him I've left him a..."

Chapter 28: So Quickly Has it Come Upon Us

The minutes Jim spent sitting with the body of the last of the Davenports were amongst the most difficult of his life. He was a bemused walk-on player in a major act, the significance of which he couldn't grasp. The waiting time seemed to drag forever and yet when he heard the sirens and saw the flashing blue lights it seemed only minutes since the two men had died.

He knew it would be difficult to explain his presence here, and even more difficult to describe what he'd witnessed but, and this was hugely reassuring, once he gave his statement he'd be able to leave the stage and walk away from this mess. No such reassurance embraced the detective who took his initial statement. Anderson knew there was no way out for him, he was in for life and perhaps longer.

Jim was detained for a surprisingly brief period. In fact, the officers he spoke to seemed keen for him to be gone, which chimed with his own inclinations. During the questioning, the unnerving storm continued to circle Skendleby, as if glued into position. It seemed contrary to nature, glimmering above the hills then returning every few minutes to deliver its preternatural ferocity over the mound.

Once the questioning finished he hurried from the scene of the crime to the cocoon of the Shogun, which he drove rapidly home to Bramhall, leaving the radius of the storm. He parked the car on the drive, shut the gates and disappeared from the stage and into his house, locking the doors and leaving Skendleby behind him.

On site, illuminated by flashes of lightening, Viv, Theodrakis and Anderson put the forensic and investigatory processes into place then gathered under the shade of an ancient oak to confer. They'd sent an officer to break the news to Lady Davenport, but not to Suzzie-Jade, Theodrakis would do that himself later.

"So much for things looking like the case is being solved then."

Viv sounded more deflated than bitter. Theodrakis put an arm around her shoulder, a curious gesture from a man who avoided physical contact. He said, "That will come later, we're approaching the climax. We need to understand what's just happened here."

Before she could reply, Anderson spoke. "Look, the white tree, it's not moving – it seems smaller."

"Jimmy?"

"The tree, it's not the same, it's changed, something's happened."

Theodrakis followed his gaze. "You're right. Davenport and Carver have fought a battle by proxy for something else. This is all about 'Devil's Mound'. Whatever happens next happens here on the mound. We need Giles and Steve." He looked at Viv. "Can you get hold of them and bring them to Skendleby Hall?"

"Yes, but why?"

"Talk about that later. Jimmy can finish off here and meet me in the Hall later."

He turned and walked towards the gate leading into the estate. He'd assumed command and Viv felt relief rather than anger at the usurpation of her case. She and Anderson watched as he disappeared through the filthy light, heading in the direction of the Hall. The storm followed after him.

The heavy iron gates that normally barred entrance to the winding drive hung open on their posts as if breached and broken. The Hall was defenceless and exposed. Theodrakis turned up the collar of his soaked raincoat and set off down the drive into the teeth of the storm.

The Hall looked its normal gloomy self and he felt this strange. He didn't know how it ought to feel but harboured a metaphysical expectation of some reaction following the pretty much simultaneous demise of its two previous owners.

What was more surprising was that there was no sign of commotion or of any activity at all. From this he assumed it would be his arrival that would break the news to Mrs Carver. How would she react? What would she feel? Could she feel? These were the speculations on which he concentrated to prevent his mind stumbling into the abyss of terror. Then, suddenly, he was at the door.

It stood ajar, he pushed and walked inside. The Hall was bathed in an occluded, submarine light, the world seemed entirely composed of moisture. Sounds of the storm ceased as it returned to whatever dimension it had been summoned from. A silence, almost palpable, hung over the large vestibule.

"In here, you'd better come in here."

The spell broke; he walked towards the voice, pushed open another door and found himself in a large room resembling a cross between a tastelessly expensive nightclub and a teenage boy's bedroom. Sitting on a sofa, which must have demanded the skins of at least half a dozen white antelopes, was Suzzie-Jade.

"You don't need to tell me, I felt it. He's dead, isn't he?"

Theodrakis nodded.

"For the best, he was well out of his depth, spent his last days in terror, never understood what he was involved in. If he'd stayed a small time, sadistic bully he'd have been all right, happy even, but he was never in her league."

Theodrakis thought he knew who the 'her' referred to, but remained silent.

"Almost feel sorry for him. Still, better off where he is than where she'd have put him if he'd survived. The mound? Did he get it?"

Theodrakis shook his head.

"What stopped him?"

"Sir Nigel."

He saw a flicker of emotion cross her face, a touch of moisture round the eyes.

"Good old Dad, he managed it then. Hoped he would. And?"

"He's dead too, heart attack we think."

"Well, at least he'll be in a better place than Si. Pity though, there aren't many like him left."

She crossed to the bar, poured a measure of spirit out of a heavy, cut glass decanter and handed it to him. "Here, drink this, looks like you need it. Are the others coming?"

He nodded. As he took the proffered drink he saw his hand shaking. She was right, he needed it, not because of what he'd experienced but because of what he still had to do. The fiery liquid burnt his throat, causing him to splutter and cough, and it was while he was doing this that she spoke the words that severed his moorings.

"Welcome to your new home."

****

Theodrakis hadn't time to question her further on this pronouncement of doom, as Viv and Giles, with a spectral looking Steve in tow, made their way into the Hall. Minutes later there was a loud banging at the front door. Giles was on his mobile trying to locate Ed stranded in France by the anarchic events in Calais. Suzzie-Jade opened the door to find Olga with a pale and unshaven Ed standing behind her.

"Well, well, talk of the devil. Come in, we've been trying to find you."

So, with the exception of Anderson, all the victims of Skendleby were gathered. They moved from the garish delights of the late Si Carver's games room to the kitchen, where they sat around the table knowing it was here they would configure the last throw of the dice.

A bizarre atmosphere compounded by two further arrivals; two police officers requesting that Mrs Carver accompany them to the police morgue to identify her husband's body. It was hard to guess whether they or Viv were more embarrassed when brought together in the kitchen of Skendleby Hall. Bureaucracy, it seemed, superseded even the supernatural. Strangely, it proved a catalyst.

Once the red-faced officers apologetically left the room there was an outbreak of laughter, starting with Suzzie-Jade then spreading round the table until it finally reached Ed, who had only seconds before learnt of Carver's death.

It bonded them and once finished they pitched into an impromptu council of war. It commenced with Giles's interpretation of the significance of the archaeological horrors beneath the city and finished with Carver's demise on Devil's Mound.

Ed grasped the significance of the bizarre tableau beneath Manchester from his experience at Quarrie. "You mean it was set up as a model for what we have to do?"

"I think so."

Giles was about to expatiate further, Theodrakis interrupted. "We know so, it was a direct communication, now tell us what the hell you've been doing."

Ed shook his head as if trying to clear it; then, "At first it made no sense, the nearest we could get to it was that we were being tested and, believe me, we were tested. Then at Quarrie a man spoke to me briefly. A strange man; indistinct yet terribly real at the same time. I can still almost see him. Fleshy faced, heavy-lidded, green eyes, old-fashioned diction with a..."

"Vassilis."

This was Steve's first contribution. He was about to say more but Theodrakis cut in, "The time for that will be later. Please, Reverend Joyce, continue."

"There's not much and what there was gives us no comfort. He said that the mound is a portal that must be preserved."

He faltered, Theodrakis pressed him. "And?"

"And that we must try the ritual again."

Giles snapped back, now sounding angry, "It didn't work last time, why try again?"

"It didn't work because we missed something out."

"Missed something out? What did we fucking miss out? The only thing we could have missed out was a real..."

This time it was Giles who faltered. Steve finished the sentence for him, "Was a real body."

Chapter 29: Women's Work

Silence. It took time for the implications of this to sink in. It was a conversational hare no one wanted to follow. Ed broke the silence. "He, Vassilis, if that's who it was, told me something else; he said there was a final link. A link of bone that must be kept safe, that can't be allowed to join and thus empower something he called 'The Throat of Death.'"

"That's her necklace, it's not ivory, it's bone, she was wearing it when she tried to seduce me. How could we have missed it?"

As eyes switched to focus on Viv, Ed said, "You're right, I think I've suspected for some time deep down, the crows tried to tell me. Oh God."

"Then it's her body that goes into the mound along with the necklace. I told you, I told you, but you wouldn't listen."

Olga's face contorted by fury seemed to have grown larger, as if it was straining against its fleshly limits.

Giles was angry too. "Claire? Put Claire in the mound, you fucking mad woman. Are you serious?"

Then they were all shouting, any concord smashed, any links severed. The babble of Babel raged back and forth across the table. Then the surprisingly measured tones of Suzzie-Jade cut through the chaos. "Listen."

They stopped mid sentence and stared at her. "This is to do with Claire or the demon within her. I know it, Ed's crows know it, we all know it. We have been led towards this moment, we've been chosen. Now we have to work out a way of getting the demon inside her body into that mound. That's what she fears, it's why she made Si try to destroy it. We have to put her in there, it's the only way."

Giles snapped back. "Oh yeah, and what about the watcher in the pit? Who are we supposed to get to volunteer to go in there? Any takers?"

The shouting started again until Olga stood up, pushing her chair to the ground with such force that the wooden frame cracked.

"While we sit here the woman I love is in the house being destroyed by that monster. I should never have left. I'm going back, I'm going to finish this."

She left the room, slamming the door and leaving stunned silence behind her. Out of the silence, Suzzie-Jade said, "She's right in a way. Viv, get your coat, we're going after her. This is how it unfolds."

Theodrakis attempted to prevent her. "But we've no plan."

She touched his shoulder, a strangely intimate gesture. "But you'll come up with one Alexis. When we need you, all of you will play your part."

As she was following Viv through the door, Suzzie-Jade paused to say,

"For now you have to wait and hope because what happens next is women's work."

****

Regardless of whose work it was, the departure of the women removed any element of consensus from the room; anger and fear in pretty much equal measure dominated proceedings. At the centre of both of these emotions was the question of Claire. Outside, the light mirrored the confusion within. It must have been past midnight but the sky was a twilight grey disturbed by occasional blue flashes.

Ed looked from Giles to Theodrakis. The latter hardly seemed real anymore, while Giles? Well, it was clear that the strain of the previous two years had eaten away all his residual strength and that the last hours had been the final straw. He sat cradling his head in his hands and talking, but talking to himself with only fragments fully audible. Steve walked over to Giles, sat down next to him and put an arm round his shoulders, before making his only verbal contribution. "He can't take this. He loved her. He can't face what she's become anymore than we can. She's way beyond anything we understand."

Then he was silent and the only sound in the room was the deranged rambling of Giles. Ed addressed himself to Theodrakis. "This talk of putting Claire into the mound is tantamount to murder."

"You can't murder something that isn't alive."

"How can you say that? You're a police officer!"

"You think she's not causing this? After what's happened to you."

"No, we have to do something, but there must be a way that helps Claire, not kills her."

"You didn't see what we saw on Samos."

Ed was on the point of telling Theodrakis about his experience with the crows. But what was the point? What was the point of anything now? He slumped into silence not hearing the question Theodrakis asked.

"What happens if she harvests the last bone and completes the necklace?"

Theodrakis left the room to return seconds later with a decanter of brandy, which, until lately, had been the property of Simon Carver. He poured them all a stiff measure then repeated his question. "And what happens when she gets the last link, the final bone?"

But it wasn't Ed who answered. To the surprise of both of them, it was Giles. "The baby, my baby, she's growing the final bone of the necklace in the baby."

****

"How old it looks, how old."

Olga's voice was no more than a whisper. They'd parked the car just inside the electric gates which hung rust-stained and broken from their moorings. Viv and

Suzzie-Jade couldn't share Olga's grief, but they certainly shared the shock. It was like looking at the ruins of Sleeping Beauty's palace a hundred years into her sleep.

Before them, at the end of the weed-infested drive, stood a derelict picture of desolation; broken roof, collapsed walls and black, empty windows. The house as it might have looked had its original late medieval self been allowed to stand empty and drift into decay across the centuries.

But whatever its state, Margaret Trescothic's dream home was far from dead, rather it pulsed with a bizarre charge of life vomiting emissions of a bluish light into the dark air. Discharges of light periodically surged up from windows and holes in the roof to join the black mass of storm cloud swirling high above. The storm that recently attacked the mound had, it appeared, localised itself to the airspace directly above the house.

The three women stood spellbound, watching, and then Olga took off, running towards the front door. The other two watched until she reached it, saw the door fly open at her first push, saw her disappear inside. They exchanged a glance then followed.

Viv reached the door first and waited until Suzzie-Jade caught her up. Inside it was intermittently dark, but it wasn't the shifting dark which halted them in their tracks, it was the smell. The house stank of something long dead and rotten. Viv reached out to take Suzzie-Jade's hand, it was ice cold to the touch. "We have to go in."

Still linking hands, they groped their way inside and across the detritus littering the floor for a few paces then waited, allowing their eyes to become accustomed to the spasmodic dark. This wasn't easy, as the light was constantly changing, something in the house was creating random surges of blue, ethereal light and spreading strange, shifting shadows.

Viv used the torch app on her phone and they slowly crept their way towards the 'Gathering' room. Of Olga there was no trace.

Inside the room a chattering, skittering sound wormed its way into their brains. Viv shone the torch towards the source where, by its light, they glimpsed animated bundles of rags. Exposed by the beam these rags slowly rose from the floor and lurched gibbering towards them.

Suzzie-Jade moved from behind Viv into the torch beam and the rags scurried back to the wall, gabbling in terror. Viv wanted to run too, there was something terrifyingly disarticulated about Suzzie-Jade's movements, but she managed to stifle the terror and held her ground.

"It's the women, Viv, what's left of the women. Whatever purpose she had for them, it's over now."

At the sound of a voice, the collections of rags began to move forward again and by the beam of the torch Viv saw it was true. Inside the filthy rags were old, broken-down women. As they drew close Viv recognised the rotten smell infecting the house.

Looking round for Suzzie-Jade she saw that, apparently without moving, she'd reached the far end of the room where she'd been joined by Olga, in whose arms was an even more dilapidated collection of rags.

"It's Margaret, it's Margaret. I found her under the table in the kitchen. Look at her, look at what's been done to her. That murderous bitch, when I find her I'll..."

There was a scream of something that sounded like laughter and the room was filled with strobing, flashing light.

"What will you do, Boxer? And how will you manage it? Look at me, look at me and despair."

Claire stood in the centre of the room, towering above them.

"It's over. In a few of your minutes I'm finished here and can move on to further good works elsewhere. You can help deliver the final bone in the necklace, then nothing will remain here, not even darkness, just nothing."

Olga made a type of sound and moved towards Claire. Claire turned to face her then continued to turn, growing with each pirouette until her head touched the high ceiling.

She smiled at them as she turned and with blue electrical light gushing from her mouth uttered one word, "Watch."

She swirled faster and faster, becoming a spinning vortex out of which sparks of lightening flew to the far corners of the room. Spirals, whirlpools of light spewed spilling from her mouth. She crackled with power.

The room began to fall apart as the universe started to split. Reality fractured, to be replaced by rapidly appearing, then disappearing, patches of dark, smoking cloud through which wild pulses of light exploded.

In the centre, holding everything together, Claire spun and spun and in her they saw the force that creates and destroys the stars and all the fabric of the universe.

****

When they discussed it later, each of them had seen a different person. Theodrakis saw Vassilis, Giles saw Choatmann, Steve saw the strange Greenman figure from Samos. As for Ed? He was never sure who it was that visited him, but if he'd been forced to speculate he would have hazarded a guess on Dr John Dee.

What they could agree on, however, was that as they sat around the table in Skendleby Hall, a figure, which they all perceived in different ways, entered the room and spoke one sentence. "Go now to the mound, open it up and dig a fresh pit facing the entrance."

Then it was gone, leaving all of them with a conviction of what was to be done. After a brief search for tools, which proved surprisingly easy to find, they set off for a final reckoning.

****

Then, as the universe seemed about to split apart, it happened.

The first indication for Suzzie-Jade, the only one capable of watching, was a change of expression on the whirling face. A moue of distaste or alarm. The light imploded, the whirling ceased, Claire gave a cry of pain and returned to what, in her case, passed for normal.

She slid to the floor where she crouched, holding her distended belly. Like any woman prior to performing the most basic and important of all human functions, she looked to others for help. It was this that gave the watching women the key to what was unfolding; the look in her eyes. The eyes were human and pleading. "It's starting, the baby's coming."

Olga, who of them all had most cause to hate Claire, recognised this first. She swept the layers of filth and rubbish from a corner of the raised dais where in happier times the women had gathered for their spiritual rituals. "Get her onto this."

They lifted her and laid her gently down. Suzzie-Jade, with a skill the others wouldn't have suspected she possessed, examined her.

"The waters have long since broken, contractions have started, there's dilation. I can see the head. It's coming, the baby's coming."

Behind her, Viv almost inaudibly, asked, "The second coming, angel or devil?"

Chapter 30: Where the Road Always Led

The storm over the house passed, the blue light pulses faded to grey darkness. The only light in the room crept through holes in the broken roof or was filtered through the filthy windows. At the rooms margins, huddled in corners, the distressed, broken-down remains of the women residents chattered meaninglessly to themselves.

"It's breathing, thank God, give it to her, put it on her breast and let it suckle."

"Don't be stupid, it's part of her, a demon, kill it, then it goes in the mound with her."

"It's a baby for God's sake, we can't murder a baby."

Suzzie-Jade ignored them both, picked up the tiny scrap of newborn humanity and placed it on Claire's belly. She moved it to her breasts where it began to suckle contentedly. For a moment the three of them watched. Then Olga moved, away muttering, "I'm going to look after Margaret. Decide about the baby quickly, we must act now before she recovers. Remember, the baby's part of her, it's not real, just a lump of evil."

Claire's eyes had been shut. She opened them and the act of doing so seemed to expend a great deal of effort. She looked down at the baby and smiled then, turning her gaze on Viv, said, "She's wrong, wrong about the baby, there's no evil in her, and you have to take her. Take her to Giles, he'll make a good father. Take her from me while I can still give her up. The birth process disorientated it but in seconds it will return. I feel it coming."

She turned to Suzzie-Jade. "I don't know what you are, I don't think you do, but there's power in you. You have to listen to me while it's still me in control. You have to put me in the mound, wall me up, it's the only way you can contain it. Take the necklace, split it..."

Viv cut in, "Put you in the mound, that's madness, you're alright now."

"There's no time, take the baby and put me in the mound, me and all the other damned souls inside me. It's your only chance."

Suzzie-Jade took the baby and handed it to Viv. "Take her."

"I don't know what to do with it, I'm no good with babies."

"Well, learn quickly."

While this transaction was taking place, there was a subtle and ominous change to the light, faint pulses of deep blue began to bounce off the walls. They turned in horror towards Claire. But it was no longer Claire they were looking at.

"Good try honey, you and your sideshow freak."

It struggled to its feet and stood tottering uncertainly, glaring at them. They could see its power returning as the light began to shine through it. Above the house there was a rumble of thunder and a dazzling flash.

It lurched towards Viv reaching for the baby. "Time to harvest, time for the last bone."

Then it was on the floor, with Olga standing over it holding a heavy silver candlestick.

"Viv, get some handcuffs. You're police, you must be good for something."

Viv rushed outside to the car while Suzzie-Jade rummaged through her bag. "One positive of living with Si was there was no shortage of drugs. This will do, strong enough to tranquilise a rhino. Help me get it into her before she comes round."

Olga forced the mouth open and watched Suzzie-Jade pour a sachet of powder into it then close it again. They ripped the necklace of bone from her neck – it was slimy to the touch and the individual links seemed to be flexing themselves. Despite the tranquiliser, Claire's body began to struggle again.

"Olga, the candlestick!"

Olga fumbled for the silver candlestick and struck Claire three heavy blows on the head. Then Viv was back. They forced Claire's hands behind her back and cuffed her.

"The car's by the door, engine running, get her into it and drive her to the mound."

"You said that would be murder?"

"What choice do we have? Just do it."

"What about the baby?"

"Take it with us, give it to Giles, it'll keep them both quiet."

Viv had taken control. They manhandled the inert body of Claire outside and into the open car, which Viv had brought up to the front door. She said to Suzzie-Jade, "Get in the back with her and when she wakes try and do what you did that night in the Bistro when you saved me. Claire said you possess powers; well use them. Olga, take the baby."

"What about Margaret?"

"This is the only way to save her and if it works she'll still be here when you get back. If not then it doesn't matter anymore."

They did what they were told. On the way to the Skendleby Mound they said nothing. The only sound, apart from the engine, being a strange, soft and unrecognisable chant from the backseat, which both Viv and Olga hoped was coming from Suzzie-Jade. Neither of them dared to turn their heads to check.

As they turned onto the track leading to the mound, the noises Suzzie-Jade was making in the back were louder and ragged.

Olga asked the question they were all considering. "But what do we do when we get there? We'll need help, how can we open it up?"

But it was too late to think of that: they'd arrived.

There were two other cars parked and by the mound the glimmer of flickering lights. Something else, dark shadows flitting across the open space and the noise of beating wings. All the elements were in place. The endgame had arrived.

They left the shelter of the car and began to drag the feebly struggling body of Claire across the field. As they approached Devil's Mound, they saw it lay open. Above them a splinter of lightening was followed by a crash of thunder and the night air was loud with the sounds of screaming voices.

Terrestrial voices too. First, Ed's.

"Here, we'll help you, it's almost ready."

"Ed, send Giles to the car, there's a baby in there, his child; he shouldn't witness this."

"Her baby?"

"No questions, just do it, Ed, do it."

"I'll get him, he's almost out of it anyway. I think it's all too much, I'll send him to the car."

Then everything became indistinct and occluded.

****

She regained consciousness: they were dragging her towards the burial chamber. In front of the tomb, Steve was crouching above a small pit and she understood that in death he'd guard her tomb so she would never escape.

The effect of the drug was beginning to wear off and the demonic entity inside her mind was waking. It knew this place and feared it. She tried to think of the baby, her baby, but there was no more time.

They'd reached the dark entrance. She could feel the fear in the men and women carrying her. They hesitated but the Shaman, Ed – she recognised his voice – forced them on.

Inside the mound was cramped and chill, the thing inside her screamed words of hate and fear, words her own lips formed but she couldn't understand. Her last glimpse of the outside world was of Steve staring down into the pit.

They dragged her inside and laid her on the cold stone floor. The Shaman bent over her with prayers and words of power. He kissed her forehead. "Forgive us, Claire, forgive us, it's the only way."

She felt the despair in his voice but also the love. He was right, it was the only way and it had been her choice. At the end she'd done the right thing, returned to what she really was. She couldn't speak but tried to show him with her eyes that she understood and welcomed this.

He placed one of the stones with the watcher's eyes across her. The other he left where it lay. Perhaps he understood that this time round there was no need for it.

Then they began sealing the tomb behind them. The watcher's eyes, which were familiar from somewhere, tormented the thing inside her and it began a strange chanted curse in its terrible language.

She watched as a hand beyond the entrance pushed the final stone into place, closing the tomb and locking in the dark. The thing inside her screamed.

She could feel the other souls inside her, which the parasite had inhabited, begin to depart with words of farewell.

Then it was her turn. Before her there was a warm light. She went towards it, at last it was over.

****

Outside there was chaos, the tumult of birds, shrieks and crashes in the night sky. A group stood around the pit, gesticulating and shouting.

Anderson watched, he knew what was happening, he'd been warned of this. They lacked the strength to perform the last act.

He wasn't sure where he'd been since he left the mound following Carver and Davenport's bodies being removed. In fact, his memory of that wasn't too certain either; everything had seemed confused and unreal.

Then he'd met the man. At first he thought it must be Choatmann because Choatmann had told him he'd recognise the moment when he had to act, and Anderson felt that the moment was close.

But it wasn't Choatmann. The face was too fleshy and the mixture of Oxbridge English inflected with a vaguely Middle Eastern filter was different.

The man must have been waiting for him, but the first time Anderson was aware of him was as he was about to get in his car, having seen everyone else off the site. The man had beckoned to him and for reasons he couldn't understand, Anderson followed him into the woods at the estate boundary.

Anderson knew they weren't alone. Amongst the trees he caught fleeting glimpses of dark shapes and shadows flitting from trunk to trunk.

Why they were in the trees he couldn't understand, nor could he estimate for how long, but by the time the hypnotic voice had ceased he found himself back by his car with the flint knife in his hand. He knew what he had to do. There were other cars here now, it must be time.

They were so occupied by shouting at each other standing around the pit, around Watkins, that they didn't see him until it was too late. It was surprisingly easy, the blade slid across the throat. Watkins even seemed to raise his chin in an act of accommodation. Like he was in on it, like he wanted this to happen. Then, within seconds, there was silence and Watkins was dead, collapsed in the pit and dead.

Anderson shouted at them what the man had told him to. "Bury him in there, bury one of the bones with him then go, go home. The Terror has moved on from here now, the evil has dispersed."

Like sleepwalkers, they picked up spades and shovels and began to pile earth over Steve Watkins. But as soon as the first shovel load of earth landed on the body the calmness that had guided Anderson in his actions deserted him. He realised what he'd done. Horror overcame him and he fled the field pursued by all the Furies. Behind him the pit was filled and the earth tamped down.

The watcher was in his place.

****

Steve found himself emerging from the mouth of something that might have been a cave into a misty, opaque landscape. All he could see surrounding him were the mossy trunks and lower branches of massive trees. He was lost in the heart of a dark wood.

He'd been following two figures, who he was sure were Gwen and Claire. It must have been them as they knew him; they'd turned and smiled. But when they drifted onto a different path through the wood he was prevented from following.

He looked round and saw he wasn't alone. The Greenman from Samos was with him, smiling at him as if satisfied with something.

"No, that way is not for you, their role is done."

Steve needed to question him, but he put up a leafy hand to prevent this, saying, "Follow the sound of the surf."

Then he merged back into the wood. So Steve continued on the path through the ethereal, mist-shrouded landscape, out of the trees until he heard the faint sound of surf on a shore. Gentle at first but growing louder until he felt shingle under his bare feet. The bare feet surprised him until he realised he was naked.

He was on a beach, a beach he recognised. Limnionas.

The light was clearer now, it was evening and warm. Before him the surf gently sifted the shingle at the shore's edge. Some metres out there was a disturbance in the water, which, as it moved closer, distinguished itself as a human shape. A woman, dark haired and naked, emerged from the water and walked up the gentle shingle gradient towards him.

He knew her now.

"Come, Steveymou, all this time I have waited for you and now we are together."

She held out a hand. He took it and together they walked along the beach towards the olive grove on the headland, where amongst the trees a soft light glimmered.

Envoi

Ed was on his hands and knees in the crypt checking the spot where he had buried the necklace hadn't been disturbed when his mobile pinged. The text alarmed Ed, not because of what it said but rather that it was anonymous. The message simply read: 'Be at Devil's Mound today at noon.'

He'd spent the last days trying to forget the mound and had been helped in that quest by a life-changing event. When he'd returned – as the first light of dawn streaked the sky – from the interment in the pit and mound to the rectory, he'd found Mary waiting. She was curled up on one of the hall chairs and in her hand she held a pregnancy testing kit showing positive.

That hadn't been the only thing going well, either: Giles, Viv and the baby had moved into Claire's cottage on Lindow Moss and he thought he'd caught glimpses of Suzzie-Jade and Theodrakis together by the trees at the fringe of Skendleby estate at dusk. It wasn't possible to be sure because of the unclear light and the very dark clothing both of them seemed to have adopted.

Best of all, Olga had told him the women's house seemed to be healing itself since the departure of Claire. Rose and Jenna had left but she, along with Margaret, Leonie and Ailsa, were going to start again. The women too were beginning to heal. Of DS Anderson there was no trace.

The text message must be from one of them, but why conceal their identity?

He walked through the woods from the estate gate, the signs of rebirth covering the ground, buds and green shoots springing up everywhere he looked. This even extended to the mound where the white tree was sprouting embryonic green leaves.

They arrived all at once. It was the first time they'd been together since that night and they stood for a moment in the sunshine exchanging embarrassed greetings, until Ed asked, "So, who sent the text?"

There was no response. In the silence, Ed noticed an oak sapling growing over the pit. How could that have happened so quickly? No time for reflection as Giles was talking. "I thought it was from you, Viv said it must be Jimmy and…"

He got no further, a voice interrupted. "Apologies for all this cloak and dagger stuff but it was imperative that I speak to you all. Although DS Anderson is currently in Athens, taking a well deserved break, he will return shortly and the seven will be re-formed."

To their astonishment, standing just outside their group was a slight, long-haired and bearded figure, which four of them recognised as Choatmann. To Ed and Olga, he resembled the images they saw in their dreams of the Elizabethan necromancer, Dr John Dee.

Choatmann favoured them with a thin half smile, then, moving closer, said,

"Now, listen very carefully."

Nov 2nd 2016 two days after Halloween

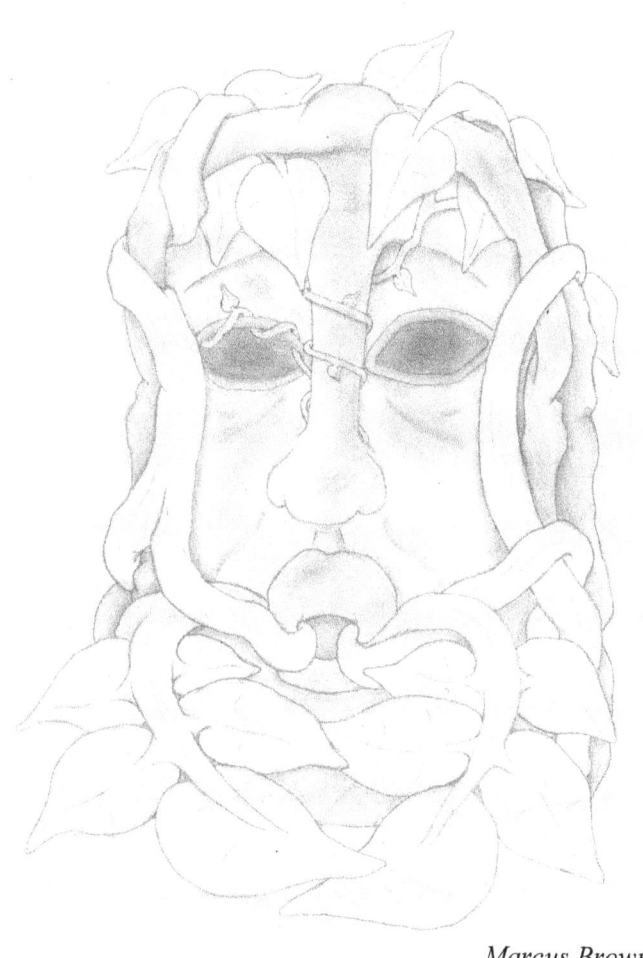

Marcus Brown

Printed in July 2022
by Rotomail Italia S.p.A., Vignate (MI) - Italy